MY ONE AND ONLY

VERY IRRESISTIBLE BACHELORS, BOOK 5

LAYLA HAGEN

Dear Reader,
If you want to receive news about my upcoming books and sales, you can sign up for my newsletter HERE: http://laylahagen.com/mailing-list-sign-up/

My One And Only
Copyright © 2021 Layla Hagen

Cover: Uplifting Designs
Photography: Regina Wamba

All rights reserved. No part of this book may be reproduced or transmitted in any form, including electronic or mechanical, without written permission from the author, except in the case of brief quotations embodied in critical articles or reviews. This is a work of fiction. Names, characters, businesses, places, events and incidents are either the products of the author's imagination or used in fictitious manner. Any resemblance to actual persons, living or dead, or actual events is purely coincidental.

1

LIAM

"Hi, Gran. All good?" I checked in with my grandmother twice a week, no matter what I had going on. Right now, I was on a short break from hearing pitches from companies that my fund was considering investing in.

"Still alive," she said.

I groaned. "Can you please find another way to greet me?"

"Why? I'm grateful every day for not biting the dust."

She had a point, but it was still too morbid for my taste.

"How are you?" I asked.

"Just left my Pilates studio. Should have tried it out years ago. Don't know why I didn't."

"Never too late to try out new things," I agreed.

"When's the last time you tried out something new?" she asked.

I actually had to think hard about that, and I still didn't come up with anything.

"I don't remember." I didn't have time for new experiences, but I liked my life.

I was running my investment fund, Harrington & Co., with my two best friends, David and Becca.

"See, that's not good. One day you'll be eighty and wondering when you let life pass you by."

I laughed. "I'll keep that in mind, Gran. Do you need anything?"

"No, no. I'm fine. That delivery service app you showed me is wonderful."

"I'm glad you like it."

One of the companies I invested in a few years ago developed an app that was a mix between existing concierge services and food delivery. The team behind it were geniuses when it came to user friendliness. As proof, Gran got the hang of it in fifteen minutes.

"I can still stop by. It doesn't replace me," I said playfully.

"Oh, I guess you could. You're still the best chess player I know."

"Happy to know I'm still a worthy opponent." We played chess for as long as I could remember. Gran thought she was better than she actually was, mostly because Grandpa let her win one too many times. He always claimed she was in a better mood afterward and that a man had to choose his battles. Gran could be stubborn and feisty, two traits I seemed to have inherited.

After hanging up, I checked the time. I still had a few minutes before the next pitch started, so I headed to the restroom. It was going to be a long day. We were in an auditorium across from our office building in the Upper West Side.

Harrington & Co. accepted proposals once a year from businesses looking for investors. We had twenty applicants this year, and they were all excellent. I took that as a compliment to our fund. It was proof that we were well known in New York and attracted a lot of interest. Usually, we signed on about three new companies each year, but this time, we were only going to take one. Our team was stretched thin already, and until we wanted to bring on more new hires, one more company was all we could manage.

Where the hell are the bathrooms? We only rented this place once a year for pitches, and the damn place was a maze every time. I went down the wrong corridor twice before stepping into the right one, then headed straight to the men's room, still playing in my mind the five pitches I already heard. I opened the door and stumbled upon a woman who was only half dressed.

Fuck. Me. She was tall with an hourglass figure and glossy hair that fell over her shoulders. I couldn't tell if it was blonde or brown—it seemed like a mix that suited her perfectly.

She'd taken off her shirt and was currently only wearing a red bra that was driving me insane.

"Oh my God. This is the ladies' room," she exclaimed, wincing when she noticed me.

Several things happened at the same time. She took a step back and tried to shield her chest, but one of the cups seemed to detach itself. I got an eyeful of a gorgeous breast before she managed to cover her front with her arms. A deep blush appeared on her cheeks, highlighting her blue eyes.

"I'm sorry. I wasn't paying attention."

"Close the door. *Now*."

I stepped back, immediately shutting the door, but it didn't close all the way. A thin crack remained, but she was completely out of my sight.

"I apologize again," I said through the door. "I was lost in thought and wasn't paying attention. I didn't mean to walk in on you." I glanced at the signs on the doors. I could swear they were reversed last year, but maybe my mind was playing tricks on me.

"Oh my God. This is so embarrassing. I, um, had to wash off a stain. I don't make a habit of stripping in bathrooms." She was rambling, speaking very fast.

"You're here for the pitching session, right?"

I recognized her because I'd seen her in the waiting room with the other applicants earlier today. I wanted to put her at ease.

"Yes. Tess Winchester from Soho Lingerie. And you're Liam Harrington, right?"

"Yes."

"Well, what a way to meet," she mumbled.

"I'll pretend I haven't seen anything."

There was a small pause before she asked in a low voice, "So you did see?"

"No, nothing," I said quickly.

"Oh, that sounds so convincing."

This wasn't working out. The more I tried to reassure her, the more she got herself in a frenzy.

"Okay, then I'll pretend we haven't met. How about that?" I asked.

She chuckled.

"Is there anything I can do to make this situation better?"

"Ending this awkward conversation?"

She sounded flustered. She was right. This wasn't helping—quite the contrary, actually. Now that she mentioned it, I realized I was just prolonging an awkward situation. After all, she was still half dressed in there.

"I'll see you in the auditorium. Good luck."

She laughed. It was more of a nervous chuckle, but it was still progress. The last thing I wanted was for her to walk in that auditorium and stumble over her own words because of this. She had one shot. I didn't want anything to jeopardize her chances of success.

I wasn't really sold on their business. I remembered from the application they sent that they had impressive sales numbers, but they had a short history. This didn't mean, however, that I wasn't going to give their pitch a fair shot.

My One and Only

"I'll try to do the same."

I smiled before ducking into the men's room, still miffed at my mistake. The auditorium building had been under renovation recently, so perhaps they changed the locations of the bathrooms?

It didn't matter, in truth. I had other problems. I might be able to pretend we hadn't met, but there was no erasing that sinful image from my mind.

Tess

OH MY GOD, THIS WAS EMBARRASSING. I SPILLED COFFEE ON MY shirt, so I'd come to the bathroom to clean it off. Instead, I flashed my boobs to Liam Harrington himself. What a way to start the day.

I recognized him from the photo on his company's website. I'd also seen him in passing this morning when we were all shown to the waiting room.

I gave up trying to wash off the stain, just holding the wet portion of my shirt under the hand dryer for a full minute. After putting it on, I also slung my black suit jacket on, buttoning it up. There, now it was hidden. I just hoped I wouldn't break into a sweat.

I smoothed my palms over my skirt before walking quickly back into the waiting room, which was actually just a long corridor with chairs lined up at the wall on both sides. The hardwood floors and tall but narrow windows gave the space a friendly vibe. The ceiling was high, and there was something majestic about it.

My sister Skye was staring at the laptop she was holding on her lap, biting her lower lip. This was a nerve-racking day for the both of us, but I'd rarely seen my sister this jumpy. Being surrounded by our competitors certainly wasn't helping. I sat next to her, determined to push the bathroom incident to the back of my mind and focus on how I could help Skye relax.

The stakes were high today. Skye and I owned Soho Lingerie, a shop selling all sorts of undergarments, and we wanted to expand. To that end, we needed financing, and we were hoping to get it from Harrington & Co. Receiving additional capital would help us expand more quickly; there was no denying that. But we'd also have to give Harrington & Co. some control of our business, and I still had mixed feelings about that. I had to take everything one step at a time though, and right now, my priority was to distract Skye.

She ran a hand through her hair, ruffling her perfectly cut bangs. Her chocolate-colored hair was in complete disarray now. Even her dark-blue suit was getting wrinkled because she was fidgeting so much.

It was usually easy for me to calm Skye down, but today I was nervous as hell too, especially after the bathroom incident.

I drew on my lifelong experience as the older sister to three rambunctious siblings and came up with an idea. Skye always lit up when she spoke about her six-month-old son.

"Did Jonas manage to sit up on his own yet?" I asked. I didn't lower my voice, because the next group was seated quite far from us.

Skye instantly smiled. "No, but he's very good at propelling himself forward on his belly. He looks like he's swimming on the floor."

"And you didn't send me a pic?" I pouted, feeling a strange tightness in my chest. I loved being there for every milestone, but this month was our busiest yet for some reason. It was mid-

My One and Only

September, which I wouldn't say was a big shopping month, but I wasn't going to look a gift horse in the mouth.

"Sorry, I forgot. In my defense, it happened yesterday when I was reading the presentation. But I have a picture." She took out her phone, tapping it twice before turning the screen to me.

I sighed as my chest didn't just tighten—something literally squeezed inside my rib cage. I loved my nephew so much. He was growing fast. Every time I saw him, he looked a tad different than the last time.

"Are you bringing him to the store tomorrow?" I asked eagerly.

Skye grinned. "Yup. Seems to make you just as happy as it makes him."

I grinned back. "That's because we have a special relationship." And by that, I meant I was holding him in my arms 90 percent of the time when I was in the same room with him. I just loved that sweet baby smell and his never-ending curiosity. I'd been a baby person even as a small kid. When my two younger brothers were born, I remembered walking with them in my arms around the house. I was pretending to help Mom, but honestly, I just loved holding them.

Skye showed me a few new photos, and her body language was more relaxed than before. Mission accomplished. To be honest, I felt less stressed too.

At least until the door opened and they called someone in to pitch.

"What's wrong?" Skye asked. "You seem a bit jumpy since you came from the bathroom. Didn't the stain come out?"

Sighing, I decided to fess up. Maybe that would really help me see things in perspective.

"So...while I was trying to clean the stain, someone walked in on me. Liam Harrington."

"What's the big deal?"

"I wasn't *wearing* the shirt," I whispered. "Just a bra. A strapless one. And then I accidentally flashed him a boob."

Skye opened her mouth wide before covering it with one hand. I still heard her giggle.

"Oh, Tess!"

"Yup. Just my luck, right?"

"That Harrington guy isn't too ugly," she whispered.

The remark was so out of character that I couldn't help but laugh. She rarely noticed any other guys since she'd gotten married. I cocked a brow at her.

"What? You used Jonas to get me to loosen up. I can use the hot-guy technique," she whispered.

I laughed despite the widening pit in my stomach. Daydreaming about a guy who caught my eye was one of my favorite techniques to relax. Not too ugly was tongue in cheek, of course. I noticed his baby-blue eyes the second I glanced at his picture on the company's website. And when we arrived today, I couldn't help but notice that he was breathtakingly handsome all around. On a scale from dreamy to hot, he was definitely on the hot-as-hell end of the spectrum, but that wasn't helping my nerves. Today, I couldn't employ my favorite distraction technique.

We received a list with the presentation order when we arrived. My heartbeat accelerated when I realized we would be the next ones to present.

I cocked my head in the direction of the auditorium just as Liam Harrington stepped out, and the whispering in the corridor stopped instantly. His presence muted the conversations the last time he came out too. I suspected he always had the effect of quieting a room, or at least causing everyone to stop what they were doing to pay attention to him. There was something undeniably magnetic about him.

My One and Only

"Okay, everyone. We're ready. Skye and Tess Winchester from Soho Lingerie are up next," he said.

All my nerves slammed right back into me.

Skye and I immediately rose to our feet, hurrying toward him. He was holding the door open for us. I carefully averted my gaze, not ready to make eye contact with him.

As I passed him, I was close enough to realize he was taller than me, at least six feet, and that his eyes weren't his only striking feature. His jawline was sharp and masculine, and his shoulders and arms were toned. He was wearing a black shirt that fit him so well it was easy to see his physique, which made me think his clothes had to be custom-made. His dark-blond hair gave him a bad-boy vibe that didn't fit the rest of him but was insanely attractive.

I juggled my belongings, taking a deep breath as we stepped inside. The auditorium was very intimidating. It was huge, with ten long rows. All the windows were covered with shutters so the presentations could be projected on the wall. The table with the projector was in the front.

Harrington stood right next to the entrance while two others who were sitting in the first row rose from their chairs as we entered. I recognized Rebecca Johnson and David Delgado because I studied their pictures and bios on their website too. I didn't know who the six people in the second row were. I assumed it would only be the three fund managers. Were they students, possibly interns?

Harrington led my sister and me to the table in the center. When he pointed to the cable where I was supposed to connect my laptop, I couldn't help but notice that his initials were sewn at the hem of his sleeve. I'd been right: his shirt *was* custom-made.

"Skye, Tess, you can start whenever you're ready. Our interns are watching this too, but if they make you uncomfortable, we can ask them to step out."

Skye and I exchanged a glance, and my sister nodded.

"That's fine. We don't mind if they stay," she said.

I turned on my laptop and plugged in the projector cable. Skye would begin the presentation, and then I would take over halfway through just as we practiced.

Liam sat next to Rebecca, and for the first time, I didn't avert my gaze. I looked straight at him. My breath caught. Damn, those blue eyes could melt hearts...and panties. I felt my cheeks heat up. Was he still thinking about the bathroom incident?

His gaze dropped to my chest—only for a split second, but I caught it—right before he flashed me a knowing smile.

Oh boy.

Two things were clear.

One: he was still thinking about me half naked.

Two: I really had to stop blushing if I wanted them to take us seriously.

2

TESS

I sat in the first row of the auditorium, a few seats away from Liam and the rest of his staff. Skye was standing right next to the desk where we propped the laptop. The screen was projected on the wall behind her. She started by presenting the financial growth we had over the last three years. Pride swelled inside me as she moved from one slide to the next. We built this business from the ground up, and last year we introduced customization options, which were a complete game changer.

Skye's final slides were about what we planned to do if we partnered with Harrington & Co., focusing on the fact that we wanted to open a second brick-and-mortar location. We also wanted money for a more robust online shop. The one we were using now was barely keeping up.

"By doing this, we'd be able to reach more clients faster. Tess will go into more detail about the type of products we'd develop with additional funding as well as show you the products that contributed to most of our growth," Skye concluded.

She sat next to me, and I squeezed her hand, whispering, "Good job, Sis," before walking to the front. Midway there, my heel caught in the gap between two pieces of hardwood, and I stumbled a bit.

Please, God, no. One embarrassing incident a day is more than enough! I was already worrying that Liam Harrington wasn't going to take me seriously. I didn't want Rebecca and David to think I was a ditz.

Thankfully, I didn't fall on my ass. I regained my balance and walked to the desk, standing next to it.

I rolled my shoulders, smiling as I spoke. "Soho Lingerie's unique selling proposition is that we have something for everyone. Ever since we introduced our customization options, it's become easier to deliver that. Customers can play with designs in our online shop. We also give them the opportunity to come to the physical store for fittings. Since we incorporated this program, the rate of returns dropped by 90 percent. We literally have something for everyone, from adult women knowing exactly what they want to young girls looking for guidance when they enter the store. They're at a fragile age, first-time lingerie buyers, and it's easy for them to question their sense of worth."

I pressed my lips together, smiling. I'd spoken too much, as I usually did when I reached this topic. I hoped it wasn't obvious to everyone how personal this was for me, but Liam's gaze had turned soft. He saw right through me. Well, that was a good thing, right? They wanted passionate business owners, and it didn't get more passionate than this. But I felt exposed, like I revealed a part of myself I'd rather have kept hidden. He was much more observant than I expected, and when I glanced from him to my sister, my protective instincts kicked in.

We both had curves early on, and that had attracted a lot of attention, but Skye had one of those crazy growth spurts, and kids made fun of her. Buying lingerie was a confidence builder for most women. When you felt good in what you were wearing, it gave you a self-assurance like nothing else could. We were determined to ease the step into womanhood for any girl who entered our shop.

I moved to the next slide, which showcased one of our hit products.

"This is an example of one product you can customize. Just as no two bodies are identical, sensory perception isn't the same. For some, velvet straps are too soft, for some too cutting. So we give them a variety of options to mix and match when it comes to straps, cup decoration, and even the inside padding of the bras. For example, I prefer cups with silk on the inside. It feels soft against my skin. Cotton just scratches me."

Unfortunately, I chose that exact moment to make eye contact with Liam, and the heat in his gaze made me blush.

Holy shit! Is it warm in here, or is it just me?

His pupils dilated a little. He was gripping his pen tight enough that I was certain the plastic would give way any second now.

Had I overshared? I thought referencing my personal experiences would help them relate and understand our business.

I carefully looked at the rest of the audience, and no one seemed as...affected as Liam. Damn. I hoped he was judging the business case, not just fantasizing about my involuntary strip show.

I chanced a glance at him again. Yeah, that heat in his gaze only intensified in the few seconds I looked away.

I willed myself not to blush even more as I moved on to the products we planned to design if we had more funding, describing them in painstaking detail.

The more I spoke, the more enthusiastic I became. I talked loudly and gesticulated a lot, and I even brought up more of my personal findings. This was just like me. I did everything at a grand scale. I was almost out of breath by the time I reached the last slide.

"Okay, well, that's it from our side," I said, glancing at the audience. Involuntarily, I lingered on Liam. "I mean, I hope what we've shown you here entices your investment interest in our business. However, if you need more information, please ask away. Any questions?"

Good Lord, his gaze was burning a hole through me, but I was determined not to look away, even though my whole body was buzzing with awareness.

Liam

I STRAIGHTENED MYSELF IN THE AUDITORIUM'S COMFORTABLE leather chair, tapping the pen against the stack of papers. I'd rarely seen anyone speak with so much passion about their clients and their products.

Sure, everyone who came in to pitch to us had pride in their financial success and accomplishments, but these ladies were different. From the way they'd spoken, this was clearly personal to them, and I liked that. I just had to stop imagining Tess wearing every design she'd spoken about.

Hell, when she said how silk feels against her skin, I nearly lost my mind. Gone were any thoughts of business. Instead, I wondered what she was wearing under her skirt. Did it match the bra I'd seen in the bathroom? I could almost feel her soft skin beneath my fingers as I took off whatever she wore.

I was *still* thinking about that. Damn it, I had to get a grip on myself. What was I, fourteen? I forced my thoughts back on the straight and narrow and told another part of my body to slow its roll. All eyes were now on me, waiting for me to take the lead since I'd been the most skeptical about their business.

We rarely got involved in the fashion industry, but their lingerie business was solid—impressive even. My previous skepticism disappeared because I realized their growth coincided with the introduction of the customization options. Their sales would continue to increase. But they had to strike while the iron was hot and get as many customers as possible to establish themselves as the go-to store when it came to customizable lingerie before others started copying their business model.

They needed a much better online shopping experience and a second brick-and-mortar store to keep up with the demand, if nothing else then to house the inventory they were powering through.

"Thank you both for the presentation," I said. "We'd known most of your numbers from the application you sent, but let me just reiterate that they are impressive. You have a very solid business. Today was just about hearing your pitch in person. We're going to get back to you in a few days with our answers and all you need to know about the next step."

"What would the next step be?" Tess asked.

"We invite you to a dinner where we all get to know each other in a more informal setting."

David spoke up. "We like to get to know the owners personally. Everything has to click; otherwise, working together will be difficult."

"Okay, well, thank you for your time today," Skye said. "We look forward to hearing from you."

While the two of them gathered their laptops and other belongings, I couldn't help but stare at Tess's ass. Damn, the woman was killing me with those curves.

When she turned around, she caught me looking and

cocked a brow. Fuck. I didn't want her to think I wasn't taking this seriously because of the encounter in the bathroom...or that I was a perverted asshole.

Neither was true.

Usually, I was far better than this at separating business from personal interests. I didn't get involved or even check out the applicants in a sexual way. Period. It was a strict rule, and I lived by it. I had no idea why it was so hard for me to control myself when it came to Tess.

Her shoulders were a little slumped as she and Skye left the auditorium.

I made a split-second decision.

"Let's take a five-minute break."

Becca nodded.

David shrugged. "Again?"

"I'll be right back" was all I said before I rose from my seat. I caught up with Tess at the building's entrance hall, where everyone could store their personal items in a locker. She was just putting the laptop in her bag, and she was completely alone.

"Tess," I said.

She looked up in surprise, slinging the bag over her shoulder. "Hey. Did we forget something inside?"

"No." I walked closer until I was standing right in front of her. "I just wanted to talk to you for a second."

"I'm listening."

There was no other way to say this, so I just laid out all my cards. "You might have caught me checking you out."

Tess gasped as color flooded her cheeks. Fuck, her reaction to me was cute.

"Might have?" she challenged in an amused tone.

"I did. Several times. I promise you I'm not an asshole. And none of it will impact the way we judge your application. I want you to be certain of that. I'm usually on my best behavior at work. It's just…very difficult to keep my thoughts straight around you. I don't know why."

"Possibly because you saw me in my bra this morning?" She was smiling now. Damn, she was even more beautiful like this. She was far more relaxed than she'd been inside.

"And without it."

She gasped again before starting to laugh. "I thought you said you didn't see anything."

"I was just putting you at ease. Or trying to."

"You failed. I was on edge the entire time."

"I could tell that by your body language," I admitted.

Her eyes widened. She cleared her throat. I leaned in close enough that I could smell her perfume. It was fruity and sweet but also had a hint of something spicy. She licked her lower lip before exhaling sharply. Stepping back, I pointed toward the front door.

"I don't want to keep you any longer. If all goes well, I hope to see you at the get-together."

"And you'll *behave* there?" she teased.

"I'll try."

"Just like you tried to pretend you didn't see me half naked?"

"I'll try a little harder. Forgive me if I fail. You make a…*lasting* impression."

Her mouth opened in an O, and she shook her head before walking past me. I couldn't take my eyes off her as she left the building. That swing in her hips was going to be the death of me.

Fantastic. I'd come out here to put her mind at ease, and I ended up flirting with her. *Way to go, Harrington.*

I'd tell myself that I'd do better during the get-together evening, but I didn't like lying to myself.

3

LIAM

For the rest of the day, we listened to twenty more pitches while my mind kept wandering to a specific lingerie business. In the afternoon, we headed back to our offices, located in a brownstone we rented on the Upper West Side. We converted the original kitchen into a welcome area. The interns worked in an open office arrangement in what used to be the living room. David, Becca, and I each had a huge office on the upper floor. The meeting room was in the basement.

We all decided to head up to the rooftop, which was the best part of the building, to discuss which of the businesses we'd invest in. Everyone loved to come up here for the fresh air, and since we weren't on a high floor, there was no wind. This September was chilly, but because of the taller buildings surrounding us, we were pretty protected from the elements up here. Every time I was inside one of New York's high-rises, I felt like I was suffocating. I didn't need a great view from fifty stories above. I needed to be able to step out whenever I wanted to clear my head.

Becca, David, and I each had two interns on our teams. One of my interns, Dexter, brought up some refreshments for

My One and Only

everyone as well as my stress ball—it's what kept me sane. When we all sat on the rattan armchairs scattered around, I asked the interns to give us their top three picks. All of them mentioned Soho Lingerie. We only had four other fashion companies in our portfolio, each tackling their market with an innovative angle.

After the interns finished giving us the rundown, they headed downstairs to their desks, but Becca, David, and I stayed upstairs.

They weren't just my business partners but also my best friends. We all met fifteen years ago when we were interning on Wall Street after college. In our spare time, we worked on an app for personal finance called InvestMe. A huge bank bought it for a lot of money. We held consultant roles on the app's management team for a while, before it became obvious that we weren't needed. We created the fund because we had a lot of cash and a burning desire to work with business owners. This fund was our pride and joy, and the three of us worked nonstop to turn it into a success. We'd been doing this for ten years now, though at thirty-six, we were still as motivated and hungry for success as we'd been at twenty-six.

Back then, there had been four of us. We'd taken another of our best friends on board, Albert. He hadn't had any money to invest, but he was brilliant, a true innovator. So brilliant in fact that it took us years to discover what he was doing behind our backs. Let's just say we don't talk about him anymore.

"So after listening to all of them, I still think we have way too many excellent applicants. A good problem to have, but still a problem," Becca said. Though we were shaded by the taller buildings, the sun shone through the cracks. It was a beautiful day to be outside.

"I agree. If we had enough people, I'd vote we take on all the projects," I said.

"Maybe we should hire that additional manpower like we talked about," David said.

I grunted, shaking my head. "No. I like our team. Training new hires takes time and resources, and we have neither." Although we'd be able to expand, training new members wasn't easy, and we really lucked out with the group we had.

"Or you're just a grumpy ass who doesn't like new people," Becca said with a devilish smile. I threw my stress ball at her. She caught it midair. "I'm not giving this back to you today. See how you fare without it."

"Becca," David practically begged. "Come on, don't do this to us. We need him to focus."

"I am focused," I assured him.

"Okay, give me your top three picks. Instinctively," David challenged.

"Soho Lingerie, Robotron, and DesignPen." I didn't even hesitate. All three pitches were stuck in my brain—Soho Lingerie's more than the others, for reasons I didn't understand.

David tilted his head. "You weren't sold on Soho Lingerie when I first suggested them. What changed?"

"The pitch was convincing. I think they can become huge if they move fast."

A smile was playing on Becca's lips. "There's something you're not telling us. You were acting weird when they came in."

They both looked at me expectantly. If I said nothing, they'd only become more suspicious.

"Fine, I accidentally walked in on Tess Winchester while she was changing her bra or whatever."

"Oh shit, that must have been awkward. Poor woman," Becca said.

"Is she hot?" David asked instantly.

I cocked a brow at him.

"Forget that. 'Course she's hot. I could tell that even though she had her clothes on. How much of an eyeful did you get?" he continued.

"Enough to make it awkward." And for me to lose control of my mind and body, apparently.

"And wait, that was enough to throw you off your game? How long has it been since you've been with a woman?" David asked with a shit-eating grin.

"I date enough," I replied without going into more detail. I didn't like discussing my private life. Not that there was much to it besides dates and no-strings-attached sex.

"Will you two stop?" Becca chastised.

"No," David answered at the same time I said, "Yes."

"Come on, man, give me a visual," David pleaded. "Just something to make my day better. And—"

I cut him off with a glare. "Let's just get back to our topic. Anyway, that has nothing to do with the fact that they're one of my top picks."

"Those are my top three too," Becca said. "But eventually we still have to narrow it down to one."

"Well, we're not choosing the finalists yet. We can invite at least twelve from the twenty teams to dinner and take it from there," David said. I could tell he still wanted to talk about what I saw.

"Let's think about this until tomorrow," I said. "I don't like spur-of-the-moment decisions."

Becca smiled devilishly again. "Yes, we all know that."

"You keep giving me shit, but you like all the processes I've set in place too." It had been my idea to have standardized procedures for nearly everything.

"I know. I just like to make fun of you. Oh, and now I see frown lines. Time to get your stress ball back." She tossed it back to me. "Well, since we're not deciding today, I'm going back down to bust my interns' balls some more."

"I'm coming too," David said.

The three of us were an unlikely group. At first glance, we didn't have much in common.

David wasn't much for following rules. He came to work wearing sneakers and jeans and would have been just as happy coaching a high school baseball team as he was running a million-dollar fund.

Becca shared his view on rules, but she liked to give *him* shit, not me...usually. She liked to indulge in the finer things in life and always showed up dressed to the nines.

"I'll catch up with you guys later. I'll think about the pitches today. In the meantime, I'm going to pay Gran a visit." Standing up, I went down to the ground floor and ordered an Uber.

Gran and my grandfather had practically raised me, and I always enjoyed our conversations. As wildlife photographers, my parents were constantly traveling, so I lived with my grandparents until I turned eighteen. My parents were currently in Kilimanjaro, and my grandfather passed away five years ago, so Gran only had me.

After losing Grandpa, she went through a phase of deep sadness for more than a year. Mom and Dad took her with them on a trip to the Grand Canyon, and since she returned, she'd been different. The change of scenery had been good for her.

During the drive to her apartment, I planned to mentally review the pitches. Instead, I found myself thinking about Tess Winchester.

The fire in her eyes and the passion in her voice were captivating even hours later. That protective look when she glanced at her sister got to me in a way I couldn't explain. I could tell a lot about a person from their presentation. For instance, Tess wasn't just involved in management decisions. Based on the things she referenced, it was clear she didn't mind getting her hands dirty...and that led me right to dirty thoughts.

My One and Only

I started thinking about her in lingerie yet again, about the peek I'd gotten of her breast. She'd been cute, all nervous in the bathroom. She'd also been delicious at the lockers, where she challenged and teased, and I'd just forgotten about boundaries or common sense. If we were going to work with Soho Lingerie, I had to stop whatever this was.

I'd always been perfectly capable of separating my personal life from my business endeavors. It was one of my strengths, and I didn't think anything could change that.

Tess Winchester was proving me wrong.

4

TESS

I loved shopping. It helped me relax, and I definitely needed that. I'd been on edge all day yesterday, even after we left the auditorium following our pitch. Today, I'd been at the store all morning, then in a meeting with our website designer in the afternoon.

Right now, I was venturing around Nolita with a mighty shopping list. I never stuck to the list, though. Typically, I finished a shopping trip with at least three more bags than planned. So far, I picked up a scarf I thought Mom might like and a necklace for my niece Avery. It was a gorgeous pendant with a blue quartz. Honestly, the jewelry shop was so amazing that I had trouble leaving it. It wasn't upscale or anything, but the pink velvet jewelry holders just made it cozy and gorgeous. I loved buying presents for my nieces and nephews the most. It was so easy to make them happy. And since my inner child was still very active, it helped me pick the right gifts.

We'd grown up in Boston in a huge house and had every convenience possible, until my parents' marriage imploded and Dad's business went bankrupt. After moving to a suburb of New York, we barely made ends meet. I learned not to ask for new things, because it made Mom sad. She would have given us the world if she could have afforded it.

I was immensely happy that I was in a position where I could afford buying anything I wanted not just for myself but also for my family. I just liked buying presents for no reason.

I loved that there were so many kids in the family. It all started three years ago when my brother Ryker started dating a single mom, Heather, who's currently pregnant with their baby. My cousin Hunter was also married to our very good friend Josie, but they hadn't had children—*yet*.

The family had grown fast when Skye got pregnant. In addition, her husband's sister also had a ten-year-old daughter, Lindsay. I still hadn't decided what kind of pendant to buy for her, though she loved just about anything I've given her. It had to be different than Avery's, so each girl would feel special, but not different enough that they would fight over whose was nicer. There were so many options to choose from that I was slightly overwhelmed. In the end, I picked up one that had an identical teardrop shape but a pink quartz.

"Pack them both in pink paper please," I told the sales associate. That was one thing the girls agreed on: pink was better than any other color.

"Right away."

I was smiling from ear to ear as I revised my shopping list. All done. I felt wildly more relaxed than yesterday. One thing was still nagging at me, though. We hadn't heard from Harrington & Co. yet; I checked my email every thirty minutes today to make sure. I was jittery every time I remembered not only my bathroom run-in with Liam but also the shameless flirting at the lockers. I hadn't expected that!

Stepping out of the store, I glanced around, deciding what to do next. A cupcake shop caught my eye, and though I was more of a chocolate cake kind of gal, the pink sign and the fluffy pillows in the window display sold me on it.

My phone rang as I crossed the street. I transferred all my bags to my right hand, searching for the phone in my purse with my left. It was Skye calling, and I answered right away, hoping she'd heard something.

"We've made it to the next round!" she exclaimed.

"Awesome, I didn't get to check my email yet. When is it?"

"They gave us three options to choose from. One is tomorrow, one Friday, and the third one next Monday. Always at seven o'clock."

"I'm free for all of those, so you choose."

"Okay, I'll reply right away. Tess, I'm so excited. I wasn't sure what to think when they just sent us on our way yesterday so quickly."

"All of us had fifteen-minute slots, Skye. I think it just seemed faster because we'd been the ones presenting."

"You're right. Well, I worried for nothing, because we've made it. I can't wait."

"Hey, I'm just looking at a fabulous cupcake shop. Want me to grab some and stop by your place to celebrate?" There was no better way to celebrate good news than quality time with my sister, her husband, and my nephew.

"Oh, I can't. We're going over to Rob's sister's for dinner."

"Just so you know, I'm pouting right now, but have fun."

"Thanks, Tess. I'm so excited about this opportunity."

I grinned. "So am I, Sis."

One would think I would have taken that as a sign to ignore the cupcake place, but instead I went over to take a closer look at the display. And what do you know? They had a slice of chocolate cake on a golden platter. I couldn't just pass that by, could I?

My One and Only

MY EXCITEMENT GREW BY LEAPS AND BOUNDS WHEN THEY confirmed we were meeting them for dinner on Thursday. That whole day, I was nervous from the moment I woke up.

I didn't have any meetings, so I worked from home. Sitting on my couch in yoga pants and a baggy T-shirt, I tinkered with a spreadsheet with budget projections throughout the day. I wasn't very productive, though.

I kept trying to imagine how the evening would go. What would they want to talk about? Our designs? Our detailed plans for the company's future? Potential questions popped in my mind faster than I could come up with answers.

I pressed a palm to my chest, breathing in deeply. I needed to relax so I could be at the top of my game this evening. I crossed my legs at my ankles, rested my hands on my knees, and closed my eyes. I tried one of the meditation techniques my yoga instructor recently taught me—visualizing that I was at the foot of a very old, very large tree and its majestic crown was sweeping in the wind. I'd been successful during the yoga class. I could have sworn I felt a light breeze on my skin.

I grinned. Yeah, I wasn't seeing any trees in my mind right now. Instead, I was seeing a pair of gorgeous blue eyes. Liam Harrington's eyes were definitely closer to aquamarine. I could visualize the rest of him in perfect detail too. Everything from his sharp jawline to those defined arms had registered in my memory. The man was seriously delicious. I could map his body with my mouth for days.

Still grinning, I opened my eyes. Well, I wasn't relaxed by any means, but it was fun.

I can't ogle him tonight, I reminded myself. I just had to make a good impression, that was all. I was hoping the hot energy between us at the locker before I left was just because of my wardrobe mishap. I was really, really hoping that, because if the man pinned me with those sinfully blue eyes again, I might combust. Just at the thought of it, I swear my panties felt on fire.

Half an hour before Skye was supposed to arrive at my place, I dressed up in yet another power outfit. This time, it was a black wraparound dress with short sleeves that I paired with dark green stilettos with silver heels and a matching clutch. I also wore huge round silver earrings. My hair fell to my shoulders in delicate waves, all accomplished with the use of a curling iron. I ran a hand through it so the blonde strands would pop out more.

By the time Skye got here, I was downright jittery. The venue for the dinner was closer to me than to her, so we decided to meet at my place and head out together.

She was wearing a gorgeous cream-colored silk dress and a black cashmere coat. I put on a matching coat; we bought them together as a present to ourselves when we'd hit our most recent milestone: one million products sold.

"Uh-oh," I exclaimed, pointing at her face. "I see worry everywhere. Don't. We'll kick ass."

Skye pouted. "I'm really hoping so. How come you're not worried?"

I laughed. "I am. I'm just better at hiding it."

With a sigh, I took my sister's hand between my palms, looking her straight in the eyes. "Sis, you have to promise to keep me in check."

"Tess, that's not possible."

"You know I can get overexcited about things sometimes."

Skye wiggled her palm from between mine, then cupped my cheeks with both hands. "You do everything on a grand scale. I don't think you even know how to do things differently."

She had a point. I celebrated good news exuberantly and generally liked to make a huge fuss about everything. Once when our brother Cole came back from an overseas trip, I waited for him with a **Welcome Home** sign at the airport. I'd wanted to buy balloons, but Skye and Ryker talked me out of it.

"Just no bathroom incidents and we'll be fine," Skye said with a smile.

I groaned. "Don't tease me about that. I'm trying to pretend it didn't happen."

"Wait a second...you're blushing. You like him, don't you? Liam?"

Why deny it?

"Well, he's superhot. But I'm just going to ignore it. Or try to."

"Why?"

"Because if they're going to invest, it's best to not mix things. With my bad record at dating, it could turn into a disaster."

I could write a whole book on bad dates. One that stuck in my memory even today was this guy Lloyd. I caught him asking for the waitress's number. When I challenged him, he said he wanted to have a backup in case I didn't go home with him. Guess who didn't get laid that night. That's right, Lloyd.

And then there was Francis, who was trying very hard to find out how much I was making at my job and how big my apartment was, because he wanted to make sure I wasn't looking for a sugar daddy.

"Oh. Okay. Good point."

"So yeah, tonight is all about making a good impression."

People who didn't know me sometimes thought I was strange. But I had to say I was a little concerned about me tonight, whether I was going to say the wrong thing or give off a weird vibe. I usually didn't care, but this time, I wanted to make a good impression. If this dinner didn't work out, we'd have to go back to searching for another partner, and we were running out of time.

"Just be yourself," Skye said. "If they don't like that, we know they're not right for us."

I gave my sister a quick hug, grateful that she just embraced my crazy-pants personality. I knew how much she wanted this partnership, so I was determined not to screw anything up. I rubbed my hands in excitement as the car slowed down, smiling at my sister as we hopped into the Honda.

"Okay, let's show them we're everything they didn't know they want and need."

Skye laughed. Even the driver chuckled, looking at us in the rearview mirror.

A while later, we arrived at The Edge, one of the posher restaurants on the Upper East Side. I tugged at my dress as I got out of the car, and then we carefully climbed the stone steps to the entrance. I'd heard about this restaurant but had never been inside it. Right next to the entrance was a high round table with a **Please wait to be seated** sign on it. There was a smaller card with the words **Ring the bell if this is unattended.** Skye touched the vintage brass bell, and a blonde server hurried toward us right away.

"Are you here for the Harrington & Co. dinner?" she asked breathlessly.

"Yes," I answered.

"Perfect. The dinner is in the room to the left."

"Thank you," Skye said.

"Chin high, shoulders straight," I told my sister with a grin. She grinned back. That had been my motto ever since kids gave her a hard time in school, and it stuck.

"What's our tactic? Divide and conquer, right?" she asked.

"Definitely. We need to talk to all three."

"I'll leave Harrington to you." She'd dropped her voice to a whisper, wiggling her eyebrows. I didn't get a chance to reply before we stepped inside the room.

It was beautiful, if a bit dark. The walls were painted a

My One and Only

modern concrete gray, and the light fixtures were vintage brass with yellow light bulbs. It was a very interesting mix, sort of *The Great Gatsby* meets modern-day New York.

There were about a dozen high round bar tables scattered around the room, and everyone was standing around them. The chatter was audible even over the faint jazz music. Although the room was crowded, I immediately spotted Liam. It was impossible not to notice him. His presence was just too intense and larger than life. Everyone in the group he was talking to stood a few feet away, as if too intimidated to get too close.

At that moment, he turned around, zeroing in on me. The second our gazes crossed, I felt rooted to my spot.

He headed our way, and that sensation of being tied to him by an invisible cord intensified with every step he took. I was tempted to avert my gaze, but that was just impolite. My breath caught and my palms became a little sweaty just as Skye shook hands with him.

"Welcome, Skye. And Tess."

He reached for my hand, and the second we touched, it was as if electricity traveled throughout my body. An inexplicable urge to be closer to him slammed into me. That time, I did avert my gaze. I swear I noticed him smile at my shyness out of the corner of my eye.

Rebecca immediately joined us, and Skye started a conversation with her, moving deeper inside the room.

Divide and conquer. That's right. I was here to impress, not melt in a puddle just because I was standing within touching distance of the hottest man on the planet.

I had no idea when I upgraded him from hot as hell to hottest man on the planet, but I had a hunch it happened in the few seconds it took him to cross the room. In my defense, in the dimly lit room, his gorgeous eyes popped even more. And he was wearing a white shirt that fit him far too perfectly for my peace of mind. I could vividly imagine all those muscles hiding underneath the fabric—and all the ways in which I'd show my appreciation for them.

"It's not as crowded as I expected," I said.

"We've divided the applicants in three groups, so not everyone is here tonight. We wanted to get a chance to really interact with everyone."

"That makes sense."

He flashed me his dimpled smile again, and I had to remind myself not to ogle him.

"Between you and me, I was mostly looking forward to seeing you," he said in a conspiratorial tone.

I swallowed, pushing a strand of hair behind my ear. "Liam! Is this you trying hard to behave?"

"This is me trying very hard," he said with a mock serious expression. "But as you can see, I'm failing already."

I breathed in and out quickly, feeling lightheaded. How could a little flirting affect me so much?

"Well, let's see if I can keep you on the straight and narrow," I said boldly, hoping he couldn't tell just how much I liked his flirty side. "Give me a rundown of what's going to happen."

"Tonight is all about getting to know each other," he said after a few seconds. "It's important in a collaboration for the parties to click. From your pitch, I could tell you're very passionate about what you do and that your business is very personal for you. I like that. Always gives business owners the motivation to go the extra mile, even when things are tough."

I nodded, happy he noticed and appreciated that. "It is very personal. It's something my sister and I built together. We're very close. Our whole family is."

"I can imagine that."

"Are you close to your family?" I had no idea why I asked that. It wasn't relevant, and yet I wanted to know the answer.

Liam's smile grew more pronounced. "That's very personal."

Damn, I knew I overstepped. "I thought that was the point of tonight. Getting to know each other."

He laughed. "True, but I can't say I saw that question coming. And to answer, yes, I'm close to my grandmother."

He didn't say anything about other family members, and even I knew it was impolite to press on the topic.

"Come on, Tess. I can tell you want to ask more. I have nothing to hide. What else do you want to know?"

A million questions popped into my mind. I wanted to know the type of person he was in his private life. Did he cross the street at a red light? Was he the type of person who saw a homeless person and thought they were just too lazy to work? Or would he give them a few dollars? I didn't know why the answers mattered, but they did. I wanted to know about his character.

Before unleashing my crazy on him, I had a confession to make.

"In the name of complete honesty, you must know something about me: I'm inappropriate 99 percent of the time. I talk too much, ask too many questions, and require way too detailed answers."

Liam chuckled, and the low rumble almost made me swoon. "Good to know. Go ahead. I don't mind."

I smiled back. Clearly, he was trying to put me at ease, but he had no idea what he was getting himself into. I eyed him intently, trying to figure him out.

"Give it a try. I don't bite, Tess. Unless you insist on it."

Holy shit. Liam wasn't only trying to put me at ease, was he? He was openly flirting with me. Did he have any intention to behave at all?

My face instantly heated. My mantra just changed from not ogling to not flirting back. But judging by that smoldering glint in his eyes, I was going to fail.

5

LIAM

Before coming here tonight, I'd been determined to be on my best behavior, and yet within minutes of seeing her, I was flirting.

I had to make an effort. A *real* effort.

"What made you decide to open an investment firm? Why not enjoy all that money you got when you sold the InvestMe app?" Tess asked.

The question was unexpected even though it was all out there for everyone to see. Our background was listed on the Harrington & Co. website, and information about our app's sale was included.

I had to think about her question for a moment before I answered. "I received advice from some people I respect a lot to be mindful about the future, not just the present. And by people, I actually mean my grandfather."

I'd thrown a huge party to celebrate the sale. My grandparents hadn't come, insisting it was for young people, but they asked me to visit them the next day for lunch. I'd been too hungover to make it in time, only able to visit for dinner. Grandpa had taken one long look at me and told me I was getting one hall pass, that they hadn't raised me to throw my life away and that they expected me to make them proud.

Tess smiled broadly, and damn, it was a good look on her. She lit up completely. I suspected that underneath all her fire and determination was a layer of warmth. The urge to find out slammed into me. Of course, I had no business finding that out. This was business, not pleasure. I didn't mix the two.

Was this what working with her would feel like? A constant exercise in self-restraint? I was going to fail; I just knew it.

I cleared my throat, pointing to one of the tables.

Servers circulated with trays of drinks, and one approached us as we headed to the nearest table. Tess took a glass of water. I did the same.

"What do you do in your free time?" she continued.

I felt like I was in a college interview, but one I was especially interested in nailing. No pun intended.

"I go for a run."

"Do you see your grandmother often?"

"Every two weeks."

Her eyes widened a fraction of an inch, and her smile widened. That was clearly important to her. I was learning more from the questions she asked than she did from my answers. Not many people would even have the guts to ask about such personal matters.

She pressed her lips together. I was betting that not only did she have a whole lot more but that they were even more personal.

But I had my own questions too. I had a standard list of them I used for all business owners. Usually, I liked to go with that, but now all I wanted was to deviate from the standard and go as personal as possible.

"Why did you two decide to open up a business?" I asked, proud that I'd stuck to the list...for now. "Per your résumé, you were both in mid-management in your previous jobs. You'd done very well for yourself in the corporate world."

Business owners usually fell into two categories. The first was young professionals, who were dissatisfied with their jobs, feeling like they could make more money on their own. The other end of the spectrum was those in very senior positions who had a lot of cash and wanted a change. Tess and Skye didn't fit in either category. Tess was only one year younger than me and had been in a well-paid midlevel management position.

"We like working together, so that part was easy," Tess said. "But I think the interest came about because I've always struggled to find the right lingerie for me. It's a tricky subject, because it's tied to self-esteem. Anyway, the right lingerie gives women confidence, and we love that we can do that for our clients."

I liked the passion in Tess's voice, and her body language. She fascinated me. There was no denying it anymore at this point. I just couldn't look away from her neck. I wanted to nuzzle into her warmth; I wanted to kiss her hard and deep, pulling her bottom lip into my mouth. I barely kept from looking farther down. She was a gorgeous bombshell in her dress. The belt accentuated her curves, and it all messed with my focus.

Back to the list of questions, Harrington.

"Do you plan to keep it indefinitely or sell at some point?" I asked.

"We're not planning on selling. Is that a problem?"

"Not at all. Just wanted to know where you stand on this." I liked working with entrepreneurs who wanted to do this long-term. My colleagues often wondered why I didn't ask about it directly in the initial application the business owners had to fill out, but it was such a personal yet important question that I wanted to look them straight in the eye when they answered. We needed time with each investment in order to make back our money, and a sale early on was not a good return for us. And knowing a client's commitment meant they'd work damn hard for everyone involved.

I nodded, fighting to not fixate on her mouth as she brought her glass up to it. Behind the rim, I noticed the corners of her lips lifted.

"You're trying to hide a smile," I said.

"Guilty."

"Why?" I moved closer to her, enjoying the way her pupils dilated.

"I thought tonight was about getting to know each other, but the questions you ask are very...stiff."

She was challenging me in a way no one else dared, least of all an applicant. I realized she did things her way. I liked that.

"Would you rather I go back to telling you all the reasons I can't stop flirting with you?"

Her eyes bulged. "Is there no middle ground?"

"When it comes to you and me, apparently not."

She exhaled sharply. On instinct, I touched her lower back, leading her toward a darker corner of the room. I couldn't miss the light shudder in her body. It made me want to pin her against a wall and kiss her until she was shaking.

"I have a list, Tess. Sticking to it is best for both our sakes. You have no idea just how personal I want to get." I looked her straight in the eyes so she wouldn't mistake my intentions.

She licked her lips, raising her glass to her mouth again as if it were a shield.

"Oookay. So, let's get on with that list, then."

I couldn't help but lean in and tease her. "Not too stiff for you?"

"Liam..."

All I could think about was how good her full lips would feel against mine. But I pulled myself together, focusing on what I needed to do.

. . .

Once I was done with my questions, I was supposed to mingle with all the applicants tonight, but all I wanted was to find out more about this fascinating woman. I wanted to lure her to someplace where we could be alone.

Becca waved at me from across the room. She was looking at me with raised eyebrows, so I knew it was time to switch conversation partners.

"Tess, I need to catch up with the rest too. It was great talking with you."

"Informative?" she teased.

"Very. Look, the servers brought food while we talked."

I put a hand at the small of her back once more, guiding her to the buffet table. She straightened, licking her lips. Damn, the way she responded to the simple touch was driving me crazy.

"Wow, you went all out," Tess murmured when we reached the table. She placed her purse on it while she grabbed a plate.

It was open, and her phone was right on top, so I didn't miss the screen lighting up with a message from a guy named Kevin. I looked away, not wanting to intrude in her personal sphere, but I couldn't miss some ridiculous heart-shaped emojis. Was she already taken? I didn't like that at all.

"We wanted to make sure there was something for everyone. Have fun, Tess."

I squeezed her arm before letting her go. I wasn't usually a touchy person, but when it came to Tess Winchester, I seemed to want to do everything differently.

6

LIAM

"This is fun," Becca said a few days later. "Just wish we'd met like three hours later."

David, Becca, and I were having breakfast on the rooftop of the brownstone. My intern Dexter was also here, but none of the other interns showed up on time. Yesterday, we went to dinner with the last bunch of applicants. After they left the restaurant, we exchanged impressions. Then we ordered some wine, and the evening got away from us.

"It's going to be a long day," I said.

Last night, we decided who we were going to sign on: Soho Lingerie.

"We need to let Soho Lingerie know. The lawyers already sent the contract. We should all double-check it," I said.

David grimaced. "That's something you usually do, Liam. The lawyers will just do their thing."

I stared down at him until he held up his hands. "Fine, fine. I'll look over the contract too."

The lawyers were great at their jobs, of course. We had a standard contract, but they adapted it to every applicant's business, personalizing it. I liked to double-check everything. It was a courtesy to everyone involved, and I insisted on it every time.

"God, can you imagine what life would look like with a more relaxed Liam?" David asked.

Becca narrowed her eyes as if considering it. "Honestly, no. He's been like this since day one on Wall Street. Always tense and a stickler for rules. I don't think he's ever even wanted to break any."

That statement had been 100 percent true until I met Tess. Something about her just made me want to disregard every rule. But Becca and David didn't need to know about that.

"Are we already deciding who will be Soho Lingerie's mentor?" Becca asked.

I shook my head. "Let's wait until after the contract is signed."

Sometimes deals fell through, and if that happened, we would need to approach our second most promising candidate. I didn't want to get into the nitty-gritty of who would mentor them until everything was signed.

"True," David said. "Well, since you're a stickler for rules and are going to make me stay here until midnight if needed, I'll get started on reviewing what's been done on the contract."

"Perfect."

Becca groaned. "Why are you indulging him? He's only going to get more insufferable."

"That's impossible."

I threw my stress ball right at David. It bounced off him and smacked into Becca's ear.

I fist-pumped the air. "Two in one shot."

Becca laughed. "Fine, I'll get started on the contract as well. But I'm claiming the rooftop for myself today."

"Good for me. Dexter, come on. Let's go downstairs."

"Sure thing." On the way to my office, he added, "I sure hope you get to mentor Soho Lingerie. That Tess is something else. I'm gonna ask her out as soon as the papers are signed."

I froze midstep. Drawing a deep breath, I turned around slowly. "No, you're not."

"What?"

"Tess Winchester is off-limits."

"There's no ring on her finger."

I stared at him, jamming my hands in my pockets. "She's going to be a business partner."

"There's no clause that says we're not allowed to ask applicants out."

My jaw ticked. I just stared him down.

"Okay, boss. Got the message. I'm backing off."

"Good."

I stalked off to my office, fully aware that I was a hypocrite. It had been five days since I'd seen her at that dinner, and I still couldn't stop thinking about her. I couldn't take my eyes off that woman the whole evening. She was a sexy goddess and an awkward goofball rolled into one, and while I never thought I'd find the latter charming, I did.

She was so refreshing, so different from any woman I'd gone out with. It was also not a coincidence that I hadn't gone on a date since the day I met Tess. I could chalk it up to my workload, but the truth was I only wanted to go out with her. And yet I couldn't, especially now that we decided to take on Soho Lingerie.

I sat down in my chair, but instead of reading the contract, I searched for Tess's number in their application and punched it in my phone. Our interns were always tasked with contacting the applicants we selected, but this time, I wanted to do it myself.

I sent Dexter a short email, informing him that I'd break the good news to Soho Lingerie. He'd probably think I was doing it because of his earlier comment. I was pissed at Dexter, yeah, but I wanted to be the one to tell Tess the good news. I wanted to be the first one who heard her reaction.

Tess didn't answer right away, and when she did, she sounded breathless.

"Hi!"

"Tess, this is Liam."

"Sorry, I couldn't find my phone. Searched the whole back room for it only to find it under a pile of panties."

I barely stifled a groan. An image popped in my mind of Tess trying on panties. Damn, I couldn't start our conversation like this. I had to pull myself together.

"Not my panties. They were...doesn't matter."

"Tess. Good morning to you too."

"Sorry, I've only had one coffee, so I'm rambling even more than usual."

She was adorable. I could picture her blush as she spoke, the way she'd try to avoid looking at me if I were in front of her.

"No problem. It was an interesting conversation starter."

She made a weird sound, as if she just swallowed her tongue.

"Good morning," she said after a beat. "Can we have a do-over?"

"Not a chance in hell."

"You like teasing me, don't you?"

"Love it."

I liked to make her blush too, but it was too early in the day for that confession.

"I have great news for you, Tess."

"Oh my God, no. Can you wait for it until I'm with Skye? I had this whole thing planned where I shared this moment with her if it was good news."

"And if it was bad news?"

"Umm…I'd process it and then find the gentlest way possible to break it to her."

I was speechless, and that rarely happened.

"You can always message me when you're with Skye, and I can call you again."

I couldn't believe I was entertaining this, but I didn't like that she labeled me as stiff. I had this inexplicable urge to please her.

"No, that wouldn't work. She'd be able to tell that I already know. I thought the calls were coming in the evening. I'm meeting Skye at six." She sounded almost accusatory.

I laughed, leaning back in my chair. "Thought we'd switch things up, shorten the waiting time."

"So we're really in, huh?"

"Yes. We're sorting out the contract, and we'll send it to you this evening. You can take as long as you want to review it, and of course certain points are negotiable. If you'd rather not take the deal, we understand. But we hope you do."

"Wow. Skye will be so happy."

Something about that sentence bothered me. Wasn't *she* happy? Didn't she want this?

"I'm going to think about a cool way to break the news."

"Are you going to celebrate?"

"Of course. In style."

"What does that include?" I was going off record again, asking personal questions, things we usually didn't discuss with our mentees.

"Champagne, of course, and a lot of food. I'm thinking a platter of French and Swiss cheeses."

"So you like your cheese."

"Oh yeah. I like even the lowly mac and cheese. As long as it's creamy and chock-full of calories, I'm in."

"And champagne? Any special kind?"

"Actually, yes. I like Bardoux's Brut Traditionnel. It's only produced in small batches, so I have to head over to Dumont Gourmet. Fingers crossed that I find it. I didn't want to buy it before I knew if we'd be accepted. I didn't want to jinx anything."

"I see you take celebrations very seriously."

"Oh yeah. I even—" She stopped abruptly.

"You what?"

"Never mind."

"Tess..."

"It was too outrageous to say out loud, even for me."

"I'm even more intrigued. Tell me. I think you and I have been past outrageous since the first time we met."

"I can't believe you're bringing that up," she whispered.

I chuckled, imagining her all flustered and blushing. "I have a confession to make. I like teasing you, Tess. Making you blush. Even if I'm not there to see it. I can picture it in vivid detail."

"You're cruel."

"No, just weak for you."

"Oh, so you don't flirt the panties off every woman you meet?"

"Only you. I promise you that."

She cleared her throat. "Well, we're going to collaborate, so we really should behave. Why don't you tell me what the next steps are?"

She was right. I needed to rein myself in.

"We'll be emailing you the contract today. We need to know within fourteen days if you want to move forward with the collaboration."

"Okay. Thank you for calling to let me know. Have a great day."

"You too. And Tess? Next time I see you, I'll get you to tell me all about your outrageous celebrating habits. No matter what it takes."

I heard her sharp intake of breath just before the call disconnected.

Instead of focusing on the contract, I opened Dumont Gourmet's website on my browser, checking where the nearest one was and then ordering a bottle of Tess's favorite champagne. I wanted to make her smile.

I had no idea how I was going to work with this woman and not make her mine.

7

TESS

"Wait, I didn't order this," I told the delivery guy from Dumont Gourmet. He stood in front of the store, holding a bottle of my beloved Bardoux's Brut Traditionnel. I'd only looked online to see if they had it available and planned to pick it up later.

Dumont Gourmet was run by my brother-in-law's sister, but she couldn't possibly know I was planning to order it.

"No, it was a gift order. Sender is a guy named..." He paused, checking a list on his phone. "Harrington."

My pulse quickened. I took the bottle from him, inspecting it closely. I was bursting to know more details. When had Liam ordered the bottle? Had he scheduled the delivery just as I was about to leave? I didn't make the delivery guy stay to question him. By the looks of his bulgy backpack, he had lots of stops to make.

The second he left, I grabbed my phone and headed to the back room; the front was packed with customers, and I didn't want to be in the way.

The front of the shop was very elegant, with velvet couches and golden light fixtures. We were determined to make lingerie shopping a pleasant experience for everyone. Girls transitioning to womanhood, adult women embracing their sensuality, or mothers learning to feel sexy again. We had something for everyone, and we were proud of that.

We'd redone the back room a few months ago because we spent a lot of time here playing around with customization options. The room was windowless, so we had half a dozen lamps in the corners as well as spots in the ceiling. It was also where we kept part of the inventory, so black metal shelves lined the walls.

The silky terracotta carpet was the centerpiece, along with the two dark-green armchairs and the ottoman. This room might not have windows, but it had plenty of life. We'd hung paintings everywhere, so you didn't even notice the lack of natural light at first.

I wasn't even trying to tone down my grin as I typed.

Tess: You sent me a bottle of champagne???

Liam: Yes.

Tess: Why?

Liam: I don't know. Impulse. I wanted to surprise you.

Tess: You certainly did. I was just about to head out to meet Skye.

Liam: I know. You said you're meeting her at six.

Wow, he was so thoughtful!

Liam: Maybe also a gift to get in your good graces. Easier to make you tell me all about your inappropriate habits next time.

Holy shit, he was being flirty again. It was so much easier to resist flirting back over the phone than face-to-face. He was going to be our business partner. There was no place for anything else. Besides, the way my relationships were going, the chances of the next one going bust were at 99 percent.

Liam: What are you doing now?

Tess: Working on more customization options.
Liam: Want to send me pictures?
I burst out laughing, shaking my head.
Tess: I'm trying them on myself.
Liam: ...
Tess: Liam!!!!

He didn't reply, so I sent another message as I sat down on the round red velvet ottoman, crossing my legs.

Tess: I meant that in a fierce tone. Does it translate into writing?
Liam: Not really. I'm picturing you trying on merchandise.

Heat spread through me like wildfire, from the top of my head all the way to the tips of my fingers and toes.

Liam: I know it's risky territory, but I like you, Tess. You're driven and determined and the most interesting person I've met in years. Kind, warm. And you're sexy as fuck.

Oh wow. I read his message a few times until every word sank in. I had no idea what to reply, so I decided to tease him.

Tess: You're still not getting pictures.
Liam: I didn't think you'd change your mind on that. I was just being honest.

And precisely because he was honest, I was completely on fire. I swear my panties just combusted. I rose to my feet, too jittery to sit.

Tess: Thank you :)

Instead of replying, he called me. I hesitated for a few seconds, because I wasn't sure how hearing his voice was going to tame the heat, but he was our investor. I had to find a way to work with him.

"Hey," I said.

"Believe it or not, I actually meant to text you about business."

My One and Only

I could hear the smile in his voice, and I couldn't help but grin. "You don't say."

"So now I'm calling."

"Think that will improve the situation?"

"I don't know, Tess. We'll see." After a beat, he added, "I want us to get to know each other better. I know it's best not to mix business and pleasure, but I can't help myself. I'm crazy attracted to you, and I think it's mutual. Am I wrong?"

"No," I admitted. Butterflies were roaming in my belly. "But I'm not sure we should…do anything."

"Think about it, okay?" His voice was relaxed, and I was thankful he was letting me off the hook, because I needed time to process this.

"Okay. I'll email any questions we have about the contract."

After hanging up, I looked at the bottle and hugged it to my chest.

I was in an excellent mood. We had a reputable investor wanting to work with us. I had a bottle of our favorite champagne. What was there not to be happy about?

Celebrating milestones was a religion in my family. I'd always insisted on that. We all had hurdles to overcome, so good things needed to be enjoyed and celebrated.

I headed to Ryker's place. Skye was meeting us there. Since my brother worked on Wall Street, we wanted his input on the contract. He'd know if the terms were fair.

On the way, I received a message, and I scowled at the phone when I read it.

Kevin: Think I've got a shot at this?

Attached was a picture of a gorgeous blonde.

Kevin was the owner of a food truck not far from our store. We met a few months ago when I bought lunch from him. I thought we clicked, so in a typically overoptimistic Tess fashion,

I asked him out. He turned me down gently, saying I wasn't his type and that we were better off as friends.

Ever since, he kept in touch—more often than not asking for advice with women. I toyed with the idea of just ignoring him, but really, I didn't want to be rude. He'd been honest. But looking at the picture, I couldn't help but ask myself, *What does she have that I don't?* It stung.

Tess: I don't see why not :)

There, that was a good reply, and it didn't invite more conversation.

He didn't send anything back, thank goodness.

My brother lived in a gorgeous apartment not too far from Soho, on the fifty-fourth floor of a skyscraper. I was excited to see my niece Avery again and to give her the gift I purchased for her in Nolita. I took it out as I stepped off the elevator, smoothing the pretty pink wrapping paper and the bow.

Ryker opened the door. My brother was a mountain of a man with permanently rebellious hair and dark-blue eyes that broke their fair share of hearts before he settled down with Heather.

He pointed at the package. "Hey, Sis. What's that?"

"A present for Avery."

"She's not here. Heather took her out for dinner. You can leave her present, though. I'm sure she'll be happy."

I pouted, holding the package to my chest along with the bottle as I stepped inside. "But I like watching her when she gets her presents."

That was one thing I loved about kids. They didn't hold back anything. It didn't matter if they were overjoyed or throwing a temper tantrum.

I gave him the package, though.

"Send me a pic when you give it to her, okay?"

"Sure." Ryker laughed, guiding me inside the living room.

I toed off my shoes in the foyer before zeroing in on the couch, where Skye was sitting all alone. "And you didn't bring my nephew?"

"No, I thought we'd need all brain cells to focus on the contract."

I sighed, resigning myself to getting no cuddle time with Jonas or Avery today. I placed the champagne bottle on the table and sat next to my sister. That was when I realized she was running her hand all over her face and through her hair. She only did that when she was worried or annoyed.

"I haven't had time to read it. Something wrong with it?"

I'd been elbow-deep in all sorts of duties at the store. Skye didn't answer. I looked between her and Ryker, who was sitting in the armchair opposite the couch.

"Nothing wrong. I just don't think you'll like it," he said.

My stomach bottomed out.

"Okay, should we go through it, or you want to sum up what I'll dislike first?" I asked.

"I'll start with the good points. They don't ask for a percentage of your company, just a percentage of profits. I don't think you'll get a better deal from any investor."

I frowned. "We knew that already. It's why we chose them as our potential investor. So what's the problem?"

"They want a lot of decision power. More than I usually see in this type of alliance. It's understandable, but it's unusual. I for one wouldn't have a problem with it, but I know you two like to be in control."

That was an understatement. Skye and I both worked full time when we opened the online shop, and we only quit our previous jobs once we opened the brick-and-mortar store. We'd done everything from prototyping to online marketing ourselves.

I looked over Skye's shoulder at the laptop. Over the next two hours, we dissected every section of the contract. My mood just kept plummeting.

"Liam did say they're open to negotiation," Skye said, chewing on her lower lip.

I gripped her hand, squeezing it reassuringly.

I'd been the one who convinced Skye years ago to go into business with me. There was a reason my family nicknamed me "the hurricane": when I put my mind to something, there was no stopping me. I talked Skye into it, and now I felt responsible for making this work. I didn't know what to say though, because our dream of expanding was slipping through our fingers. No way could we agree to these terms.

"Tess, we have sixty-five points we want to discuss. I don't see how we can reach an agreement."

I was tempted to just reject the deal, because these negotiations would likely take time, and we didn't have any to spare.

"Okay, I'll send him an email with our comments, asking for an appointment," I said.

I sent the email right away, keeping my fingers crossed that he would want to meet soon.

"Come on, girls. Let's go out to dinner. My treat. You two need something to cheer you up," Ryker said.

"Have I told you I love you recently?" I teased, getting up from the couch and kissing his cheek.

"Only a couple of times."

"We planned on ordering a cheese platter," Skye said.

I vehemently shook my head. "No, that's for celebrating. Let's not spoil that by turning it into comfort food."

Needless to say, we hadn't opened the champagne.

To my astonishment, Liam emailed before we left the apartment.

Liam: I can see you and Skye tomorrow at eight and discuss your worries.

"Perfect," Skye said when I read her the content. "Works for me."

I emailed him back right away.

Tess: We'll be there.

I tucked the phone in my bag, determined not to be swayed tomorrow by those baby-blue eyes or his sexy-as-hell ass. I planned to keep it all business.

"Okay, it's all set. We're meeting him tomorrow."

"Let's take our dear brother up on his offer, then," Skye said.

"Yes. Hey, here's a thought. Why don't we go to the same place Heather took Avery? Think they're still there?"

"For sure," Ryker replied.

"Perfect. That way I get to see Avery too and give her the gift myself. I need extra cuddles tonight."

8

LIAM

The first thing I did upon arriving at my office the next morning was download the document Tess had sent me on my computer. I'd only read her email last evening, asking for a face-to-face meeting. I stared at the PDF, scrolling to the end of it. Sixty-five comments. They were roasting our ass worse than anyone we'd done business with.

I tapped my fingers over my desk. I had a bad feeling about this. Mentees who wanted to negotiate every line of the contract were a time-suck. But I wasn't prepared to let go of Tess without a fight.

"Not of Tess, of Soho Lingerie," I corrected myself. This was about bringing in another solid company for our portfolio.

There was no time to go through all the comments, but I started reading them anyway. At five to eight, Dexter poked his head inside the office. I hadn't even heard him come in. The brownstone had been empty when I arrived at seven.

"Liam, Tess is here."

"Just Tess?"

"Yes."

"Okay, show her in. Thanks."

I stood up, pacing around my desk.

When Tess stepped into my office, I couldn't help drinking her in. Her body was just perfection. She was wearing a black skirt and white shirt that were snug around her generous curves. *Is she wearing one of their sexy-as-hell designs?* I couldn't ignore the way her curves looked in her pencil skirt or how damn attracted I was to her.

This was one of the reasons why I kept my personal life separate from business. Yes, personal chemistry was necessary for a good business relationship. But when I said chemistry, I meant being on the same page, not wanting to kiss her until she moaned every time I saw her.

But I wasn't going to fight my attraction to her any longer. I already knew I wanted her. "Good morning, Tess. Is Skye joining us too?"

"No. She was supposed to, but her son wasn't feeling well this morning, so she went to the doctor with him."

"I hope it's nothing serious."

"She doesn't think so."

"Let's sit. Do you want any coffee? Water?"

"I'm good, thank you. Let's get straight to it."

She'd barely sat down when she took a stack of papers out of her bag. A second later, I realized it was the agreement with all sixty-five comments. She wanted to go through every point in person.

This woman was killing me.

"I want us to clarify the points I marked," she said the second I sat down.

"Tess, going through all those comments will take hours. I only have forty minutes."

She stared at me, pressing her lips together. "Then why did you agree to this meeting?"

"I hadn't opened the document when I replied. I assumed

there were a few big things you wanted to negotiate. I like discussing delicate issues in person. I told you we don't invest in companies; we invest in people. We believe in interpersonal relationships, in building trust and having the right chemistry."

I was sure that would earn me points, even charm her a little. It didn't. She glanced down at the stack of papers.

"Well, personal chemistry or not, a contract is what dictates the terms of a collaboration." She tapped her pen against the papers, looking back up at me. Her eyes were full of fire and determination. She wasn't going to ease into this.

I pinned her with my gaze, letting her know I could play just as tough.

"Those are standard terms in this industry but also negotiable."

"That's exactly what I'm here to do. Negotiate."

"Tess, I've read the first twenty comments. Your position isn't that of someone who wants to negotiate. It's of someone who doesn't want an investor at all."

She straightened up, rolling her shoulders. "I just want a fair deal," she said after a beat.

"You think I'm out here to scam you?"

Her determination faltered for the first time, vulnerability replacing it. I was on to something that explained her overly defensive behavior. I wanted to get to the bottom of this.

Every instinct in me wanted to move to the other side of the table and sit next to her, to touch her and reassure her in every way possible, but I didn't want this to turn personal. Not yet, anyway.

"No, I don't think that," she replied softly.

"Talk to me, Tess. Did someone try to scam you before?"

She sighed, crossing her fingers in her lap. "In the early days, yes. And then a few years ago, an investor was interested in us. He pulled out at the last moment, and we'd already promised our suppliers that we were growing our business, and as such, they prepared for more orders. Needless to say, it gave us headaches."

And no doubt it left them with a sour taste too.

"Tess, I'm not here to make false promises or scam you."

"I think you're out to maximize your profits."

"Everyone who pursues business is. Profit maximization does not come at the expense of the entrepreneurs." I looked her in the eyes. "Tess, why don't we schedule another meeting, one where I can allot a few hours and where Skye can attend as well?"

"Okay."

"Also, I've noticed that some of your comments are about legal lingo. I can give you the number of our lawyers, or you can ask one you trust. That way, we save time and focus on the important points."

"We have a lawyer in the family. I'll arrange for that." She nodded, rising from her chair.

I wasn't ready to end this.

"Tess, I have a proposition for you. Let's grab breakfast together. No talking shop, just getting to know each other."

"Why?"

"I want you to trust me, and we're not going to get there just by negotiating."

"Well, that's true. This is going even worse than I imagined."

"How did you imagine it?"

"Never mind."

"Tess, every time you do that, you make me even more curious. You know that, right?"

She gave me a small smile, and I took that as a good sign that we were moving from enemy territory to a more neutral place.

"You were saying about breakfast?"

"I know a few great places nearby."

She nodded, placing the stack of papers in her bag.

I led her out of the office right away, not wanting to give her time to reconsider. Putting a hand at the small of her back, I guided her down the corridor.

"Wait, didn't you say you only have forty minutes?" she asked.

I leaned in, bringing my mouth to her ear, clamoring to be closer. "I'll clear my schedule for you, Tess."

"Ah, you'll clear it for breakfast but not for discussing the contract?"

"As I said, it's best if Skye is here too when we go through it. For breakfast, however, I want only you."

She turned her head, looking straight at me. "But—"

"No but."

"If you have work—"

"I'm taking the morning off, and we're going to eat breakfast. No discussion."

She chuckled. "And you think this is the way to convince me you'd make a good business partner?"

"What is the way, Tess? Tell me."

"I don't know," she whispered, pressing her lips in a thin line.

The urge to kiss her just slammed into me. I barely kept from leaning in even closer. That was not the way to win her trust.

On the way out, I stopped by Dexter's desk.

"Dexter, cancel my next meeting."

His jaw dropped, but he had the good sense not to contradict me.

Once we stepped outside the brownstone, I mentally reviewed the nearest eateries.

"I know a place with great cheese. Your favorite food, right?"

Tess sighed. "Liam, charming me is not on the table."

"We said no talking shop, so charming you is absolutely on the table. How else can I win you over?"

I was far too close again, touching her lower back.

Tess drew in a sharp breath, pointing at me. "You're flirty again."

"Yes."

Her mouth formed an O, and it took all my willpower not to lean in even closer. What was it about Tess that made me so impulsive? I was calculated and liked to plan everything, yet I canceled a meeting at the last minute without a second thought.

"Don't. It can get messy."

"I agree. But I can't stop myself. Every time I see you, I tell myself I'll do better. And every time, I fail."

"Liam..." She shook her head, glancing around. "So, where's that breakfast place?"

"Come on, I'll show you."

After a five-minute walk, we reached a small restaurant that could only seat about ten people at a time. David, Becca, and I were regulars here. Besides the great food, the vibe was also relaxing with armchairs next to floor-to-ceiling shelves full of books. I led Tess to a round table in one of their nooks. We had complete privacy here. She hesitated, looking down at her feet, fidgeting in her spot.

"What is it?" I asked.

"Okay, so I've thought about it. Charming is on the table. But nothing else."

"Are you sure?" I teased.

"Yes. This is about establishing trust, and—"

"I meant are you sure you can keep it to just being charming? What if your inappropriate side kicks in?"

"Liam..."

"You're lucky I find that side of you adorable."

She blushed but held my gaze, as if determined to make a

point. After a few seconds of eye contact, she looked down, twiddling with the strap of her bag.

I spoke in her ear. "Sit down, Tess. Let's order food."

I didn't want to make any promises, because I was sure I'd break them all. Outside the confines of the office, it was even more difficult to keep this insane attraction in check.

I heard her sharp intake of breath before she sat in one of the chairs. I sat in the other and ordered my usual selection when the waiter came.

Tess asked for a cheese platter and some special coffee with many extras.

"Let me just check on Skye," she murmured once the waiter left, typing on her phone. "She was supposed to be done by now. I really hope it's nothing serious."

Damn, this woman was too sweet.

After a moment, her phone chimed, and she focused on the screen. She smiled from ear to ear, sighing. "Yes! She just typed back. Doctor confirmed it was just colic. He's okay, just cranky."

"Is he your only nephew?"

"Yes. I have a niece named Avery and also another niece, the daughter of my brother-in-law's sister."

"I'm losing track."

She grinned. "Already? I didn't even give you a rundown of the whole family."

"How big is it, exactly?"

"Well, there's Skye and me, obviously. My brother Ryker and my other brother Cole. Our cousin Hunter also lives in the city."

"Big family."

She nodded. "Oh yeah. And it just keeps growing with everyone getting married and giving me nieces and nephews."

She lit up completely. I didn't think I'd ever seen her smile like this.

"Speaking of your family...I did some digging because I kept thinking your last name sounded familiar. Your family organizes the Ballroom Galas."

"Yes."

Even though the events were raising funds for charities, the family was known to have a lot of money.

"I know we said we don't want to talk shop, but your cousin Hunter runs one of the biggest real estate companies. Why don't you ask your family for funding?"

She shook her head. "I don't want to mix family and money."

"Fair enough. I respect that."

"How about you?" she asked. "Just you and your grandmother?"

"My parents too, but they're never here. They're wildlife photographers and travel constantly. I think they're in New York about ten days per year. I grew up with my grandparents, but my grandpa passed away a few years ago. Since then, I'm keeping a closer eye on Gran. She's a strong woman, but since Grandpa passed, she's having a hard time."

"She was used to sharing her life with someone for decades. Perhaps she's feeling a bit lost since it's just her. If they were two peas in a pod, then I think her life is a bit out of balance. It can take time to find a new purpose."

"That's exactly it. She's feeling unbalanced. It takes time to reacclimate yourself after you lose someone."

Her remark was surprising. Not only because she was spot-on, but because she'd understood Gran's situation so quickly. Tess was like me in many ways.

"Gran's been trying out new things that she wouldn't before. She still loves some of her old favorite pastimes, like playing chess. I've been letting her beat me too often. Thought it might improve her mood."

We both chuckled at that, and then Tess said, "Wouldn't have thought you had it in you, with all your rules and everything."

"I always have clear lines for everything. I don't cross boundaries. But you have no idea how many times I've thought about breaking my own rules since meeting you."

Tess laughed but immediately brought her cup to her lips. When the cheese platter arrived, she dug right into it.

"Someone was hungry," I teased.

"I only had time for a quick coffee this morning."

"So you came to my office hungry and semi-sleepy?"

"Hangry, more likely. And not too sleepy. I was full of adrenaline. I got up very early this morning and worked on a few bra designs we're testing now. Trying all of them on was a bit too much for my sensitive skin. It's red all around—" She groaned. "Too much information. Why do I always make a fool of myself around you?"

I chuckled at her dismay, because honestly, I was thrilled she was so comfortable around me. "It's part of your charm."

She was so open and unrestrained when we weren't talking shop. But when we talked seriously about business, she put up a wall. I wanted to get past it, but for now, I was enjoying our breakfast. So much, in fact, that I was starting to think it would be better if we didn't strike a deal. Then I could just ask her out without worrying how it might impact our collaboration.

Tess was a fun conversationalist, easy to talk with, and I enjoyed that about her. We were talking about our favorite restaurants, and I loved finding out how similar our tastes were. Tess had ordered a pancake with maple syrup too, and I liked watching the syrup escape her mouth as she brought out her tongue to capture the sticky droplets.

After she finished, I asked, "Are you in a hurry?" We asked for the bill, but the server hadn't returned yet. We both rose to our feet, allowing someone else to take the table while we waited.

"Yes, I am actually. I have an appointment with a supplier."

"Damn, I was hoping I could get you to tell me about your outrageous celebrating habits," I teased.

She tilted her head, her cheeks heating with a lovely shade of red. "We aren't there yet. You have to work harder for that information."

God, I loved our banter. "Careful, Tess. I'll take you up on it. Work so hard for it that you'll have no choice but to..."

"What?"

"Give in."

She licked her lips, probably enjoying the lingering sweetness that was still there, then twiddled her thumbs. It was all I could do to prevent myself from pulling her into my arms. "Liam...I don't like mixing things up."

"By the looks of it, you're kicking us to the curb, so that won't be a problem."

I was grasping at straws, but I wasn't giving up; I needed to kiss her too badly. She wrinkled her nose, drawing in a deep breath. I just had to ask, "Tess...are you seeing someone?"

"What? Why would you ask that?" Her response was almost defensive.

"Because I want to kiss you so damn bad, and I don't like to share."

"No, I'm not seeing anyone."

I leaned into her the next second, pressing my mouth against hers. The moment she parted her lips, an urge to claim her slammed into me.

I wanted to kiss this woman until she didn't see anything other than me, until she wanted no one but me.

I savored her lips before deepening the kiss, needing to explore her in all the ways possible. She whimpered deliciously, and I couldn't hold back any longer. I wrapped one hand in her hair, keeping her as close as possible as I inhaled her response. I skimmed my other hand down the side of her body, lingering on her waist. She rolled her hips, pressing herself against my already stiffening cock, and I groaned, tightening my grip on her waist. I wanted to touch more of her, all of her, and taste her everywhere too.

The sound of someone clearing their throat broke the moment. I stepped back, drawing in a deep breath. Tess pressed her lips together. Her cheeks were red.

The server was looking between us. "I have your bill ready."

Tess reached out for it, but I caught her wrist midair, pinning her with my gaze.

"I've got it. This morning is on me, Tess. All of it."

9
TESS

"Oooh, you brought me goodies. Gimme, gimme. Wait, is that fruit? No, no. You can keep that. I want the scones," Skye exclaimed. I'd gone to her house in the suburbs after the meeting with the supplier, buying snacks along the way.

I laughed. We'd had the same conversation since Skye was a kid. I'd never been successful in convincing my sister to choose fruit over treats, but that didn't keep me from trying. Her eyes were a bit swollen, but other than that, she looked like her usual self. Jonas was okay; he'd just had colic and kept her up. Her brown hair was wild around her head, and she was smiling broadly.

"Can I cuddle him?" I pointed to my nephew.

"He just fell asleep. I'm afraid he'll wake up if I move him." Jonas was soundly asleep in a small mobile crib next to the couch where she was sitting.

I pouted but didn't insist. I'd fallen hook, line, and sinker for him from the first moment I held him. He was tiny and cute, and that newborn smell still hadn't changed. Whenever I visited

Skye, I was glued to him. I really wanted a small bundle of joy for myself. At thirty-five, my biological clock was ticking.

"How was the meeting with Liam? You didn't text me."

"No, I thought it best to just tell you everything in person."

I sat next to her on the couch, opening the bag of scones and putting it between us.

"Oh no. The meeting didn't go well," Skye murmured suddenly.

"How can you tell?"

"You've got guilt written all over you."

"Skye, honestly, I didn't mean to roast his ass. I wanted to go through all the notes I made on the contract, and he didn't. He was all broody and full of swagger."

"Wait a second. There's more to this."

Damn, my sister was giving me that *knowing* eye.

I sighed, pressing my chin to my chest. "Yes, we went to breakfast, all his idea. Liam suggested that getting to know each other would make it easier to build trust. And it seemed a good idea, since business-wise we're at odds."

"But?" Skye questioned, drawing the word out. She knew me too well.

"We ended up kissing." I said it all so fast that it was a wonder she understood me.

Skye gasped before grinning. "You what? Oh, Tess."

"I know." My face warmed. Ugh, I knew I was turning red.

She continued prodding me while I tried to calm myself. "I mean, I was teasing you about him looking at you with sexy intentions, but I didn't think you'd actually kiss him."

"Neither did I. Can we please forget about it?"

Skye wiggled her eyebrows. "If you insist."

"I do. I feel guilty enough as it is."

"I just have one question."

"Shoot."

"On a scale from one to ten, how good was it?"

I threw one of the fluffy pillows from the couch at her and then squeezed another one to my chest. Skye was a pillow freak.

"Ten all the way," I confessed. How could I lie? She was my sister, after all.

She opened her mouth, but I pointed at her. "You said one question. That's it."

She narrowed her eyes, shrugging. "Okay. So, what are the next steps?"

"Well, he suggested you and I talk to a lawyer about all the legal stuff we've highlighted and then meet again with him to discuss our business concerns."

"That makes sense. A lot of our questions were of legal nature. Harrington & Co. certainly has a detailed contract."

"I've already messaged Josie. She said she has time at three o'clock." That was in two hours. Josie was not only our cousin's wife and our best friend but also a fantastic lawyer.

"Okay, we can review the document until then," Skye suggested.

"That's what I thought too."

We analyzed it right until it was time to talk to Josie. We spent two and a half hours on the phone with her, going through the contract line by line, and she was extremely helpful. The first time I read it, I flagged everything that sounded even a little bit vague. I could see now how that could annoy anyone. Josie patiently explained every legal question we had in layman's terms, which was exactly what we needed.

In the end, we reduced the number of issues we wanted to discuss with Liam from sixty-five to eighteen. Josie also pointed out that they had a silent partner, Albert McDowell, and encouraged us to ask what his involvement would be. I was worried about the clause that said they could pull out of the deal within six months in case of force majeure, but Josie assured me that was just a precaution and the chances of that happening were slim.

"You still have some work ahead of you until you can reach an agreement though," Josie commented, "but I think you're on the right track. They're offering you a solid deal, ladies. If you can smooth out those few things, you should have a great partnership."

"I think so too," Skye said.

"Thanks so much, Josie," I told her sincerely. Just having her approval made Skye and me feel more comfortable. I could see my sister's relief in her posture, and I'm sure it was reflected in mine.

"I'll keep my fingers crossed for you two," she added before disconnecting the call.

I turned to Skye. "Okay, so I'll email Liam, since I was the one who met with him."

"And you kissed him."

"Well, technically, he kissed me."

She was smiling. Hell, *I* was smiling, because I usually *lived* for details, and I recounted every date, even painted a vivid picture of any guy I liked. But things were complicated with Liam.

I sent him an email right away, asking for another meeting and attaching the version of the document Skye and I had worked on.

"Okay, this was a productive day!" she exclaimed.

"I know, right? Want me to peel some of those oranges?" I pointed to the untouched bag I brought.

Skye pouted. "I say we're productive and you want to celebrate with fruit, not scones? Who are you, and what have you done with my sister?"

"Well, I was just trying to do the right thing."

Before I could add anything else, Rob arrived.

"Hey, Tess."

"Hey."

He kissed my sister and his son, then stared at the bag of fruit.

"Tess, you brought that?" he asked.

"Yup. Couldn't talk her into eating any, though. Maybe you can help me convince her?"

He nodded. "Leave it to me."

"Oh great. Now you're ganging up on me," Skye griped.

I winked at Rob before standing up from the couch. It was time for me to go. As much as I loved spending time with them, I didn't want to be a third wheel or impose.

My heart gave a mighty sigh watching the three of them just *being* so happy together. One day, I was going to have a little family of my own; I was sure of it.

I was pretty hopeful and romantic, even though my dating life wasn't giving me reasons to be that way. But hey, being positive and optimistic had always been my way of life, and it helped propel me in difficult times, such as when we'd just opened the store and worked crazy hours.

I had a lot of love to give—though sometimes I thought it was too much and it might be overbearing—and I wanted to share it with someone.

I headed straight home afterward, and just as I entered my apartment, my phone buzzed.

It was my brother Cole. I plugged in my earbuds before answering so I could go about taking off my shoes and my coat. Even though it was only the third week of September, the weather had changed fast.

"Hey, Sis," he greeted.

"Hey!"

"I have a question for you, and you can of course say no."

"That's a strange way to start a conversation."

"As you know, Laney and I finally set a wedding date. We've also found a wedding planner, but we'd love your input in the organization. You did such a great job with Josie and Hunter's wedding—"

"Yes, yes, yes! I accept your invitation to be your secondary wedding planner," I practically screamed into the phone. That was me, the perpetual planner, and I *loved* it.

"I knew you'd be psyched."

"I don't know if you can hear me grinning, but I'm grinning." I strutted deeper inside my entrance hall with a little shimmy in my hips.

"You have great taste, and I know your organizational skills are the best. We would have asked you to oversee everything, but you have enough on your plate as it is."

I pouted. "I really do, but thanks for the vote of confidence."

My brother proposed to his fiancée on the Fourth of July, and they'd recently decided on the wedding date.

"I'll discuss some things directly with your wedding planner so you don't have to explain things twice," I said.

"Thanks for doing this."

"My pleasure." Did I mention that I *loved* planning weddings? I helped with our cousin's but had been too caught up with the store when Ryker got married. That one ended up being a double wedding, because Skye had just discovered she was pregnant, so I was even more upset that I hadn't been involved in the planning. I had plenty of experience in organizing events, because my family hosted a few charity events each year. They were elaborate galas we held in a ballroom, and weddings were similar, except there was so much *heart* in them. I couldn't wait for Cole's.

After ending the call, I took out my laptop and made myself comfortable in the chair in my living room. I loved my home. The apartment was nothing special except that it was the right size for me and had become my very own relaxation oasis. It was a mix between bohemian and hippie, with bamboo coffee tables and dining set and frilly, colorful pillows stacked on the couch and the armchair. I had a huge bow lamp hanging right overhead in a mix of brass and silver. My armchair was one of those fancy ones with a remote. I lifted my legs, leaning all the way back and starting the massage function while I searched for wedding locations online.

I was startled when my phone vibrated on the armrest. Glancing down, I saw it was a message from Liam.

Liam: Tess, I can shift things around in the afternoon. Does five o'clock work?

I double-checked with Skye first, who replied instantly that it was okay.

I texted Liam next.

Tess: Yes, five o'clock works for both of us. How much time do you have? I think we'll need two solid hours.

Liam: I've cleared the whole evening. We can go to dinner after that.

Hmm. Did he mean this as a business dinner…or not?

Tess: Skye has to be back home right after the meeting.

Liam: You and I can go. I know a great place for dinner. And another kiss.

And just like that, my whole body was on fire. I smiled, pressing a fluffy pillow against my chest.

Tess: I don't think that's a good idea.

Liam: The dinner or the kiss?

Tess: Both.

The next time my phone buzzed, it was with an incoming call.

"If I take the kiss out of the equation, is that a yes to dinner?" he asked.

"My God, you're a great negotiator."

"I know." The sudden roughness to his voice did nothing to help me stay strong.

"Liam...let's just focus on getting to an agreement tomorrow, okay?"

After a brief pause, he said, "Whatever makes you comfortable."

"Thanks." I kind of hoped he'd press me more, because I knew it wouldn't take much to make me say yes, but honestly, this was for the best. I still wasn't sure how we could work together and date. But I wanted it so, so much.

"What are you doing right now? I can hear you clicking. Tell me you're not adding more comments to the document." His tone changed to teasing, and I had to chuckle.

"I'm not. Just clicked on an article that claims it's the ultimate source for wedding planners."

"You double as a wedding planner?"

"Only for my family. My brother asked me to oversee the preparations for his," I explained, bursting with pride. "I can't wait."

"You're a fascinating creature," he said softly. "See, details like these just make me want to take you out to dinner even more. And ki—"

"Liam!" I interrupted before he finished that word. I was smiling from ear to ear. Could he hear that in my voice? "No talk about dinner or our breakfast or any other activities tomorrow, okay?"

"Activities," he repeated in an amused tone.

"Yes. I'm not big on rules, but I think it's sensible to just focus on one thing at a time."

"I agree. And as you know, I'm all about rules. The problem is I keep wanting to break them when I'm around you."

10

TESS

The next afternoon, I arrived first at the brownstone, and one of the interns showed me into Liam's office. He wasn't inside, though.

Skye came in two minutes later, winking at me. We sat in front of his desk waiting. My nerves were already stretched thin, and this didn't help. I kept tugging at the hem of my black dress. It must have shrunk in the wash—or maybe I'd been eating too many scones.

The second he entered the room, I felt a shift around me, as if the air charged. I turned around slowly. My heartbeat intensified when our gazes met.

Skye was closer, and he shook her hand first.

"Skye, I'm glad you could make it today."

"Life with kids is just one surprise after another."

He extended his hand to me, and I shook it.

"Good to see you again, Tess." The way he said my name made me even more aware of him. Damn. I refused to react to him this way.

Liam went on. "As I told Tess last time, the contract is open to negotiation, but discussing every line you highlighted wasn't a productive use of our time. I appreciate that you narrowed down the list of questions."

"We like to be thorough and wanted to bring everything to your attention," Skye said.

"The questions we removed, we reviewed with a lawyer, and we're now fine with those items," I added.

He nodded. "It's good to cover your bases."

"We have a question about your silent partner. What is his involvement?" I asked.

"Zero," he said immediately. "He's just that, a silent partner. We pay him, but he isn't involved *at all*."

We began discussing every point after that. Liam had printed a handout for each of us. I took a pen out of my bag, making notes in the margin. Skye did most of the talking until we reached paragraph seventeen. I was carefully avoiding Liam's eyes, because I wanted to focus fully on this, and I happened to lose track of my thoughts when our gazes crossed.

"It states here you want us to decide on the number of designs we want to develop at the start of every quarter. This is not how we do things," I said.

He leaned back in his chair, looking between the two of us. "Okay, walk me through your process. I want to know."

This was encouraging. "We always keep in mind what excited our customers the previous season, as well as what brought in the most sales, and we build on that. But we can't tell beforehand how many products we want. We may have a general idea, but that often changes. What if we just decide the overall budget together, and you leave the number of designs to us?" I asked.

"That could work." Those deep blue eyes pinned me without mercy. I became hyperaware of every inch of my body. Not even Skye's presence seemed to help diffuse the strange tension in the air.

We went through the next few paragraphs with a fine-tooth comb. Liam was calm and collected, explaining the reasoning for every demand and agreeing to discuss the changes we wanted with Becca and David.

We finished the document hours later. Skye clapped her hands, checking her watch.

"This is perfect timing. I'm just going to step outside really quick to call and check on my son, okay?"

"Sure. Take your time, Skye."

My sister stepped out of the room, and I suddenly realized I'd been wrong. The tension instantly magnified until it was so thick I didn't know how to act.

Liam's eyes were trained on me. They were dark, sinful, demanding. He watched me silently for a few seconds. My skin simmered under his focus. My mouth suddenly felt dry.

"You seemed very opposed to this partnership last time."

"No, I'd just been a bit overstressed reading the contract, but now Skye and I are on the same page."

"You shouldn't agree to this just for your sister's sake. You have to want this too."

"I know. I do."

He tilted his head, as if he wasn't quite convinced.

"You have very good arguments for everything you want," I said. "Besides, you grew on me a bit yesterday during that delicious breakfast. I liked that you were open and didn't mind sharing personal details."

"I liked our breakfast too. And the kiss."

My breath caught and my pulse went into overdrive.

"Liam...we set rules, remember?" I whispered.

"You broke them first."

I narrowed my eyes. "I just brought up breakfast."

"Really? And I thought breakfast was code for kiss and you were paying me a compliment."

He stood up from his chair and moved around the desk until he was just a few inches away from me. His eyes were relentlessly trained on me.

I searched my brain for a safe topic. "When will we receive the revised contract?"

"I'll discuss all your comments with David and Becca, and draft a new contract by the end of the week. I'll send it to you as soon as I have it."

"Thanks."

"Tess...don't sign anything if you're not 100 percent sure it's what you want. Not even for Skye's sake."

"Don't worry; I won't."

"By the way, I'm still waiting for your assessment of our...breakfast."

I laughed even though my heartbeat was intensifying again. "You just can't stick to the rules, can you?"

I rested one hand on the back of a chair. He leaned in slightly, covering my hand with his. Oh my God. My skin was on fire. My mind just went blank. This slight touch was enough to remind me how delicious the kiss had been. It made me long for more. All I wanted to do was touch and kiss him.

But one thing at a time. This was a business meeting.

"I could...but why do that when the alternative is so enjoyable?"

A knock startled me. Skye opened the door, poking her head inside.

"Call is over. Did I miss anything?"

"No, Liam was just telling me that he'll send us the modified contract soon," I said. Skye nodded before tapping on her phone, probably ordering an Uber. I turned to Liam, asking, "Is there anything left to discuss?"

He gave me a knowing smile. Stepping closer, he said in a

low voice, "Many things. But I know how to bide my time. Strike at the right moment."

Liam

"You cheater," my grandmother exclaimed later that night. "You're letting me win. How long has this been going on?"

She'd just declared checkmate before her outburst. Instead of coming up with a smart answer, I asked, "What gave me away?"

"Liam Harrington, I raised you better."

"You didn't, though. Remember how you always pretended to need more time than me for puzzles?"

"You were seven."

"True."

We were in the winter garden of her penthouse, our usual place for chess. She drummed her fingers on the marble table, shaking her head.

"Something's up with you," she said.

"How can you tell?"

"You've been fake-losing for years, and this is the first time I caught on. Means you're off your game."

"I was bound to give myself away at some point." Gran was very intuitive.

"Trouble in paradise? You, David, and Becca always made such a good team."

"No, we're good. We're in the process of signing a deal."

"That's right. And you haven't talked my ear off about all the exciting companies you're going to take on. I wonder why."

Possibly because I'd been too consumed with one particular mentee. I'd been thinking about Tess ever since she left my office.

"We're just taking on one this year. It's in fashion." We already told the others that they weren't in the running anymore, except our second choice. If Tess and Skye decided not to sign, we were going with DesignPen.

Gran sipped from her glass of wine. "Fashion? You rarely take on anything in that industry. I believe this would only be your fifth investment."

"That's right."

That was one of the things I loved most about my grandmother. She didn't ask questions just to make conversation. She listened and remembered.

"It's good to spread risk and challenge ourselves," I went on.

"Good for you. You know who else likes challenges? I do. Liam, you don't need to coddle me. I've been through a rough time, and I came out on the other side. You certainly don't have to lose on purpose. I like a good challenge. You know that."

To a stranger, my grandmother would appear no older than her sixties. Her hair was dyed black and always cut to her chin—it was her Chanel look, as she often told me. She was agile in movements and quick in wit, and if you didn't know her, you'd think she never had a difficult day in her life, let alone that she lost her husband. But I wasn't a stranger, and I was observant. She still kept the painting of a sunset in Santorini because he'd liked it so much, even though she hadn't. She was still adjusting, just as Tess had said. I missed Grandpa too, every single day. He'd been a larger-than-life character, always up for a challenge, always stoic. He was a man of few words and rarely expressed any emotions.

He never shied away from doing handiwork around the apartment. I aspired to be like him my whole childhood. He worked on Wall Street as the director of a bank. I wanted to step into his shoes, which was why I started working on Wall Street right after college. I realized it hadn't been for me even before we sold the app. I just didn't fit in that environment. I liked playing by my own rules. I always thought he might be disappointed in me for veering off my original career track, but the day I told him I was leaving Wall Street, he said, "Everyone has to find their own way. There's no shame in that."

"No, you're right," I said. "I'm sorry. I don't know why I did that."

"Because you care about me," she replied simply. "And now, before you leave, I want another game. A real one."

"I promise."

She beat my ass for real this time.

After finishing the game, I headed home. I took out my phone to text Tess about Gran figuring out my chess tactic. I had no idea why I wanted to share it with her, but I just did. I had a dozen messages in the group chat I shared with Becca and David, but I wanted to text her first.

Liam: Gran caught on that I've been letting her win on purpose. It's all your fault.

Tess: Why mine?

Liam: Instead of focusing on the game, I was thinking about you. I still am. Is that crazy? The first thing I wanted to do was share this with you.

Tess: Hmm...this is you biding your time?

Liam: I want to see you. Not in the office, somewhere else.

It was true; I did tell her I'd be biding my time, but I just needed to see her again. Taste her again.

I watched the phone as the words **Tess is typing...** appeared. They stayed on for so long that I wondered if she was deleting and typing again. I could push, suggest a meeting point myself, but I wanted this to be on her terms so she'd be comfortable. I just wanted her; the where and when didn't matter.

Tess: I'm going to a fashion week event in two days. Proenza Schouler. I have one spare ticket, because Skye can't come. Want to join me?

I would have preferred a more intimate setting, but I sure as hell wasn't going to say no.

Liam: Yes. Absolutely.

Tess: Great. My goal is to get some inspiration for designs and network a bit.

Liam: I have other goals. Making you blush. Kissing you. Learning you.

Tess: Be careful what you wish for, Liam. You might get more than you're bargaining for.

I laughed at her unexpected reply. I'd been counting on her telling me I had to behave again, not tease me like this.

Images flooded my mind of Tess and me in a secluded corner, anywhere I could explore her soft skin with my mouth, her curves with my hands. I'd been fantasizing about tasting that perky nipple I noticed on our first encounter. I wanted to please her in every way possible.

Liam: I'm up for anything. Absolutely anything.

11

TESS

The next morning, I woke up to a text from Liam.

Liam: Morning! How's the search for panties going today?

I grinned, remembering that embarrassing conversation.

Tess: Hey…I'd been searching for the phone. Which was under the panties. And I don't start all my mornings like that :)

I didn't confess that I was still in bed. It felt too intimate.

Liam: So I just got lucky?
Tess: Or unlucky. Depends how you look at it.
Liam: When it comes to you, I'm always lucky.

OVER THE NEXT TWO DAYS, LIAM TEXTED ME IN THE MOST unexpected moments, asking me what I was having for lunch or even just what I was doing. He was constantly on my mind.

On the night of the Proenza Schouler show, I was all nervous and jittery as I arrived at Spring Studios on St John's Lane in Tribeca twenty minutes early.

I loved the endless opportunities New York offered, especially when it came to fashion events, and especially Fashion Week—which was more like fashion months, really, with events spread throughout September and October. I felt so fancy in my cocktail dress and light coat. I was shivering a little, because though it was mid-September, it was pretty chilly, but I wasn't going to spend much time outside.

The crowd was thick in front of the entrance. It was a great opportunity to meet important people, but this wasn't the best time for striking up a conversation. After the show, everyone was more relaxed and open. Magazine and industry heavy hitters were all here, but I was leaving the socializing for later. Right now, I was a little starstruck as I spotted Gisele Bündchen and her husband walk in. A few seconds later, I noticed two actors from my favorite superhero movies.

I was so busy trying to spot other celebrities that I didn't notice Liam until he was standing right in front of me.

He was wearing a dark-blue suit and bow tie paired with a white shirt. I couldn't take my eyes off him. He always dripped masculinity and sex appeal, but right then, he was just off-the-charts sexy. The man could easily be the cover model for *GQ*. I wanted to kiss every inch of his skin.

Holy shit, if my thoughts darted down that dirty road so early in the evening, how much dirtier could they get at the end of it?

"Hey! Here's your ticket." Our fingers brushed when he took it from my hand, and I swear I felt that touch in all my intimate places. How was that even possible? I quickly lowered my hand. It wasn't the first time my body reacted to him like that. Every time I saw him, I seemed to become even more susceptible to his touch.

"This is my first time at a fashion show," Liam said.

"Really? It'll be fun. And no talking about the contract, okay?"

"Great. When does the networking start? Now or after the event?"

"After."

"Okay." Abruptly, he looked over my shoulder. "Is that Tom Brady over there?"

I chuckled. "I like that you noticed him first. Most men would see Gisele before him."

He returned his focus to me. "I'm only interested in one woman tonight."

Holy. Shit.

I cleared my throat. "Anyway, Proenza Schouler is very talented. I'm hoping to pick up some inspiration from the theme for my brother's wedding too."

He smiled broadly. "I haven't met anyone who thinks about their family as much as you do."

"I just want to make them happy. So anyway, that's one of my goals. The other is to add any new trends to our customization options."

"I believe I made my goals clear," he said. His eyes smoldered.

I swallowed hard, licking my lips. Oh, I remembered his goals.

Making me blush. Kissing me. Learning me.

Yeah, I read that message until the words were etched in my brain.

"Which one would you like to start with?" I teased. I had no idea what I was doing, but I was enjoying this too much.

His eyes flashed. "Which would you prefer?"

"I get to choose?"

"Of course."

I fidgeted in my spot, biting my lower lip.

"You're nervous," Liam said. "Why?"

He leaned into me, as if inviting me to whisper in his ear.

On impulse, I tilted forward and confessed, "I'm not sure what I'm doing."

Laughing softly, he straightened up. "How about we just figure it out as we go?"

"Hmmm...sounds risky."

Liam was silent for a beat, just pinning me with his gaze. "I like you, Tess. I mean it. I like that you're strong and know what you want. I like that you'd do anything for your family even though you have zero time. I like that you asked all sorts of inappropriate questions during the get-together evening and wouldn't let me off the hook until I answered."

Oh wow. If I thought my pulse was quick before, now it escalated to another level. It pounded in my ears, reverberating through my whole body.

Just then, the crowd started to move toward the entrance.

"Let's go inside," I whispered.

"Whatever you wish." His tone was still playful, but his eyes didn't lie. They were still as smoldering as ever.

As we stood in line, he placed a hand at the small of my back. Even through my jacket and dress, I felt that touch as if it was skin-on-skin contact.

After taking off my jacket and leaving it in the designated spot at the entrance, I tried to focus on my surroundings, on anything but the sexy man next to me.

Spring Studios was a glamorous location, perfect for a fashion show. There was a green marble bar to one side with round high seats along the counter. On the opposite side was a huge glass window overlooking Tribeca.

The string of spotlights above cast a pleasant glow in the room. There were five rows of seats on each side of the runway. Liam and I were sitting in the fourth.

Even after we sat and the chatter died away, I was still very much aware of the handsome man next to me.

Focus on the runway, Tess. Focus.

Just a few rows in front were the representatives of giant industry magazines like *Vogue* and *Cosmopolitan*. Every aspiring designer wanted a chance to talk to them, pitch their ideas. But I wasn't one of them. Those publications weren't really our targets. I approached this differently. We contacted fashion and lifestyle bloggers, YouTubers, Instagrammers. Some of the more influential ones scored invitations to these shows, and I was trying to see where they were seated. Some sported at least a tote that showed off their brand, but some were incognito. I did note a few in the crowd though, and I made a mental note to approach them later.

Once the first model strutted out on the runway, I was completely fascinated.

I loved Proenza Schouler. They had a perfect blend of urbanism and feminine delicacy in their collections, sometimes in the same outfit. They paired jeans with silk or even lace. A tiny clutch could completely elevate even the most laid-back outfit.

I was bursting with ideas. As discreetly as possible, I took out my phone. I typed as quickly as I could, hoping my notes would make sense.

After putting my phone away, I focused on the runway again. Liam trailed his fingers up my forearm before placing his arm on my shoulder. Oh Lord. I was hyperaware of every spot where we touched.

"What's next?" he asked after the last model came out. "Already know who you want to approach?"

"I've noticed two influential Instagrammers and a blogger I'd like to meet."

"I've seen an advertising exec I've worked with before. And also the director of *A La Mode*. It's not as big as *Vogue*, but in my opinion, it's a better place for you to advertise. I can introduce you to him."

"That would be great. Thanks."

"Want to go around together? That way we can let them know we might work together. It could help you out if they know you have additional backing."

"We haven't even signed yet and you want me to brag about it?" He was right; that would make a huge difference, but it didn't feel right, since we hadn't sealed the deal.

"I think it'll make some people pay more attention. Besides, I don't want to risk losing you. I have plans for you and me later."

"Oh?"

"Rounds first."

"Then let's win this crowd over, Mr. Harrington."

ALMOST EVERYONE STAYED HUDDLED AROUND THE BAR. The chatter was so loud it sounded like background music. While we walked around, I was extremely aware of my body, as if it suddenly operated at another level. Everything was heightened. He held his hand at my lower back, touched my shoulder or my arm at every turn. The result was that I was on edge the entire time.

I approached my favorite Instagrammer, LorelaiInLingerie, and we spoke a bit about how we could collaborate.

"You're very natural at this," Liam remarked once Lorelai moved to someone else.

"I like socializing. And I like Lorelai's account a lot."

"I could tell. Everyone likes honest praise. And liking to socialize is an important quality in a business owner."

"Am I still on probation?" I asked, batting my eyelashes.

He leaned in, whispering, "Am I?"

I shrugged a shoulder playfully. "Maybe."

"Then let me show you how good a partner I'd make as an investor."

We headed straight toward the owner of the advertising company he mentioned earlier. After introducing us, Liam talked about Soho Lingerie.

"They've got passion in spades, and you can see it everywhere from their products to their customer relationship," he finished.

"Well, that sounds like someone who can take the industry by storm. Drop me an email, Tess. I'll be happy to help you any way I can," Jerry, the head of Eastside Advertising, said.

"Thank you."

We actually emailed Eastside Advertising last year, asking for a proposal, and they replied that they don't work with small shops. I shook my head, smiling to myself. *It's all in who you know.* Now, because an investor was interested in us, they didn't view us as the new kid on the block.

As Liam introduced me to several people he knew, I realized he wasn't trying to sell me on his abilities as an investor—he genuinely believed in our business. We needed him on our team. I swear, I swooned a little every time he spoke about us, and therein lay my problem: Could we collaborate *and* act on this crazy attraction?

"You're tense," Liam whispered.

How could he read my body so well?

I nodded.

"Let's see if my plan will help with that."

A flirty smile played on his lips. His eyes were trained on me, hot and demanding, and my thoughts spun out of control with all the things that plan could involve. He brought a hand to the small of my back before skimming it all the way up to my neck. My whole body was on edge, as if he just trailed his mouth at the back of my neck, first giving me his lips and then his tongue.

"I'll buy you a drink and convince you to give up all your secrets," he teased.

There was that confidence again. I loved it.

I licked my lower lip, trying to steel myself against the charm that was just oozing out of him. Spending more time with Liam heightened the odds of slipping into risky territory. As it stood, I was already having risky thoughts (How long would it take me to yank the shirt off him and lick all those delicious muscles?) and risky body reactions (My pulse was definitely quickening every time he touched me).

"Sure, why not? I'd like a glass of white wine."

"Sit here. I'll take care of it." He pointed to two empty bar chairs.

"I like the sound of that."

I climbed on one of the chairs, taking out my phone. I reviewed my notes quickly, correcting the words I mistyped while I still remembered what I wrote.

"White wine for the lady," Liam said.

"Thanks. That was fast."

Our hands brushed when I took the glass from him, and I swear I felt that touch all over my body. Damn, I was in trouble.

"So, why are you tense?" he asked, sitting in the chair next to mine. Was I imagining it, or did the chair and Liam seem closer than before? I licked my lips, then sipped from my glass.

"First, let's talk a bit about you," I said. "We always talk about me."

"Let's make a deal. I answer any question you want. And then you answer any of mine."

He was looking at me so intently that there was no way I could say no. I didn't want to, either. I shrugged a shoulder playfully. "Okay. Tell me about you, David, and Becca. Are you just partners or also friends?"

"They're my best friends. We all started working on Wall

Street together after college, and we became very close. We created the InvestMe app more for fun, even though I think we would have left Wall Street anyway. It wasn't our scene. Too many rules and too many standardized processes."

"But you like that. Didn't you have the same list of questions for all applicants?" I teased.

"You sound like David. He always gives me shit about being too...stiff."

"And liking rules? Or breaking them? I'm very confused on that topic." I meant to sound serious, but I was grinning.

He leaned in, bringing his mouth to my ear. "I only like rules when I'm the one making them, Tess. And the only rules I'm breaking are the ones involving you."

I felt every breath of his on my skin, and it seemed almost as intimate as kissing. For a brief second, it seemed we were the only ones in this crazy busy room. Then the chatter ramped up, as if someone had poked the bubble surrounding us.

I cleared my throat, and Liam pulled back. I couldn't take my eyes off him. Everything from the cut of his shirt and suit jacket to the determination in his gaze was dripping with sex appeal. I clasped one hand tighter around my glass and the other around the edge of my chair to keep from touching him.

It was so tempting to find an excuse to just open that top button of his shirt. I mean, wasn't he the least bit warm?

"Why work on Wall Street at all, then?" I asked, pulling myself together. I wanted to know everything about him.

"Growing up, I always wanted to be like my grandfather. He worked on Wall Street almost his whole life."

"Almost?" Something in the way he said that word made me think there was a story behind that.

"Right until he unexpectedly got laid off. He saved enough money, so that wasn't an issue, but he just wasn't the same. He became depressed and just didn't seem like his old self. Then I asked a therapist how Gran and I could help, and he suggested we have strict routines and schedules, like he was used to at the bank. It actually worked. He got better and eventually did start liking his early retirement, but I got used to that sort of strict routine in the process."

I was stunned, to be honest. He'd done all that for his grandfather? I think I fell for him a little right there and then.

"My turn." His eyes flashed. He leaned forward, placing a hand on my knee. Holy shit! My body instantly lit up. My nipples perked up. Heat shot between my thighs.

What is happening to me?

"That's not fair. I have more questions." I pouted, blinking slowly.

"Fuck, Tess, stop with that cute pout or I'll kiss you right here in this bar."

My breath caught. I had no doubt he'd do it.

"Tell me why you were tense earlier." His voice was so demanding that I had no choice but to give in.

"Because I like you so much, and..."

"Talk to me, Tess. Tell me what you're afraid of."

"I'm not even sure."

"You mentioned the collaboration a few times. I promise I'm a professional. No matter what happens, it will not affect my work ethic. If it makes you feel better, David or Becca could even become your primary mentor. You'd only see me in a professional capacity during strategy meetings."

Wow, he really thought about this? Just to put me at ease?

"What else is worrying you?" he asked.

Getting my heart broken. I couldn't say that out loud, though. We hadn't even gone out on a date. I didn't want to scare him away with all my romantic ideas. I'd always been a dreamer and an optimist, but fifteen years of dating taught me it wasn't easy.

"Lots of things, but I really like your suggestions." I couldn't believe he was so considerate.

I started playing with my glass of wine to give my hands something to do. His gaze dropped to my lips, and I could swear he tilted forward a fraction of an inch.

Before he could say anything else, someone knocked into me from behind.

I spilled the glass of wine on my dress, soaking it. I jumped from the chair, smoothing my palms over the fabric out of instinct. It didn't help. Glancing at the woman who knocked into me, I saw her apologetic face along with her grimace.

"I'm so sorry. I'll pay for dry cleaning."

"No need. It could happen to anyone."

"Are you sure?"

"Don't worry about it."

We chatted a bit more before she went on her way, and after she left, I turned to Liam. "I'm feeling cold already. It's soaked all the way through. I need to go home."

"I'll walk out with you."

Putting his hand on the small of my back, he led me out to the entrance where the coat room was. There was a short line, but I received my coat in a few minutes. Thank God, because I was shivering from the cold wind coming in every time someone opened the entrance door.

Liam held my coat, and I tried not to react as his fingers brushed my shoulders while I put it on.

"Not how I pictured our evening ending," he whispered in my ear from behind while I fastened the belt around my middle. "Seems I'll have to put the rest of my plan into motion another time."

My stomach flipped as I turned around, facing him. "It seems so."

Damn wineglass. It was keeping me from a very promising night. But maybe it was for the best.

"Come on. There are cabs outside."

He walked one step behind me, and I swear I could feel his presence even though he wasn't touching me. Once outside, we saw the last two cabs leaving right before our eyes. The concierge of the event assured us a new one would arrive in a few minutes.

"Are you cold?" he asked.

I nodded. I was rubbing my hands because they felt icy. He took them in his, which were warm and felt amazing. I liked this far too much. My breath hitched when I caught him looking at my lips. Holy shit, I suddenly felt warm all over, not just where our hands were touching. I couldn't look away, couldn't do anything to break this spell between us. And the man was warming my hands, for God's sake. Was he trying to make me swoon on purpose?

I had no idea who leaned forward first, but the second his mouth was on mine, I couldn't think about anything else except *him*. His lips were firm and soft at the same time. He was exploring me slowly, as if there wasn't anything else he'd rather do right then than kiss me. As if that was all he wanted to do for the rest of the evening.

Letting go of my hands, he grabbed my waist, holding me tight. When he deepened the kiss, I just couldn't hold back and ran my hands through his hair. Urgency coiled through me. I whimpered involuntarily, and he deepened the kiss. I was aching for him.

The way he kissed me made me feel like I was the only thing that mattered tonight. He pulled me flat against him and feathered his lips down the side of my neck. Every kiss sent little shockwaves of pleasure reverberating through my body. His cologne, juniper and pine, overwhelmed my senses. I slipped my hand under his suit jacket, moving toward the button that had been teasing me all night. I wanted to rip it away, along with all the other buttons. I wanted to—

Loud honking made us jump apart. I blinked for a few seconds, disoriented. Then I noticed the cab and the smirking concierge.

"The cabbie honked three times before you noticed," the concierge informed us.

I wasn't even sorry, because that kiss was worth being honked at.

My legs were a little shaky as I walked toward the car with Liam at my side. He opened the door for me. As I lowered myself into the cab, he tilted forward, kissing my cheek before bringing his mouth to my ear.

"Next time I see you, I'll make sure there won't be any glass of spilled wine or honking cabs getting in our way," he said.

When he pulled back, the promising glint in his eyes was just pure heat, and I was certain that next time, nothing would keep him from going after what he wanted: me.

12

LIAM

I wasn't the type to linger over moments, playing them over in my mind. It just wasn't who I was. But I couldn't forget my evening with Tess. If kissing her felt that way, how would exploring her in bed be? I wanted to keep her with me the whole night.

Spending time with her had been intoxicating. She actually listened to me when I spoke about Grandpa and that tough period of our lives. No one usually asked, and I wasn't used to talking about it, but it felt so easy with Tess.

I sent her and Skye the revised contract that night after the show, but I hadn't heard from them since. Granted, I sent it Thursday evening and today was Monday, but I was getting impatient. I didn't want to be the one reaching out, though. I knew when to push, and I knew when to wait. I wanted the contract to be signed. Then I'd have free rein to pursue Tess.

"You getting old or something? You're running slow today," David said.

We met at seven o'clock three times a week, running before we started the day. We had showers at the brownstone and kept fresh clothes there so we could still be at work at a decent hour.

"No, just have a lot on my mind."

"That hasn't stopped you from beating my ass before."

We always raced the last mile. I wasn't going to let David beat me. He'd never stop bragging about it.

My lungs were struggling with the chilly air. Damn, it was cold for the end of September. If this weather trend continued, I'd only be able to keep up the running routine throughout October and November.

I pushed my thighs to move faster, then even faster on the pavement. I only looked back once I reached the front door of the brownstone. David was right behind me. My whole body was burning, but even that effort didn't drown out thoughts of Tess.

"Only five seconds faster," he said through loud panting. "I'll catch up to you one day."

I punched his shoulder. "No you won't. Let's get to work."

David went to the shower first, and I headed to my office to retrieve the fresh clothes.

When I passed Dexter, he said, "You got a few calls while you were running."

I always left the phone inside when I went on a run, and the intern's first task was to check for any missed calls.

"I'll look at them later."

"But there is—"

I didn't hear the rest of the sentence, because I closed the door to my office. Tess was inside it. That was probably what Dexter was trying to say.

"Tess, what a surprise."

I was drenched in sweat, and my shirt was clinging to me. Tess didn't seem to mind as she slowly looked me up and down. I cocked a brow. She blushed.

Since she was so openly checking me out, I saw no reason to hold back. She was wearing a black dress, the same coat from the fashion show, and stilettos. All I wanted was to strip her of everything...except those red shoes.

"Sorry to barge in here like this, but your intern said you didn't have any appointments this morning."

"What can I do for you?"

She put her bag on the desk, taking a stack of papers out of it and placing them next to my laptop. "Skye and I signed the contract."

"This is great news. Fantastic. But you didn't have to bring them in person."

"I know. I wanted to. I'm just so excited." She clasped her hands together, smiling from ear to ear. "So, what are the next steps? When do we get the ball rolling? When can we show you the space we're thinking about leasing? And start working on the new online shop?"

I smiled, reaching for the gym bag in the corner. Taking out a towel, I put it on my shoulders. "You don't do anything in half measures, do you? First, you roasted my ass, but now that you've signed, you're all in?"

Her smile dimmed a bit. "Yes, well, I am kind of known for doing everything...enthusiastically."

She sounded a bit uncertain. Dropping the gym bag to the floor, I walked closer to her. "I like that a lot about you, Tess. Just as I like everything else. I'll sign this morning, along with Becca and David. Then we can have a general meeting."

"So, should I come back later with Skye? When you...have more clothes on?"

I smirked. "You have a problem with my outfit?"

"Yes. Your abs are on display. You know how distracting that is? All I can think about is touching them. Licking them."

Fuck, is she trying to kill me? I was going to get a hard-on if she continued. Something told me that not only was Tess all on board with the contract, but she'd also made up her mind about us. And she was letting me know in her usual overexcited way.

I stepped even closer. "Tess...you can't say those things to me right now."

"Why not?"

"Because I'm not going to have you on my desk while I'm sweaty from a run."

Her eyes widened before she narrowed them. "I see. So you like flirting, but only on your terms?"

"Yes."

"See, that doesn't work for me." She wiggled her eyebrows. "You don't know how to handle me right now, do you?"

"No," I admitted with a laugh.

She lifted her hand, touching my chest. I clasped her wrist and then the other. Her eyes widened as I held her arms to one side and covered her mouth with mine. She tasted like maple syrup and coffee, and I wanted to taste her all over. I explored her mouth until I felt her squirm, then heard her moan. I held her hands firmly, kissing her on my terms. I also didn't want her touching me like I knew she wanted, because I had a raging hard-on already. She parted her thighs, accommodating me. I groaned in her mouth, letting go of her hands. I needed to explore more than her mouth. And I desperately needed her to do the same with me.

I pulled back only long enough to say, "Touch me. Tess, fuck. Touch me," before kissing her again.

She slipped her hand between us, touching my erection. I nearly exploded at the contact. She teased me, rubbing two fingers up and down. I pressed her ass against the edge of the desk.

This was torture. Pure torture. Kissing her felt so good, but touching her waist and thighs was not nearly as satisfying. She had too many clothes on. I moved my hand lower from her belly, applying pressure as I went farther down. I touched her clit over her clothes, and her knees buckled. She whimpered, tugging at my drenched shirt with her free hand. Then she slipped her hand under it, tracing the lines of my abs with her fingers, just as she'd promised. I was determined not to let her mouth anywhere on my body, because there would be no holding back then.

It wouldn't take much to make her come. She was even more on edge than I was. But I didn't want the first orgasm I gave her to be like this—quick, while she was still clothed.

I wanted it very dirty and very hard, but not here in the office. I moved my hands back up her body. I was learning every curve even over her clothes, and I couldn't wait to explore them again when she was naked. She protested, taking her own hand away as well...but then she rolled her hips, grinding against my erection, and I nearly toppled over her.

"Tess, babe."

She brought her hand to the waistband of my shorts, but I stopped her, looking her straight in the eyes.

"Not here." My voice was rough, like I hadn't used it in a while. I wanted to do things the proper way with her, and a quickie at the office definitely wasn't the way to start things. She deserved better. We were both acting on instinct right now, but I wanted to romance her a little first. I'd never even done that before, but I was certain she'd like it. She was special to me in a way no one had been before.

I pulled away, taking a step back so I wouldn't completely lose my head. "Tonight, I want us to celebrate signing the deal. Just you and me."

She nodded, eyes slightly hooded. I felt victorious. The ink was dry on the papers, and nothing was going to stop me from making Tess mine.

13

TESS

The rest of the day was a little insane. Liam texted me right after I left that they all signed, and we agreed on the following morning for the general meeting. I had Liam on my mind constantly, and there was no getting him out. I still felt his lips on mine, his hands on my body. We agreed to meet at seven o'clock in front of the store, and I might have been counting down the hours...and minutes. I was so giddy!

I thought I'd have all day to play around with customization options and reminisce about that sexy-as-hell way he pushed me against his desk and kissed me like there was no tomorrow.

But in the afternoon, I discovered we had one hundred mismatched orders. Our online shop hadn't recorded some sales. The girls had double-checked all of them and inserted any missing items, but I had to repack them. I was really looking forward to having a better website. This one often crashed or just registered orders wrong. Since the orders had to be shipped tomorrow, I only had today to sort them out. No way was I going to be ready at seven.

I didn't want Liam to think I was playing hard to get, so I snapped a picture of the boxes and sent it to him.

Tess: I don't know when I'll be done with these. Rain check on the celebration?

I smiled when the words **Liam is typing** appeared in the small box. Was he always so fast to respond, or was I getting special treatment?

Liam: No.

Liam: I want to woo you tonight.

Oh my God.

Tess: Don't tempt me. Pleeease.

Liam: Hell yes, I will. Cheese? Champagne? A kiss? My naked abs?

I laughed, holding a hand to my belly. I eyed the pile, then the armchair, and then the phone. Okay, so since I was my own boss, I could allow myself a flirting break. Grinning, I sat down, legs up on one armrest, dangling my feet in the air.

Tess: Is this a negotiation?

Liam: Only if I'm winning.

I shimmied in the armchair. I'd only been looking for a little flirting. How was I simmering already?

Tess: Not how negotiations work.

Liam: Tell me your terms.

Tess: Do they have to include kissing?

Liam: Yes. I'm not budging on that.

I was on pins and needles as I wrote three texts before deciding on one. I pressed Send before I could talk myself out of it again.

Tess: What exactly do I get to decide?

I wasn't just simmering now. I was on fire. I held my breath as the words **Liam is typing** popped on the screen. *What's taking him so long?*

Liam: Where and how many.

Tess: I'll think about the terms and get back to you.

That's right; I could tease too. I could flirt.

My One and Only

Liam: Tess...the longer you wait, the more kisses I'll demand. One for every hour you make me wait.

Holy shit. Clearly, I couldn't beat him. He was a master at this.

Liam: You're not working on those orders alone, are you?

Tess: Yes, I am. Skye is meeting a supplier, and the sales associates are busy with customers.

Liam: Okay. I understand.

I laughed, wondering if I should point out that he told me he'd *demand* more kisses for every hour I took...but perhaps it wasn't the best idea to remind him. Who knew what other *requirements* he'd throw at me.

Liam didn't write anything else, and I was grateful for that, because this man's flirting skills were dangerous enough to make me forget my tasks.

My hands were numb after the first twelve boxes. I was going to be here even after closing time, and I couldn't ask the girls to stay; they'd been on their feet all day and were even more tired than I was.

About one hour later, I heard Liam's voice in the front and jumped to my feet. I told the girls we just signed with him as an investor, so they'd probably send him to me right away.

OhGodOhGodOhGod. My stomach was full of butterflies as I heard heavy footsteps approach. I swear my heart stopped when he entered the back room.

He pinned me with those sinful eyes. Heat flashed through me, and he hadn't even said anything. The man was simply delicious. He was wearing washed-out jeans, a black shirt, and leather jacket on top of it. His hair was disheveled, as if he'd run his hands through it.

"Hello, Tess."

"Hi!"

He was carrying a paper bag.

"What's that?" I asked.

"Tacos. And your favorite champagne. We don't have to go out to celebrate. We can do it here. That way I can also help with the boxes."

"You want to help me?"

"Yes."

"Why?"

"I'm a partner, remember?" His eyes were playful.

"That's the only reason?"

That playful glint turned hot in a fraction of a second.

"And to claim all those kisses I negotiated."

I gasped, covering my mouth. "I forgot to answer."

He winked again. "I know. Lead the way, Tess."

He shrugged out of his leather jacket, leaving it on the back of one of the armchairs.

Surveying the room slowly, he frowned at the pile of finished boxes.

"Tell me you didn't make all of those on your own."

"'Course I did. Easy-peasy. I just have to rotate my wrists a bit. They're stiff."

I flexed them, doing a bit of wrist gymnastics.

Liam put the paper bag on the coffee table in front of the armchairs. I thought he might start on the boxes, but instead he came right for me. He captured one wrist, then the other, pressing his thumbs exactly where I was sore. I closed my eyes, letting my head drop back a bit.

"Mmm, this is too good," I murmured. My whole body was relaxing even though he was only working my wrists. With my eyes closed, my other senses became hyperalert. The faint aftershave smell was wickedly sensual. The heat of his body was just

My One and Only

too much. I blinked my eyes open and almost whimpered when I realized how closely he was watching me.

"Better?" he asked.

"Yes."

"Let's sit down and eat. Then you relax a bit, and I'll get started on the boxes."

"Oooh, I won't say no to that. Let me show you exactly how I do it before we start eating."

Liam gave me a half smile, pointing to the small piles of unfolded cartons.

I tried focusing on the box and not how close he was, or the fact that his lips would brush my ear if I leaned backward just a smidge.

I finished the demonstration as soon as possible, then watched him do the next one.

"Okay, you've passed the test."

"Thanks for the vote of confidence," he said with a laugh.

"Hey, I want our customers to feel important."

He sat in an armchair, and I took out the tacos. There were three of them each packed on a separate paper plate. I also grabbed the bottle and hurried to one of the shelves where I kept champagne glasses.

He laughed when he saw them.

"What? Skye and I like to celebrate milestones. But maybe let's open it once we're done with the boxes."

"You got it, boss."

"There's a thought. Me bossing you around. Hmm...that has so much potential."

He cocked a brow.

"Oops, did I say the last part out loud?" I teased.

"Yeah you did."

"Well, I didn't mean to." He was still looking at me expectantly, so I added, "Hey, let's eat fast so you can start on the boxes. No slacking. I'm the boss, remember?"

Chuckling, he bit into a taco. We both ate in silence, practically inhaling our food.

"These tacos are so good," I said once I was done, putting the empty plate on the coffee table. Liam mirrored my movement, as he finished too. "Kevin's really talented."

Liam stilled. "You know him?"

"Yes."

When I didn't say anything more, he asked, "Did you two... date or something?"

"No. Why?"

"During the 'get to know each other' dinner, I saw a message from him. It had heart emojis."

I blinked, caught off guard. He was looking at me expectantly. I wasn't sure what to say.

"So, we didn't date, but...I did ask him out. He just turned me down."

"What?"

"Said we're better off as friends. So...we're friends, I guess. He keeps asking my advice about how to date other women."

"He's a fucking moron."

I smiled, feeling a bit self-conscious.

Liam rose from his armchair, sitting on the armrest of mine.

"But *you* asked *him* out," he said, more to himself. "Do you still have feelings for him?"

His jaw clenched. His eyes were hard.

"No, of course not. Unless you count feeling inadequate every time he messages me."

Liam cupped my cheek. "Moron. Forget him. Never buying his tacos again."

I laughed, shrugging.

Still eyeing me intently, he moved to the floor, finishing the box. By the time he started the second one, I decided I was done resting and crouched next to him.

"I can do this myself, Tess. Rest for a bit."

"No, no. I'm not a mean boss. I love doing things myself."

"I know. One of the things I really like about you."

My stomach somersaulted. "What else do you like about me?"

He leaned into me sideways, bringing his mouth to my ear. "I could tell you, but then we'll never finish packing."

"That's how little faith you have in me?"

"No, in me. I'm hanging by a thread, Tess."

I was caught up in his spell, unsure what to say.

He pulled back a little, looking me straight in the eyes. "Let's make a deal. We finish packing, and then I'll tell you everything in detail. And then I'll claim those kisses. Every single one of them. What time do your sales associates leave?"

He spoke every word against my lips. I was barely hanging by a thread too.

"Ten o'clock," I whispered.

"We'll be done with the boxes by then." He swallowed hard, looking at me for a few seconds before returning his focus to the task at hand. The next few hours flew by fast, and once ten o'clock passed and the girls left, I doubled my efforts. We only had a few boxes left.

Even though I was bone-tired and my wrists were aching again, I didn't pause or even slow down.

"Someone's in a hurry," Liam whispered playfully.

"You gave me a good incentive."

"The compliments or the kissing?" Once again, his mouth was so close that we were almost touching. My body was completely on edge.

"Not sure," I teased just as I glued the red silk bow to the last box. "All done."

I sat on my ass, legs curled at my side. Liam mirrored my stance. His eyes were pure fire, and I wasn't sure I could navigate this tension between us anymore.

"So...you were saying something about me asking questions?" I whispered.

"Anything you want."

"Elaborate on the things you like about me."

He cupped my cheek. The touch set me on fire.

"How about I first claim all those kisses I want?" he asked.

"You mean those I owe you?"

"No. Those you owe, plus all the extra ones I want."

Holy hell! I was drunk on this man.

I nodded, leaning in until our lips brushed. The second his mouth was on mine, I couldn't even breathe. Emotions rolled into me, and I couldn't tell one from the other. I was consumed by the way his lips felt on my mouth and then the side of my neck. One of his hands went to my waist, the other down my thigh. He feathered his fingers at the hem of my dress where fabric met skin.

Pleasure shot right between my thighs. I whimpered, pulling him closer by the collar. My position wasn't the most comfortable, so I stumbled onto my knees, straddling him rather clumsily. I pressed my knee into his thighs before parting my legs a little wider. His lips curled into a smile *while* he was kissing me. I punched his shoulder lightly. His smile widened at the same time he slipped his hands under my dress. He moved them upward in slow motion until I was trembling in his arms.

Liam was going to rock my world tonight.

14

LIAM

I fucking loved kissing this woman, and I planned to take my time. I liked exploring her, knowing there was no timer on this.

She was mine.

This was better than anything I imagined, and I imagined Tess like this quite a lot. Her body was exquisite. Those toned legs, the trim waist. I couldn't decide what my kryptonite was: her breasts or that round, perky ass. I planned to explore both thoroughly before deciding. Her brown-and-blonde hair was falling around her shoulders, and I didn't hesitate to wrap my hand in it, feeling it silky and smooth between my fingers.

I only stopped kissing her long enough to take off her dress. I threw it to one side, drinking in her slim silhouette and that pearly white skin.

She was seductive with a hint of vulnerability. I wanted to get to the bottom of that. To learn what made her feel that way and change it.

I couldn't believe I was lucky enough to be here with her. But first, I needed to get her somewhere more comfortable. I spotted a couch near the changing rooms.

I pulled back, interrupting the kiss. She jutted out her lower lip and was so damn adorable that I nearly captured her mouth again.

"Up we go, beautiful."

Gripping her ass with both hands, I lifted her off me and then rose to my feet, pulling her up along with me.

I stepped behind her, kissing the back of her neck before tilting her head to one side. I turned rock-hard as I moved my mouth down the side of her neck, then tipped my pelvis forward, pressing my erection against her ass. Tess gasped, rocking right back into me.

"See what you do to me?" I murmured. "You're not even touching me, and I'm losing my mind for you."

She laughed softly before bringing a hand between us and squeezing my erection over my jeans. My vision blurred. I groaned, moving back and forth. She attempted to turn around, but I gripped her hips, stopping her. I quickly discarded my jeans, then the rest of my clothes. I didn't want anything between us. Once I was naked, I kissed down her back, lowering myself until my face was right in front of her gorgeous ass. She was wearing black panties that only covered the upper part of her backside.

I kissed one cheek and then the other before turning her around and looking up at her. I skimmed my thumbs up her inner thighs, right until I reached the hem of her panties. Her skin was pebbled with goose bumps. She sucked in a breath. The muscles in her stomach contracted. I liked seeing her like this, barely able to breathe from anticipation. Looking her straight in the eyes, I stroked my thumb over the fabric. Her knees wobbled as she gripped my shoulders with both hands. I wasn't just rock-hard now. It was painful.

I grabbed my cock, squeezing, looking for some relief. I

found none. I needed her to touch me, but later. Now, it was all about her.

I tugged at the waistband of her panties, pulling them down, then patted the edge of the armchair, directing her, "Put your foot up here."

She did just that, opening herself up to me. I kissed up her inner thigh, slowing down as I neared the apex. I smiled when she threaded her fingers through my hair.

I pressed the flat of my tongue against her clit. At the same time, I strummed my fingers against her opening. Tess moaned, tugging harder at my hair. Her soft flesh was drenched. She was ready for me already, but I wanted to bring her even closer to the edge.

I wanted to sensitize her so much that when I entered her, she'd barely be able to breathe from the pleasure. I wanted her to get lost in me, but with every touch, I was the one losing myself in her.

I was becoming addicted to her scent, her soft skin, and her reactions to me.

"Liam," she murmured, rolling her hips.

I wanted to make her come with my mouth, but I wanted to kiss her too badly. I needed to feel closer to her. I kissed up her body, stopping right at the edge of her bra. I took it off in a single move and pulled back a few inches. The sight of her naked breasts was enough to drive every instinct in me crazy.

I drew my fingers on the pink skin around her nipples, then traced the same path with my tongue. Tess moaned right before I pulled her to me and captured her mouth. I trailed my fingers down her abdomen, past her navel, until I reached her clit. I coaxed her tongue with mine while moving my fingers in circles around her clit. My erection pulsed, and every inch of my body was on edge. She was inching closer to her climax, her muscles contracting under my touch. The kiss turned more urgent. She was desperately chasing her release.

Then she exploded beautifully, rocking against my hand. She cried out my name, throwing her head back and holding my shoulders tight. There was no sight more extraordinary than Tess overwhelmed by her climax. Her cheeks were flushed, and her legs were shaking slightly. I was holding her firmly with both hands, kissing her neck while she rode out the wave of pleasure. Every instinct in me wanted to claim this woman. When she rocked back and forth from her heel to her toes and then back to her heel, I gave in to that urge.

I needed to be inside her, to completely own her pleasure and thoughts. Hooking my hands under her ass, I lifted her up. She wrapped her legs around me, trapping the tip of my cock between her pussy and my pelvis. I groaned at the shot of desire that rippled through me.

I carried her to the couch between the changing rooms and lowered her onto it.

She glanced at the jacket I draped on the armrest, licking her lips.

"Tell me you have a condom in here." She patted the jacket.

"Yes, I do."

I took the wallet out, holding the condom between two fingers and ripping the package with my teeth. Tess gripped my erection with one hand and held out the other for the condom. I nearly lost my mind when she slowly rolled the condom over my cock. Then I lowered myself between her spread thighs. I smiled when she clenched them, trapping me there.

"Not letting you go," she muttered with a sated smile.

I entered her all the way to the hilt, grunting at how unbelievably good she felt. Tess cried out, her inner muscles pulsing around me, the small aftershocks from the last orgasm. I wanted to intensify her pleasure while I chased my own. I drove in and out of her relentlessly, watching between our bodies. She felt so impossibly good, as if she'd been made for me. Desire rippled through me again, this time in waves. My muscles were burning, but I wasn't ready to succumb to an orgasm yet.

I slowed the pace, smiling against Tess's mouth when she rolled her hips faster, trying to make up for the change in my rhythm, and then I pulled out abruptly. Her little pout was so damn delicious that I almost lost my resolve.

"Turn around," I whispered in her ear.

Eyes wide and still pouting, she complied with my order.

"When you're so close you can't take it anymore, I want you to touch yourself, okay?"

She gasped a little, nodding again. I parted her thighs wider, sliding in hungrily.

"Fuuuuuck!" I gasped. How could this feel even better than before? A burning sensation coiled through me. Every muscle strummed tight. I was walking on thin ice here.

I was learning her body with every touch, memorizing what made her moan or cry out. She had a sweet spot between her shoulder blades and on the back of her neck.

She cried out, moving one hand to her pussy, just like I told her to. It was such a turn-on how she followed every instruction. She gasped in the pillow, calling out my name the very next second, and I was a goner. I started to come even before her inner muscles tightened around me; just the sound of my name from her mouth pushed me over the edge. I pushed in and out of her, every time deeper, then harder, until we both surrendered to our climaxes.

When we were both spent, I lay on top of her, holding my weight mostly on my knees. I caressed the side of her breasts with my fingers as I kissed the back of her neck. Her skin was flushed, her hair a bit sweaty at the nape. Damn, she was a fine sight, sprawled like this, sated and happy.

I moved to one side before lowering myself to the floor.

Tess pouted. "Why did you go so far away?"

"I can see you better."

"But I can't fondle you like this." She rolled over, and I only realized what she was up to when she fell on top of me. We both burst out laughing while she moved into a more comfortable position, half straddling me.

"My clumsy girl."

She grinned. I couldn't stop looking at her, taking in every detail.

"Why are you smiling?" she asked.

"Before, I was wondering if your boobs or ass was my kryptonite."

"And what's the verdict? Wait, hold that thought. I'll bring some wet wipes."

She went to the back room, returning after a moment, and we cleaned off quickly before lying down on the couch.

"So...what was that about your verdict?"

"Don't have one yet. Need to explore you some more before I make up my mind."

"Well, then, I'll tempt you with both, and you can tell me which one's the straw that breaks the camel's back."

Grinning, she turned on her stomach completely, exposing her delicious bottom. I palmed her right ass cheek before moving to the left one.

"You have the most gorgeous ass."

She wiggled it right under my hand. Goose bumps broke out all over her body.

"Okay, I believe this was enough ass appreciation. Time to give the girls some attention so they don't feel neglected."

She rolled on her back, bringing those gorgeous breasts right in front of me. I leaned right in, sucking a nipple into my mouth. She moaned in surprise, and her back arched off the floor.

I pulled back, looking her straight in the eyes.

"I still can't decide," I said as seriously as possible. "I think I'll need several rounds of this."

"That's all right with me. Do I need to be naked or dressed?"

"Naked, of course."

"Hmmm...just wait until you see me in some of my smoking-hot lingerie. You'll change your mind."

A sound escaped my throat as I imagined Tess stripping for me. Hell, I'd be a happy man if she just modeled lingerie for me.

"Oh, that was a growl. How damn sexy. I can't wait to see what you do when I actually wear it. I have a few perfect outfits in mind." She tapped her temple, smiling sassily.

"Come here, you." I leaned over her, kissing her long and deep, until I felt her smile against my mouth.

"It's code red," she taunted.

"What's that?"

"Skye and I have a code. Green means period lingerie. Yellow is normal lingerie. And red is super sexy."

"It's all you wear, isn't it?"

She chuckled. "Umm, no. What I had on today was code yellow." She looked at me and quirked a brow. "Don't give me that look. I wanted to wear red for our first time, but how was I supposed to know you were going to seduce me so shamelessly today?"

"Our morning meeting didn't clue you in? Or the texts today?"

She wiggled against the floor, drawing her fingers down my abs.

"Well, yes...but then I thought I'd have to cancel tonight. But it was so romantic, how you just showed up here and swept me off my feet." She sighed. "Oh, and speaking of our emails and texts, we need some rules." Her expression was serious, but I could tell she was fighting a smile.

"Oh, really?"

"Yeah, maybe a heat code or something. If we go by the one I use for lingerie...we need to keep all our emails code yellow."

"Or what?"

"Or we'll both get distracted and be unproductive."

"Small price to pay. Every fucking message made my day."

"Still, rules are good." Her tone held a hint of a challenge. She was teasing me.

In response, I pulled her under me. Her eyes widened as my lips nearly touched hers.

"I know that. I live by strict rules. But with you, I just want to break all of them."

She grinned widely, shimmying her hips under me. "So, Mr. Harrington, did you claim all those kisses you were after?"

"Not by a long shot. But that's what the rest of the night is for."

15

LIAM

The next morning, I felt like a college freshman. I'd gone to sleep at two o'clock in the morning after dropping Tess off at her apartment.

She looked just as exhausted as I felt, and we exchanged conspiratorial smiles as we left the room after the first general meeting about our new partnership.

It had been a productive one, where we set our immediate goals. We were going to start with radio ads right away. Tess and Skye would give us a list of their requirements for the new online shop, which we'd then send to the website-building companies we used in the past.

Dexter and Becca were also going to assess their Facebook and Google ads. We decided that I would be Soho Lingerie's official mentor, since I'd been in contact with them the most.

And right now came my favorite part. Tess was going to show me the location of the space they wanted to lease for their second shop.

"Okay, everyone, great job," I told the team, Tess, and Skye once we were all back on the interns' floor. "We all have our tasks, so let's get the ball rolling."

Everyone was going to think I was just being a hardass, as usual, but instead, I just wanted to get out of here with Tess.

Everyone except Skye, who was looking between me and Tess with a smile. The three of us left the brownstone together.

Skye shook my hand. "Liam, I'm sorry I can't come with you to see the space, but I'm sure Tess will be great company."

"Yes, she will."

Skye was looking at Tess with a huge smile, then whispered something in her ear as she kissed her cheek before getting in the Uber she ordered.

"So, what was that about?" I asked once it was just the two of us.

"Yeah...this morning my sister asked for a rundown of every little detail from last night. I promised I'll update her today."

"You say that like it's normal." I didn't discuss my personal life even with David and Becca, and they were my best friends.

Tess burst out laughing. "It is. We have a no-secrets policy in my family. I'm the chief enforcer," she said proudly.

"I learn something new about you all the time."

A black Mercedes slowed down in front of us. It was our Uber. I opened the car door for Tess. She wiggled her eyebrows at me as she lowered herself inside. "I love that you're always opening doors and such. I've only ever seen it in old movies."

I laughed and climbed in next to her.

We arrived in Soho quickly. The location they planned on leasing was only a few streets away from their original store. It was smart, keeping the two spaces so close to each other. It would make logistics easier, and their name was Soho Lingerie, after all. Tess was beyond excited as she showed me around inside. The realtor had given us a quick tour and now was smoking outside.

"So, we can model this after the original store. The layout of the room is perfect. It would strengthen the brand, I think."

I was only half paying attention to her words, too busy drinking in her exuberance, the way she just lit up when she spoke about her dreams. I wanted to make every single one of them come true.

"Hey, focus," she admonished, poking my arm.

"Or what?"

"Or you might make the wrong decision."

"The space is great, Tess. When will you be able to open?"

"If we sign this week, probably in the beginning of December."

"Let's get the ball rolling, then."

Turning around, she headed toward the door. I caught up with her midway, kissing the side of her neck from behind.

She yelped in surprise before turning around. "You, sir, have a playful side I like very much. You kept it hidden until now."

"I don't think I was aware of it," I said truthfully.

She grinned. "So it's just for me?"

"Just for you, I promise."

She leaned in for a quick kiss, then smoothed the collar of my coat. "Well, let's go finalize things with the realtor. Then you can go back to the brownstone, or David will hand me my ass."

I growled. "First, David's going nowhere near your ass. It's mine."

"And second?"

"I want to spend the day with you."

I had no idea where this came from, but it was an impulse I wanted to follow.

"But I remember you and David going on about all the things you had on your to-do list today."

"I know how to sell this to David. I'll just tell him I'm getting to know your business better. Honestly, he'd probably approve. He'd also show me the middle finger for skipping work, but he's always making fun of me for being so stiff about schedules and lists."

Tess grinned again. "So I bring out the playful side of you and make you want to skip work? I'm not so sure I'm good for you."

"I guess we'll find out."

"Okay. Our store is covered by two sales associates, so I don't necessarily have to go there."

We both headed outside, and while Tess talked to the realtor, I texted David. As I predicted, he answered with a middle finger emoji.

Laughing, I dropped the phone back in my pocket.

"It's all done," Tess said as the realtor left. "So...how serious were you about spending the day with me?"

"Dead serious. What was your plan?"

She blushed. "I was going to pick up some fabric from the store, then head home and experiment a bit. The back room is full of orders waiting to be shipped, not exactly spurring creativity."

I wiggled my eyebrows. "I'll gladly watch. Or help."

"And how exactly do you plan to 'help'?" she asked with air quotes.

"Any way you want me, Tess. I'm very good at taking off your lingerie."

She gasped lightly before pointing at me. "You will do no such thing. Promise."

I cocked a brow.

"Not until I'm finished with the experiments," she amended.

"That's better."

"Okay, then. Let's go."

We stopped by the store first before heading to her apartment near Bryant Park.

I only walked her to the door last night when I dropped her

off, so this would be the first time I'd gone inside. She glanced over her shoulder several times as she unlocked the first door. *Is she nervous?*

We left our coats and shoes at the entrance, and then she led me to the living room.

My apartment looked empty compared to hers. She had pillows and furniture everywhere. It was warm and inviting. It fit her.

"So, this is my place. You're the first guy in here in...forever."

That caught my attention. "How so?"

She shrugged, unloading the bag she filled with supplies at the store straight in the middle of the living room floor.

"I've had shit luck dating these past few years. I think the last time I went out with the same guy for longer than a few months was when I was still at my corporate job. I thought it was more serious than he did. He made that clear when he started dating a coworker immediately after breaking up with me. Anyway, when I just get to know someone, I prefer to go over to their place. Bringing someone here...it's just personal."

I saw red at the thought of Tess going home with any other guy. Fuck no. I needed that image out of my mind. She was mine.

I chose to focus on the fact that she brought me here.

"So, um, I'm not sure how good I am at this dating thing."

"Tess, tell me what you're afraid of. I want to know." I took her hands in mine, lacing our fingers.

"Getting my heart broken," she whispered.

I kissed her temple, working my way to her forehead. "I can't promise I won't make mistakes, but I won't break your heart. Can you trust me on that?"

She nodded, leaning into my touch. "I do. How about you? Why aren't you taken?"

I shrugged. "No particular reason. Last serious relationship I had was right before I sold the app. She broke up with me because she wanted to move across the country, and since then, I haven't had anything serious."

She pulled out of my arms, wiggling her eyebrows. "Well, mister, seems we're both in the same boat."

"We are. " I grinned, pointing to the pile of bras. "How does this work?"

"I usually play with—"

She stopped talking when a phone buzzed from the entrance.

"I think it's your phone," Tess said.

"I'll just go silence it."

I went to the front. As I took the phone out of my coat, I heard Tess come in too.

It was my grandmother calling. Shit. She rarely called. Usually, I was the one doing it.

"I have to take this," I said and immediately answered.

"Liam, hi. This is Ellen's friend, Hilary."

She was a neighbor who often played chess with my grandmother. "Is something wrong?"

"So, Ellen had a fall."

"What happened? Did you call an ambulance?"

"She doesn't want me to. Says with a bit of ice, everything will be fine."

"What do you mean, she doesn't want to? Okay, okay. I'll be there as soon as possible. Can you stay with her? I'll need about fifteen minutes."

"Of course. But don't worry. It's just her knee hurting a bit. Nothing more serious."

"What happened?" Tess asked after I disconnected the call.

"Gran fell down, and she doesn't want to go to the hospital. That was one of her neighbors calling. I'm sorry. I really wanted to spend this whole day with you, but if I don't check on her, I'm just going to keep thinking about her. The neighbor says she's okay, but I want to make sure."

"Of course. Want me to come with you?"

I was stunned. My shock must have been obvious, because she quickly said, "It's just...you look super tense. I thought maybe it would help."

"It would, actually. And Gran would love meeting you."

Tess blinked rapidly.

"Why do you look so surprised?" I asked.

"Let's just say you're unlike any guy I've ever known." Coming closer, she took my fist between her hands. I hadn't even realized I clenched it.

"You're going to cut your palm," Tess whispered. She unclenched my fingers.

I left marks on my skin. Tess lifted my hand and kissed my palm gently. I wasn't used to anyone soothing me—I always licked my wounds alone—but right then, all I wanted to do was more of this. More of Tess.

16

LIAM

I couldn't calm down on the drive to the Upper East Side. Tess kept my hand between her palms, looking sideways at me.

"I have an idea. My brother's fiancée is a doctor. I know for a fact that she's not on shift right now. I could ask her if she can stop by your grandmother's place to check up on her, if you want."

How had she guessed that I was worried sick that my grandmother didn't want to go to a hospital? That I needed the reassurance of a doctor?

"That's a great idea, Tess. Thank you."

"I'll call her right away." Taking out her phone, she brought it to her ear and spoke quickly. "Hey, Laney. I hope I'm not disturbing you. I have a huge favor to ask. The grandmother of a very good friend fell down. She appears to be okay, but he'd be much happier if you checked on her. She doesn't want to go to a hospital." Tess had my hand in her lap, caressing it. "Okay, perfect. Thanks. I'll text you the address." Hanging up, she half turned to me. "We have a doctor."

"Thank you."

"Just tell me the address."

She typed as I spoke, and I couldn't take my eyes off her. I didn't like that description of me—a "very good friend"—but this wasn't the time to bring it up.

We arrived in front of my grandmother's building ten minutes later. I led the way, keeping a hand at Tess's back. I couldn't stop touching her, and honestly, I wasn't even trying. I was calmer whenever we were connected.

I rang the bell, even though I had a key, just to give Gran and her neighbor a heads-up. I unlocked the door, and Tess and I stepped inside the narrow and dark corridor.

To my astonishment, I heard my grandmother's laughter from the living room. Had they not heard the bell?

"Someone's in a good mood," Tess whispered.

Nodding, I led the way, right until my grandmother and Hilary came into view. They were both sitting on the flowery couch. Gran had her leg up on a wooden chair with a pack of frozen peas on her knee. Hilary, a white-haired wisp of a woman who always dressed in dark colors, had her face scrunched in concentration at the chess board in front of her. They both startled upon seeing me and Tess. Clearly, the doorbell wasn't working. I made a mental note to fix it.

"Liam, darling. Who is that lovely creature you've brought to see me?"

"Gran, this is Tess. We were together when Hilary called to tell us about your fall."

Tess smiled at her. "Nice to meet you, Ms. Harrington."

"Call me Ellen." Then she turned to me. "Liam! Tell me you didn't interrupt a lovely day just to check on this bag of bones. I clearly heard Hilary tell you I'm okay."

Hilary merely waved at us before focusing on the board again. She lost against my grandmother every time, and to my knowledge, she wasn't faking it.

"Don't chastise him, Ellen. He was too worried not to check on you personally. Especially since you didn't want to go to the hospital," Tess said.

Gran scoffed. "I didn't even scratch my knee. You don't go to the hospital for a fall."

"If you're eighty, you do," I said, losing my patience.

Tess winced. Gran narrowed her eyes.

"Liam Harrington! You don't get to lecture me."

I shook my head. "Okay, that was uncalled for. I apologize."

Gran softened immediately, looking between Tess and me.

"Ellen, I have a family friend who is a doctor. Liam was so worried about you that I offered to ask her to come over. Is that okay?" Tess asked.

Ellen waved her hand. "Fine, fine. I can't fight both of you."

Tess smiled. "She'll be very quick, and that way, you don't have to go to a hospital and your tyrannical grandson will be appeased. It's a win-win."

"She's coming here at this hour?"

"Yes. I told her it's for a very good friend of mine."

There she went with that label again.

I could barely keep from smiling. Tess was good at this, wording everything as if she was asking for permission. I'd forgotten that Tess's friend was on her way. I could only imagine Gran's reaction if a doctor appeared at her door out of the blue.

"I'm going to check on my friend," Tess continued.

"Make yourself at home. I'm sorry I can't get you a drink—"

"I'm on it, Gran."

Putting an arm around Tess's shoulders, I guided her to the dining area. It was a separate room around the corner, where we were out of earshot. My grandma kept a bar here.

"What would you have done if she said no?" I teased.

Tess laughed. "I'm sure you could have convinced her...or just played your tyrant card."

My One and Only

"I don't have your ability to sweet-talk everyone."

Tess placed a hand on her hip, batting her eyelashes. "I have four siblings and a cousin. Mastering family politics was a vital skill."

I moved my hand down her back, then up again, wrapping it in her hair. I traced her lower lip with my tongue, kissing the corner of her mouth. Tess sighed deliciously. I barely kept myself from pinning her against the bar and kissing her senseless. I was so damn happy she was here. Just being near her filled me with this sense of calm that was foreign to me. She was balancing me out. I gripped her waist with both hands, skimming my mouth from one corner of her lips to the other. She held on to my shoulders, digging her nails in the fabric to my skin. Her breath turned shaky.

"Kiss me," she whispered.

"I can't. I'm afraid I won't stop. I just want to hold you like this."

"And torture me?"

I smiled against her mouth. "Possibly."

"You have no qualms about being in your grandmother's home, huh?"

"Tess, I've kissed you against walls in public. Nearly had you on my desk. I think I'm actually on my best behavior right now."

She laughed, glancing down at my hand. It was on her ass. I must have slipped it down unconsciously.

"Well, you're groping my ass, so I'd say that's debatable." She walked backward a few steps, narrowing her eyes. "I'd say this is a safe distance. I'm not in the receiving area of those pheromones rolling off you."

I burst out laughing. "What?"

Tess tapped her cheek as if considering something. "Actually, you know what? We'll be even safer if you go behind the bar. I do want a drink anyway. This bar is so damn sexy."

Laughing, I stepped behind it. "What do you want?"

"No clue. I'm a wine person, but this bar screams cocktail."

"I'll mix you one. What do you want?"

"Surprise me."

"Will do."

She sat in one of the chairs, inspecting the rows of drinks.

"I thought you wanted to check on your friend."

"Yes, but she already texted me that she'll be here in twenty minutes. Does Ellen expect us back?"

"Actually, it's best if we stay here. She likes to focus on her game. My grandfather loved this bar."

I started preparing a Tequila Sunrise, mixing Don Julio with orange and pomegranate juice.

"You miss him," Tess stated.

"Yes. In many ways, they were more like my parents. I grew up with them. I lived here."

"So your parents have always been traveling?"

I nodded, sliding her the drink.

"Yes. The only way to keep at the top of their game was to always take photos of the next big thing, then sell it to magazines. Now, their blog rakes in enough income that they don't even need the magazines anymore, but back then, things were different. They came home a few times a year and tried to be here at Christmas, but it didn't always work out." I looked at the drink I just gave her. "Let me know if you don't like it and I'll mix you something else."

The Christmases they missed were the only times I felt really lonely. Opening the gifts they sent only drove home that they weren't with me.

I always thought that if I had kids, I'd do things differently. I'd be there for them, teach them handiwork and help them fill out college applications. I'd do all those things my grandparents taught me.

"That must have felt a bit lonely." Tess was looking at me with soft eyes.

Right, time to change the subject. The last thing I wanted was her pity.

"You haven't tasted your drink."

"Oh, right." She wrapped those plump, perfect lips around the straw. The sight sent a jolt right below my belt. She sipped half her drink at once.

"Babe, there's tequila in there. You might want to slow down."

Her eyes widened. "Oops. I couldn't tell. I just tasted the orange juice."

"You didn't see me pour Don Julio?" I teased.

"No, I was too busy admiring the bartender's sexy arms and hands."

"You like this bartender, huh?"

"Quite a lot. He's got mad skills behind a bar, and in bed, and outside of it. And he steals kisses with *so* much style."

I came out from behind the bar, heading to her. Tess scooted so far back in the round chair that she nearly fell off. I caught her ass in my hands, pulling her toward me until we collided.

"What are you doing?" she whispered.

"I want to kiss you."

"But I thought this cocktail thingy was supposed to distract you." She pointed with her chin to the glass on the counter.

I pressed my fingers on the top of her ass cheeks, wanting to rid her of the thick fabric, to feel her bare skin.

"That was before you admitted to liking that I steal kisses."

"I don't know what you mean. I was talking about the bartender."

A deep sound reverberated in my throat.

"Was that a growl? Oh my God, you're jealous of yourself?"

Yes, I was jealous of myself. I was losing my mind.

She grinned, right until the moment I kissed her.

She rested her hands on my shoulders, her legs dangling around mine. She tasted like oranges and tequila, and I wanted to kiss her all night long. I explored her mouth until she pressed her entire body against mine, craving contact just as much as I did. I pulled her even closer on the edge of the chair, spreading her thighs wide. She grinned again when I pulled back, closing her eyes and humming.

"This was one for the books," she whispered. "I think it's even in the top three kisses."

I laughed. Only Tess. "You have a top?"

She opened her eyes lazily, still keeping me trapped between her thighs.

"Oh yeah. I started counting when you gave me the first one, then sort of lost track after today. But this one was definitely among the best."

I opened my mouth to dig deeper into that statement, but Tess's phone rang on the counter, interrupting us.

"Oh, Laney's here. That doorbell really isn't working."

She slid down the chair, heading toward the entrance. I followed her, lost in thought. One stood out, though: I wanted to give her the best kisses she'd ever had. The best *everything* she'd ever had.

LANEY BECAME ONE OF MY FAVORITE PEOPLE WITHIN FIFTEEN minutes of meeting her. At first glance, she seemed soft-spoken, what with her blonde wavy hair and round eyes, but she managed to check on and then scold my grandmother for not going to the hospital in a way that made her cower a little.

"You're lucky to have such a caring grandson," she finished, prescribing something for inflammation.

"But it wasn't hurting too much," Gran protested. She'd only reluctantly given up on the chess game.

"You were lucky, but you could have torn a ligament without noticing. I've been in many surgeries caused by exactly this behavior."

Gran sighed. "Thank you for coming at such short notice. I really appreciate it. How much do I owe you?"

Laney smiled. "Absolutely nothing. Tess is family."

My grandmother looked between me and Tess, then Laney.

"Then stay for a drink, Laney," Gran said.

"I suppose I can do that. But just one."

We all moved to the bar area, and after fixing everyone drinks, I excused myself, wanting to check the doorbell before I forgot.

My grandfather had done most of the repairs around the house, and I learned to fix everything from pipes to electrical systems by the time I was fourteen.

I had a fancy alarm system installed for Gran, and the bell was wired into it. I identified the issue quickly enough, a simple electric overload. I flipped the circuit breaker back on and tested the bell. It rang loud and clear. *Perfect.*

I returned to the bar, grinning when everyone raised their glasses to me. They were sitting at the round table just next to the bar. Gran used an extra chair to elevate her leg.

"When you said you were taking a look at it, I didn't think you'd actually fix it," Tess said.

"It was quite easy."

"He's very handy to have around," Gran informed Tess. "My Hector taught him to fix just about everything. Anything needs repairing, he's your guy."

The tips of Tess's ears turned red. Gran noticed it and winked at me.

"Well, this drink was delicious, but I really have to go now," Laney said. "I have an eager fiancé waiting for me."

"We can't compete with that," Gran said, then turned to me. "But you two are staying, right? Tess offered to play a game of chess with me."

She offered to what?

She could have turned Gran down, come up with an excuse. But she wanted to stay here. She didn't mind spending time with my grandmother. I couldn't wrap my mind around that.

After Laney slung her huge bag over her shoulder, Tess and I walked her to the door.

"I really appreciate you coming," I said.

"Anything for Tess...and a *good friend* of hers." She emphasized the last words in an amused tone.

Tess blushed.

"I'm glad she didn't have anything more serious," Laney continued. "It was good you called, Tess. It never hurts to double-check."

I opened the door for Laney, waving as she left. Tess was still blushing, and I seized my chance. Closing the door silently, I pinned her with my gaze.

"A very good friend?" I teased.

Tess licked her lips, pushing blonde strands behind her ear.

"I didn't know what to say."

I stepped closer until I was in her personal space.

"You want to keep us a secret?" My whole body went rigid at the thought.

"No! No, I don't want that. But I didn't know..."

"We're dating, Tess. As soon as we actually get a moment to breathe, I'm taking you out. But just so we're clear, we're dating. Seriously dating."

Her eyes widened a little. I'd gone out on a limb there, and now I held my breath for her reaction. Her eyes widened even more, and then a huge smile spread on her face. Tess was transforming right in front of me.

I claimed her mouth the next second, sealing this step, capturing the joy of the moment.

She giggled when we pulled apart.

"Seriously dating? I like the sound of that."

"We probably should have some rules."

"Why, so we can break them?" she asked seductively.

"Exactly."

17

LIAM

$\mathcal{T}$ess and I ended up spending half the day with Gran, and then we want back to her place, where I watched her work on her lingerie. I spent the night there, and as a result, I only slept a few hours yet again. I felt as if I was hungover, but it had been so damn worth it.

I was already looking forward to when I'd see Tess next. We didn't make any plans—we'd been too busy devouring each other—but I wanted to actually take her out somewhere she'd like. I needed some intel on what would make Tess happy, and I was certain Skye would have no problem sharing info.

I was in a great mood when I reached the brownstone and was determined not to be an ass to anyone today. Unfortunately, I realized something was amiss the minute I stepped through the office doors.

The interns were all quiet, which never happened. And Becca was on the interns' floor, huddled on a beanbag with her laptop. That also never happened. She liked to be alone when she was working, insisted she couldn't focus if others were around. She was wearing David's bulky noise-canceling headphones. I looked questioningly at Dexter, who just nodded to

Becca. I went straight to her, lowering myself to my haunches so she'd see me.

She startled, taking off her headphones.

"What happened to make you work in public?" I asked.

Becca frowned, pointing at the interns. "I need people around to keep me from going inside your office."

"Why?"

"Albert's there."

A vein pulsed in my temple. We had a simple agreement with Albert: we sent him a check every month, and he never, ever showed his face here. "What's he doing here?"

"I don't know. I didn't ask. David left the second he found out Albert's here."

Which meant I had to deal with him, as usual. I rose to my feet, patting Becca's shoulder.

"I'll get rid of him." I just had to remain calm and civil.

I took my time, making myself a coffee and then drinking it slowly. Dexter was looking at me with raised eyebrows. Even the interns could tell I was procrastinating. I always took the bull by the horns, but usually the opponent wasn't someone who used to be a close friend. I didn't take betrayal lightly.

After finishing my coffee, I went upstairs. Prolonging this wasn't going to do me any favors, so it was better to just get it over with.

I opened the door and stopped in my tracks. Albert was sitting in my chair. That pulsing vein threatened to explode.

"Get up from my chair," I barked. So much for keeping calm.

"Hello to you too, Liam."

"Get. Up."

He held his hands up in defense, rising from the chair. I hadn't seen him in three years, but he looked just the same. Bald, expensive jeans and shirt, sunglasses on top of his head, even though there was no sun today.

"I was just testing the...amenities. You're spending a pretty penny on all this."

"Why are you here?"

I sat in the chair he just vacated.

"I haven't paid you a visit in three years."

"Which suits us just fine. That's the deal. You stay away, the checks come in your mail."

Albert paced the room, looking out the window. "It's all getting to be very boring."

"What? Partying on money you're not working for? I can't imagine how that feels."

He turned around. "It wasn't my choice to leave. You three chased me away."

"Because you were treating our partners like shit. You were treating *us* like shit. Like this company's capital was your personal trust fund."

"I made one mistake."

"It was a choice. What do you want? Coming back is not an option. David can't even be in the same building with you. Becca is still hurting every time we talk about you."

"That's not my problem."

I waited for him to continue, refusing to be baited into whatever he was after. If he didn't want to outright say it, I wasn't going to beg him.

"I'm bored of being a silent partner."

"Tough luck. We're not budging on this. You signed the contract."

He smiled sardonically. "I did, but contracts can be amended."

"We are not interested in doing that."

Was he really here because he was too bored spending all that money? Once upon a time, I'd known Albert well. He'd been my best friend in college. We had big dreams for this company. And then he tried to steal from us by pretending to use that capital for clients. So perhaps I never really knew him. He was a thief, and the only reason we didn't sue the shit out of him was because we didn't want any of this to be public knowledge. No one would want to work with us if word got around that Albert had been misappropriating funds.

"Just think about this for a few days. You can convince David and Becca to do what you say. Everyone knows you run the show. What you say goes."

I straightened up, placing both forearms on the desk and leveling him with a glare. "And what I'm saying is that you'll never work here again. Ever. In any capacity. Don't show your face here again."

"That's not stipulated in the contract."

"I can have our lawyers add it in a heartbeat."

"You're that petty?"

"No. I just protect the people I care about. David spirals out every time you show up here, and Becca's not doing any better."

I rose from my seat, pointing to the door. I had no patience for this anymore. He clearly hadn't come here with a goal, just to annoy us, and this was unacceptable.

"I can talk to David and Becca," he said.

"Don't, or I'll tell our lawyers to work on a restraining order too."

He shook his head so vehemently that his stupid sunglasses fell off. He caught them midair.

"You have no grounds for that."

"We'll see. Get out. And don't even think about stopping to talk to Becca."

I didn't even blink until he left the room. *What a fucking asshole.* I counted to twenty before heading downstairs.

Becca was already on her feet at the coffee machine. Her

hands were shaking slightly. She had her back to the staircase, probably in an attempt to not even make eye contact with him.

"What did he want?" she asked.

"Why don't I take you out for a real coffee?"

She turned her head abruptly. "It's that bad?"

"No, but I think it would be good for you to get out of here."

She smiled, nodding. "Okay, then, let's go."

She put on her coat, and I took my leather jacket. Once we were outside, she added, "You always know what to do when I'm pissed."

"We've been friends for a long time."

"Should we call David too?"

"No, he's probably running sprints. I'll deal with him later."

We each had our coping mechanisms. Becca put up a wall between her and everyone else while David exercised until he was exhausted.

"So, tell me," she beckoned.

"He just wanted to annoy me. Said he was bored not coming in to the office."

"I hope you told him to fuck off."

"Of course I did. I also added that we're going to get a restraining order if he shows up again."

"I don't think we can do that."

I chuckled, putting a hand around her shoulders. "I don't think so either, but I wanted him to understand that no means no."

"I'm always so on edge when he shows up. Reminds me how shitty it felt to realize he was an ass. Stealing from us. Lying to me. I thought we were in love, you know?"

I knew. It was why Becca was so beside herself whenever he showed his face.

"He's not going to bother us again."

"How can you be sure?"

I wasn't, but I just didn't want her to worry. If he did, I'd just deal with him when the time came.

I took her to the same coffee shop where I went with Tess the other day. It was chock-full today with teenagers wearing uniforms.

We sat at a table that gave me a direct view of the spot where I kissed her. I instantly felt my limbs relax, like I just downed a shot of tequila. My mood changed while I replayed the kiss in my mind, and then last night.

"What are you thinking about?" Becca asked. "You know what? Don't even tell me. Just keep doing it. You look happy suddenly."

"I am."

She tilted her head, smiling. "You've always known exactly what to do to help me and David cool down, but we've never figured out how to help you."

That was because I hadn't known how to cool down either. But thinking about Tess had this unbelievably positive effect on me.

Becca ordered a latte, and instead of my usual black coffee, I asked for the sugary drink Tess ordered last time. It wasn't something I'd ever order, but I wanted to do things differently for a change, taste life from Tess's perspective.

"Okay, now I'm suspicious," Becca whispered after the waiter left. "You're changing your coffee order? Did aliens body swap you or something?"

"Ha! Can't I change things from time to time?"

Becca tugged at her necklace, grinning. "You've had the same car for ten years."

"It works, and I don't need it in Manhattan. It sits in the garage all the time anyway."

"I mean, change isn't exactly your thing," she said on a laugh.

When we received our order, it became clear why I didn't

like change. This drink was atrocious. Nothing but sugar and milk. I barely swallowed one mouthful. Becca burst out laughing.

"Oh my God, you should see your face. Wait, can you grimace again while I take a picture?"

Cocking a brow, I wiped my mouth with a napkin, leaning back in the chair.

"Okay, you have to tell me. What made you order that?"

"I'll tell you on one condition."

"Okay..."

"Don't laugh."

She narrowed her eyes. "I'll try. But that warning means this is one hell of a story."

"I came here with Tess, and she ordered that. We kissed." It had tasted delicious on her.

"So you ordered that because she ordered it? That's sweet, Liam."

"You're not going to comment on the kissing part?"

She shrugged, but her smile was infectious. "You liked her the second you saw her. I like her too. She's good people."

"Yeah, she is. She even came to Gran's with me yesterday."

Becca's eyes widened. "You already introduced them? Wow."

"Gran fell, and I was worried. Anyway, she came with me."

"Is Ellen okay?"

"Yes."

Becca was grinning from ear to ear. "I can already hear wedding bells."

I groaned. "See? That's why I don't discuss my private life."

"Okay, okay. I won't give you shit." She watched me intently while she ate the whipped cream off her drink with a little spoon.

"I haven't seen you date seriously in years. Unless you're better at keeping your private life quiet than David and me."

"No, I haven't. Just..."

"The usual dates that don't pan out for anything more than some sex?"

"This conversation is uncomfortable," I replied.

She grinned. "And why is that?"

"The three of us never discuss this."

She took a large sip from her cup, wiggling her eyebrows. "No, David and I do. We just don't bring it up to you. You're so...uptight."

My eyes nearly bulged out of my head. "I'm not... Okay, I wouldn't use that word, but I'm not chatty."

"Liam, everyone has their own way of doing things. I'm not judging, just making an observation." She slid lower in her armchair, looking very pleased.

I was glad she was more relaxed. Now I just needed to track down David.

"You're thinking about David, aren't you?" she asked.

"Yeah."

"Well, your work with me is done. I'll just ask them to put this in a paper cup, and I'll go back to the brownstone."

"Are you sure?"

Nodding, she rose to her feet. "You're a great friend, Liam. Thanks."

She made kissing sounds before leaving. I cocked a brow, and she pointed a finger at me. "No, you don't get to take this joy away from me. I will forever remember this as 'the day when Liam ordered the same drink as the woman he likes.'"

Better than "the day Albert showed up at the office."

After she left, I sent David a message, asking where he was.

David: Recovering. I would have kicked your ass today.

Liam: I'm at the bookstore coffee shop. Come here when you feel human again.

David: Yes, boss.

I knew it would take a while until he came, but I wasn't in the mood to go to the brownstone and get my laptop.

Instead, I called Tess. She answered after five rings.

"Hey!"

"You sound flustered. Were you hurrying from searching your phone again? Was it under a pile of panties...again?"

"Umm...no. I'm trying on bras right now."

A visual of Tess in a mouthwatering bra popped into my mind. I barely stifled a groan.

"Tess, you're going to kill me one of these days."

"No, no, no. Not my goal at all."

I grinned. "What is your goal?"

"Like I'm just going to tell you."

"You're determined to make me work for everything, aren't you?"

"Well, to be honest, you don't have to. But it's so much more fun." She said that last part in a lower voice.

"Why are you whispering?"

"I don't want the sales associates to hear me."

I felt even more relaxed than before. How could just hearing her voice affect me like this?

"I'm at the coffee shop where I took you for breakfast. I ordered your drink."

I heard her suck in a breath before whispering, "Why?"

"I don't know," I replied, but that very second, it became clear why I did it. I missed her. I was searching for the right words to tell her, because I wasn't used to expressing feelings. I'd been raised that way, and it was fine by me, but I wanted Tess to know.

"I miss you."

"Oh, wow."

"And I wanted to taste things from your perspective. I'd much rather taste you."

"I can't believe you're so good at flirting even at ten o'clock in the morning. Especially after getting so little sleep last night. I'm still half asleep, and you're in top shape. Are you trying to melt the panties off me?"

"No. Only when I'm in the same room." Last night, we'd both been too tired to make plans, but I wanted to rectify that. "I want to see you, Tess."

"Today?"

"No, but soon. I have a standing date with my grandmother tonight. I wanted to check in with her anyway."

"Oh, let me know how she's feeling. Tell her hello. And that I'm jealous."

Only Tess could say that in a conversational tone.

"Everything okay with you? You sound a bit different."

She'd picked up on that? I debated telling her about Albert but decided against it. She'd worry for no reason, and that ass had nothing to do with her or her business. The fucker was my problem.

"Now, as much as I'd like to keep talking to you, handsome guy, I just spotted a teenage girl entering the shop. She looks intimidated, so she's going to need me to ease her into this. Oh, poor thing, she's not even going near the bras."

I couldn't believe she cared so much for every customer. I'd never met anyone with so much empathy.

"Go charm her, Tess."

After hanging up, I searched for a place to take Tess tomorrow. I wanted to please her, pick something she'd really like. She completely lit up when she was happy, and I wanted to bring that out in her as often as possible.

On impulse, I texted Skye, asking her if Tess would like anything in particular.

After that, David arrived. His grim expression instantly brought me back to the problem at hand. I was going to call our lawyer today too, double-check that Albert's hands were tied by the contract he signed. I also wanted them to dig into everything and come up with something we could hang over his head in case he really did want to come back.

When I told him that I protect the people I care about, I didn't mean just Becca and David but all our partners. They put their faith in us, not Albert.

I grimaced just imagining Tess's disappointment if Albert managed to weasel his way back into the office. I wasn't going to let her down.

18

TESS

After a busy morning at the store, Skye and I met with the realtor, signed the deal, and got our keys.

"I can't believe we've finally signed the lease!" Skye exclaimed as we left her office. It was in Soho too, and we headed straight to our favorite ice cream shop to celebrate. As we sat down at the table, Skye pointed at me.

"So, it's super cloudy and overall shit weather, and you're usually moody when it's like that. You've been grinning the whole day. Did something more happen with Liam yesterday?"

I grinned as I got out my laptop. We were supposed to be working on our post-investment operational list.

"Well..."

"Wait a second."

My grin widened. We'd only sat down a few minutes ago, and she was already on my case. Today was going to be fun.

"I'll make you a deal. Let's blow through our to-do list, and then I'll tell you everything in a lot of detail." I lowered my voice to a conspiratorial whisper. "A. Lot."

Skye pressed her lips together, nodding, and we both focused on our screens.

Honestly, our to-do list was insane, because we were also putting everything in motion for the second store. But for now, we were focusing on blasting the news about our investor to everyone. If I'd learned something from the fashion show, it was that even people who turned up their noses at us before would take a second look now.

We were also putting together a list of all the functions we wanted our new website to have. Midway through making the list, I received a text.

Kevin: Saw you passing with Skye by the food truck. Something special bringing you to this side of SoHo?

Tess: Yes, we just signed the lease to our second store.

Kevin: Wow, that was fast.

Okay, no congrats? Whatever. I pushed him out of my mind.

Forty minutes later, Skye cleared her throat.

"Sorry, I can't focus. I tried, but my attention span is nonexistent. I'll focus much better if we get this out of the way first. Pinky promise. I swear on my ice cream."

I laughed, attempting to steal her cup, but she moved it out of reach. My sister had good reflexes.

"Okay. You win," I said, barely keeping from laughing. To be honest, I'd been about to spill my guts the second we met, but I wanted to amp up the anticipation a bit.

In a low whisper, I told her in exquisite detail about yesterday.

Skye finished her ice cream halfway through my story.

"Wait. I want to restock. This is so good that I need another ice cream with it."

I laughed as she practically ran to the counter, asking for two more scoops.

The owner immediately gave her a refill.

His parlor was practically our office, and we made sure to buy enough beverages, ice cream, and the occasional snack to

My One and Only

make up for occupying a table the whole day. We didn't like staying in the back room if it wasn't creative work.

"Okay, continue," Skye said the second she sat down.

I was super-giddy recounting everything. I mean, what was there not to be giddy about?

It had been so long since I had anything other than silly pickup lines to share, or epic date failures.

"I like that huge smile on your face," Skye said.

"I like it too."

"I'm happy that you aren't letting the fact that he's our investor deter you."

I sighed, pointing to my temple, then to my heart. "I'm still worried about that, but the heart won."

"And the hormones."

"Those too."

It was more than that, though. I could resist purely physical attraction but not a deeper connection.

"Just promise me one thing," I told Skye. "Don't let me talk about Liam during the working lunch." Once upon a time, we'd done our working lunches with the family weekly, but lately we only managed to all gather every three weeks or so.

"Why not?"

"Because I might get carried away and go into even more detail than now, and that would be too much information."

We had a no-secrets policy, but sexy details were definitely outside the scope.

"Duly noted."

"Now, let's get back to work, please."

"Sure thing, boss."

I worked on making a to-do list for store number two. I searched in my archives for the master to-do list from when we opened the first one. Opening it, I scrolled all the way down, then broke out in a cold sweat.

"Holy shit, I'd forgotten how much work opening a store is," I murmured. We could cross off a few things, since we already had payment and stocking systems in place, but that still left us with a truckload of tasks.

"Tess, we have assistants now, remember? We don't have to do everything by ourselves. Plus, we can hire more. We have money."

Yeah, but I had a control problem, so that was going to be a challenge. I was much better now than a few years ago when I micromanaged absolutely everything, but delegating still wasn't my thing. I had this bad habit of double-checking everyone's work, which took longer than if I just did it myself.

The two of us set up a timeline. Between ordering furniture, and the factory producing all the extra merchandise we needed, we couldn't open any earlier than December.

At lunchtime, Skye and I headed to lower Manhattan, to Cole and Hunter's office.

Since we were running late, we asked them to order for us so we wouldn't wait a million years for the food to be delivered. Sometimes, lunchtime deliveries at some of these restaurants could be super slow.

When we approached the meeting room, I smiled at the sounds of their voices. Ryker and Hunter were bickering. Cole said something in a voice too low for me to hear, but my money was on him putting more gasoline on the already heated discussion. When both Hunter and Ryker exploded, I laughed to myself. I knew my siblings well. Which was why I was fairly sure I knew exactly how today would go.

"Hello, hello," I greeted, entering the office.

Ryker, Cole, and Hunter were sitting next to each other. Looking at them, you wouldn't say they were related, except for their height and well-built physiques. Where Ryker's hair was dark-blond, Cole's was jet-black, and he had more angular cheekbones.

Hunter smiled, pointing at the chairs in front of them. His wife was sitting on the other side. I was happy that Josie was also here.

There were two plates with burritos for me and Skye. I ate mine the second I sat down. I hadn't been in the mood for ice cream, which was weird for me.

"Someone skipped breakfast," Josie said disapprovingly.

Of course she was immediately on my case. I had no choice, because a certain seductive someone kept me up until late, and I'd been in too much of a hurry to eat.

I confirmed with a nod, then wolfed down another burrito.

"You look like you want to tell us something, Tess," Cole said.

I glanced at him, startled. *Holy shit.* Cole was usually the last one to catch on about anything.

Cole laughed. "Shit, that was a shot in the dark, but you really have something on your mind, huh?"

I narrowed my eyes at him. A shot in the dark, huh? That was akin to confessing that he'd been actively trying to shift the focus from him onto me.

"Hmm, you know, I actually do, but I'm going to keep you all a bit in the dark. It's just more fun," I declared.

Ryker glanced at Skye. "You know something about this, don't you?"

Skye bit her lip. "No. I don't think so."

He cocked a brow. "How can you not think so?"

She winced, turning to me. "Help."

"Don't gang up on her!" I exclaimed.

"Someone's got to give in," Hunter said.

"There's nothing for you to worry about."

Cole winked. "That's not how this works, Tess."

And didn't I know it?

Skye straightened up, glowering at the table. "We do have news, so lay off Tess. She'll share when she's ready."

Hunter leaned forward, looking at Cole and Ryker. "I don't remember Tess granting us the mercy of sharing when we're ready."

My brothers shook their head.

"Yeah, I don't remember that either," Josie added. "But let's hear their news."

"Well, as you know, we're moving forward with the investor," Skye said quickly, standing super straight and smiling from ear to ear. "And we just signed the lease for the second brick-and-mortar shop."

There was a chorus of congrats, and then chairs screeched as everyone came to hug us. I sighed, just soaking in all their affection.

"I already knew that," Ryker said. "I spoke to Mom before coming here."

I grinned. We called Mom the second we signed the lease today.

"Just let us know if you need anything," Hunter said. They'd been very supportive every step of the way, from helping us get the first store ready for launching to actually taking shifts on Sundays so Skye and I could take a day off.

"We've got things under control this time," I said. "At least, we think we do. We might have to cut back on our tasks for the galas, though."

That was breaking my heart a little, because I loved those with a passion, but until we got the store up and running, I couldn't split my focus.

"We're going to tell the event planner immediately," Hunter said.

Cole frowned. "Tess, why didn't you say that? You don't have to do anything for my wedding."

My One and Only

I shook my head. "No, that's okay. Your wedding is next summer. With the first gala already behind us, the next one will probably be in January, and we're hoping to open the store at the beginning of December, so..."

The first gala was always in the beginning of September, and it had been a success. We raised a lot of funds. But with everything going on, I couldn't spend any time on the organization.

"Are you sure?" Cole asked.

"Yes."

"So, anyone else have news?" Skye asked, glancing around the table.

Everyone shook their heads, but I thought Josie looked a little guilty. Hmm...I could push, but it wasn't right after she took my side.

We just chatted about the store, then about Cole and Hunter's expansion in Europe. Their real estate company was huge in the US, but they'd just branched out in Europe, building a shopping center in Rome. They were kicking ass, and I couldn't be prouder.

One hour later, Skye, Josie, and I left the office. As usual, these lunches seemed too short.

"Hey, girls, can I talk to you?" Josie asked while we were in the elevator.

"Of course." I was all giddy, wondering if she was letting us in on whatever she hadn't shared before.

"So, Isabelle is trying to organize some events for her clients and asked me for ideas. I'm terrible at this stuff, so I was wondering if it's okay for her to ask you?"

Isabelle was a dear friend of ours. She was also Josie's sister. She'd moved to New York a couple months ago and was still adjusting. As a freelance therapist, she had some trouble growing her client base. I sympathized with her, as I knew all too well what it meant to struggle with your business. Skye and I worked fifteen-hour days in the beginning trying to kick it all off. We were lucky enough that it took off and that we had so much demand that we actually needed an investor to expand. But I didn't forget those early days, and I wanted to help Isabelle in every way possible.

"Of course," Skye answered. I nodded excitedly, even though I was 100 percent sure this wasn't what Josie held back before. Instinct told me not to push on that topic, though.

"Are you sure? Because you two are super busy—"

I linked an arm with hers. "Yes, but giving advice to a friend is no biggie. I'm a bit upset Isabelle didn't just outright ask us."

"I think she just doesn't want to bother you."

"Hmmm...so she hasn't gotten the memo yet that she's part of the family," I said as the elevator doors opened and we stepped out. "No worries. I'm gonna change her mind."

We always had a close relationship with Josie's siblings, Ian, Dylan, and Isabelle, and since she moved to New York, we all embraced Isabelle, but clearly she needed more proof.

"I'll call her," Skye offered. "Okay, girls, I've got to go pick up Jonas from Mom's place." She got into an Uber, and then Josie flagged down a passing cab.

As she waved to the car, she placed a hand on her belly in an oddly protective way, and I was pretty sure I knew what the secret was.

She's pregnant! Oh my God, oh my God. My eyes became a little misty, and I blinked rapidly, hoping she wouldn't notice anything. I barely refrained from saying anything and hugged her quickly before she opened the door to the cab. Ryker's wife was pregnant too, which meant we'd be having a baby boom soon.

I was grinning from ear to ear at the thought of having a new niece or nephew on the way.

After we said our goodbyes, I ordered an Uber to SoHo. Holy

My One and Only

shit, I was just so happy you'd think I had a full night's sleep. Lunch with my family usually had that effect. Add Josie's potential news to that and I was bursting with energy.

I went straight to the store, helping our sales associates in the afternoon in between managerial tasks. Around closing time, I got a text message from the shop next to our new one, informing me that UPS had dropped a package with them. Crap. I'd scheduled it to arrive tomorrow, when I was also going to be there. After texting her back, I noticed I had five missed calls from Liam. I dialed his number right away.

"Hey, Tess."

"Hi, sorry. I just now saw the missed calls."

"I was starting to think you were kicking me to the curb."

"No, no. I just didn't look at my phone. What's wrong?"

"Nothing's wrong. I just wanted to hear your voice."

Wait a second. He'd called five times just because he wanted to talk to me? My lips stretched into a grin all on their own.

"I want to see you tonight."

"Your date with your grandmother was at lunch?"

"No, dinner. But I moved it earlier in the afternoon, because you said you're free this evening, and I really want to see you."

He changed his plans for me? Wow. I felt so important to him!

"How can I say no to that?" Holy shit, I wanted to jump up and down.

"Where are you?"

"I'm heading to the new store. UPS delivered a huge package today instead of tomorrow. They left it at the neighboring shop, and I don't want to leave it there overnight."

"I can be there in half an hour and help you carry it."

"Mr. Harrington, you're charming me. Just thought you should know. I'm already thinking about how to spoil you in return. I'd suggest a wrist massage, but that made me drop my clothes last time. Not sure what effect it'll have on you."

He laughed softly. "I'm game for whatever you want, Tess. I have some ideas of my own. I'll share them with you...in person."

I tingled all over at that.

"My phone's battery is dying. See you soon."

I still felt like jumping up and down as the call disconnected.

Grabbing my coat and bag, I bid our sales associates goodbye before practically running out of the store.

19

TESS

I was walking quickly, hoping to get to the fragrance store before they closed. It only took me fifteen minutes on foot to get there. The downside was that I passed my favorite ice cream shop, pancake stand, and waffle station on the way. This girl had little self-restraint, but today I was in a hurry, so it wasn't even an option.

SoHo was so vibrant. The streets buzzed with visitors, New Yorkers and tourists alike. It had a different vibe at night than during the day, when everyone hurried from shop to shop. Everyone was more relaxed in the evening, enjoying a cocktail and dinner.

I headed straight to the fragrance shop, a very hip, artsy place where you could even mix your very own signature fragrance.

"I'm so sorry they dropped it off here," I said when I came in. "I had no idea. It was supposed to come tomorrow."

"It's not a problem," Deborah, the sales associate, said with a smile. She was a beautiful woman with silky black hair that was always braided on one side and big brown eyes.

She pointed to the corner where the huge-ass package stood.

Luckily, it wasn't very heavy, so it didn't make sense to wait for Liam. Not that I didn't want to watch him flex his muscles... buuut I could think of many other ways to do that. Much less clothing. Much sexier.

I managed to push it out to the street and into my own store without a problem. As I placed it on the floor, I noticed a few messages from Cole's wedding planner. We exchanged quite a few emails and texts regarding wedding locations, and I did a little happy dance when I saw all the locations in the top five were available on the date we needed it. Now Cole and Laney just had to look at them and tell us which they preferred. I would totally go for the one that had a fountain at the entrance, mostly because I could imagine taking perfect pictures at the edge of it, maybe jumping in at the end of the party for fun.

Oh, no, no. No daydreaming about my wedding. That was just dangerous!

I'd just started unpacking the box when I heard a knock at the front door. I looked up with a smile, which immediately dimmed. I expected Liam, but it was Kevin.

"Hi," I greeted as he stepped in. I'd really found him attractive? He seemed so insipid now with his gray eyes and blond hair.

"Hey. Saw you pass by the food truck. I called after you, but you didn't hear me."

"Oh...I was just lost in my own head, as usual, I guess."

He looked around the empty shop before focusing on me. "Am I interrupting something?"

"I need to unpack this box." I wasn't in the mood to speak to him. Actually, I just realized I wasn't in the mood for this so-called friendship anymore.

"You've certainly done well for yourself, opening up a second store so quickly."

Something in his tone was off.

"Thank you."

"Do you have time for a late dinner? Or a cocktail?"

"No, not really." I didn't mention Liam, because it wasn't any of Kevin's business. Instead, I just pointed to the box.

"Come on, Tess. You've wanted to go out with me forever. Now's your chance." He winked in a very self-assured way.

"Excuse me? This is my chance? Who do you think you are?"

I felt blindsided. The last time I heard from him was when he asked about his chances with that bimbo weeks ago.

"You kept sticking around."

"What the hell do you mean?" Okay, now I wasn't just blindsided but mad.

"That you were hoping I'd eventually give you a shot. Well, I'm ready."

Oh my God, this man is beyond annoying. How did I miss this? I pointed to the door. "Out."

He frowned, jerking his head back. "What? Why?"

"I have no interest in going out with you. Now or anytime."

"Well, it's not really going out. We could go in your back room if you prefer. You look like you need a good fuck."

What. The. Hell? He'd just played that friendship card so he could have me on call for a quick lay? Sometimes I wondered how I was still so naïve when it came to the games men played to get someone in bed. Even after years of bad dates, the occasional asshole still managed to surprise me. I couldn't believe this. I was so pissed.

"You can't talk to me like that."

"Come on. This is New York. What do you want, flowers?"

"I want you to get out and never contact me again. You're an asshole."

"Why are you being difficult?"

I clenched my fists at my side. "You're treating me like shit, and I won't have any of it."

"Jeez, I knew you'd be high maintenance. That's why I said no in the first place. Women like you always think they're better than the rest just because they make good money."

Wait a second. That was his problem? He couldn't deal with my success, so he put me down?

"Well, then, I'm high maintenance, and you're an asshole. Get the hell out of here."

My face felt hot as anger coursed through me.

When he didn't budge, I walked to the door, opening it for him.

"Out! Don't text me again, and don't you dare show your face at either of the stores."

"I pity the idiot who thinks fucking you is worth putting up with all your crazy."

He smirked right before leaving.

I wanted to call out "Fuck You" for the entire street to hear, but I didn't need a bad rep before we opened for business. Instead, I shut the door violently before leaning against it. I was fuming, and I still had to finish unpacking. I ordered some office supplies so Skye and I could work from here. We also ordered desks from IKEA, because they had the fastest delivery times, but those hadn't been shipped yet.

As I was taking out the supplies, I had an idea. I should put an "Opening Soon" sign in the window. That way, passersby would already know something new was coming here. The sign with **Soho Lingerie** was nowhere near done, but a teaser would still help. I was also going to put the link to our website, advertising that people could subscribe to our newsletter if they wanted to be notified when the store opened.

The sound of the door opening caught my attention.

If Kevin had returned...

But thankfully it was Liam. The corners of my mouth instantly lifted.

"Hello, handsome. The box wasn't heavy, so I brought it here myself. Your carrying skills aren't necessary anymore, but I can think of a few fun ways in which you can show me those muscled arms."

Liam wasn't smiling. Something was off.

"I saw a guy leaving the store."

My good mood plummeted. "Yeah..."

"Who was it? Kinda looked like that taco guy."

"It was him. Kevin."

Liam put his hands in his pockets, cocking his head to one side. Was he avoiding looking at me?

"Do you see him often?"

"Actually, no." I was in no mood to talk about Kevin.

"I don't want you to see him anymore."

I bristled. "What?"

"There's only one reason a guy plays the friendship card with a woman who's asked him out. He wants to get you in his bed."

"You're trying to tell me who I can be friends with?"

I wasn't quite sure why I was lashing out at him when he was completely right. Perhaps precisely *because* he was right. He hadn't even met Kevin, yet he guessed his intentions when I'd been completely blind.

Liam came closer until there were only a few inches between us.

"No, I'm telling you that I don't want to share."

I put my hands on my hips. "What exactly do you think, that I have you both on speed dial and call each of you for quickies? What is wrong with everyone today? What did I do for people to treat me like crap?"

My face was blazing hot. My eyes were burning.

His expression changed from cold to concerned in a fraction of a second.

"Babe, what's wrong?" he asked, reaching out with both hands.

"Just what I said. I must be doing something very wrong. You come in with all these accusations—"

"Tess, baby. I wasn't accusing you of anything. I just...I'm crazy jealous when it comes to you. I can't help myself. Just the thought of anyone wanting you makes me sick. Maybe I'm wrong about the guy—"

"You're not. That was what he was here for."

"What?"

"Yeah. Apparently, he thought I was going to jump in bed with him if he snapped his fingers. Got pissed at me that I didn't. I told him never to show his face around me again. I can't believe I didn't see through him. How could I be so stupid?"

Liam closed the distance, touching my waist with one hand, my face with the other.

"Tess, you're not stupid. You're the most amazing person I've ever met."

I smiled a little, soothed by his touch. "Are you trying to charm me so I'll say yes to whatever you have in mind?"

"I mean it. Most people I know just assume the worst of everyone before they even meet them. You don't. I think that's refreshing. The downside is that you're going to give idiots the benefit of the doubt, but now you have me. I'll be happy to get them out of your way."

"Want to be my personal bodyguard?"

"Fuck yes."

"Does that mean you're going to want to vet all my friends? I have strong opinions about that."

"Only friends you've asked on dates."

"Well, problem solved. I didn't ask anyone recently, and right now, I only plan on asking out a certain sexy-as-hell investor who also wants to moonlight as my own personal knight."

My One and Only

He feathered his thumb up and down my temple, skimming his lips over my forehead. "I'm sorry about my outburst. I just thought about you with another guy and I saw red."

I leaned into his touch, soaking up all that alpha thing he had going on. I loved it.

"You're quite possessive," I teased.

"With you, I can't be any other way. I want all of you all the time."

He kissed my temple before moving down my cheek. And right there in his arms, I realized that I always held a bit of myself back when I'd been dating. I didn't know if it was because of my parents' divorce or because my intuition had been on point with those other men. But with Liam, I also wanted all of him, all the time.

My heart was beating fast. I wrapped my arms around him too, burying my face in his neck. I took exactly two breaths before he burst out laughing.

"You're ticklish there?"

"Apparently so."

"I'll keep that in mind."

He pulled back a notch. "No, you won't."

I wiggled my eyebrows. "It's important information. I might need it. And now that I know, I likely won't forget."

He touched his mouth to mine before capturing my lips altogether. The kiss was electrifying. He moved his hands all over my back, and I felt hot at every point of contact. And when I pressed my hips into his and realized he was hard? I nearly jumped him right there in the middle of the store.

Reluctantly, I stopped the kiss.

"You think that's going to make me forget?" I teased. "Because it's not working."

"I've only just started." His eyes were playful, but that glint of desire in them was unmistakable.

"Hmm...well, I feel compelled to tell you there's no couch here or any soft surface. So don't tempt me too much."

He threw his head back, laughing. "I wasn't going to."

"What's the plan, then?"

"I only have one for tomorrow, but I can't move it to today. I just knew I wanted to see you. I needed to."

Oh, that gave me butterflies. I barely kept from pressing my palm to my stomach. He *needed* to see me? Could he be any more swoonworthy?

"So, since we're here, why don't you show me around SoHo? You always rave about it. I've been around plenty of times, but I want to see it from your perspective."

"You want to explore SoHo with me?" I couldn't explain why I was excited, but I felt it like a huge personal victory every time I convinced someone that SoHo was the very best part of New York City.

"I just want to spend time with you. Doesn't matter what we do."

Perfect. I could finish unboxing tomorrow. I'd only come here to relieve the neighbor of the huge package.

I grinned from ear to ear. "In that case, prepare yourself to get a very unofficial tour from yours truly. A word of warning: it'll take forever, and at the end of it, you'll have to agree with me that this neighborhood is the best in New York."

"Demanding, aren't we?"

"Oh yeah."

He pinched my ass, and I pinched him right back.

"Fine, I'll agree, but on one condition: you'll say yes to anything I want once it's over."

I laughed, shimmying my hips as I nodded. "Your negotiation skills are a little too good, you know that, right?"

20

TESS

The next evening, I was meeting Liam at an address he texted me, along with the instructions not to google it. To my astonishment, I actually managed not to snoop! I tried my best yesterday to make him tell me what we were doing today, but he didn't give anything away. Since he went to so much trouble to keep it a secret, I wanted to be surprised.

The Uber brought me in front of a cute restaurant at the entrance of Prospect Park. The brick-and-wood facade was simple but beautiful.

Liam was waiting for me, gazing down my body slowly as I exited the car. The man didn't even need words to make me simmer. One look and I was done for.

"Mr. Harrington, you look even more handsome than I remember."

Taking one hand, he pulled me against him. Cupping my face, he touched my lower lip with his thumb. I opened my mouth slightly, sucking in a breath. He kissed me the next second, deep and wet, and I nearly climbed him on the spot. He lowered his hands down the sides of my body, resting briefly on my waist before sliding to my bottom. I smiled against his mouth, pulling back a little.

"You're not even trying to hide your dirty intentions," I murmured.

He palmed my ass cheeks, wiggling his eyebrows. "Why should I?"

"I don't know. You were all about talking and getting to know each other."

"The two things aren't mutually exclusive."

I laughed, tilting forward and kissing his Adam's apple. "Good thing I have a similar plan. And I want to start by kissing you."

He groaned slightly. I loved that sound; it was so primal and damn sexy. He grinned before kissing my jaw, then each corner of my mouth before feathering his lips against mine. I shuddered, feeling that light touch all over my body, including between my thighs.

Ah, first rule of the game. Don't reveal your intentions.
Lesson learned, Liam. Lesson learned.

I pulled back, holding a finger in front of me.

"Maybe we should just head inside."

Liam pressed his thumb at the corner of my mouth, trapping me with his gaze. "Maybe I should just change the plan completely. I don't feel like sharing you with anyone tonight."

"No, no, no. I've never had dinner on the docks. I'm excited about it."

Something flickered in his eyes. He took my hand, kissing it before leading me through a gate next to the building.

We aren't going inside?

A wooden pathway snaked ahead of us between thick trees. A pair of servers stood behind a huge table on the side of the pathway. It was packed with picnic baskets.

My One and Only

"Hi, I have a reservation under Harrington," Liam said.

The blond server nodded, handing him a basket. "The number on the basket is also the one for your blanket."

"Thanks," Liam answered. He carried the basket on one side, taking my hand in the other one and leading me down the wooden staircase. I had this ball of energy and happiness lodged in my chest, and I felt like I might explode if I didn't let it out. I shimmied my hips, taking in deep breaths. The air was chilly, and I knew it was going to be one of those evenings where I needed a thick blanket to keep me warm.

Or I could ask Liam to warm me up. I was sure he wouldn't mind.

I soaked in our surroundings, the pink-orange sunset and the yellow and red leaves. On the docs were ten glass constructions, like small greenhouses, spread around, separated by rows of pampas grass. Inside each one was a table for two and some cozy swings.

"Wow, this is beautiful," I murmured once we were inside.

We sat down on the swing next to each other. It was warm inside from heaters, but Liam threw a blanket over me anyway. The swing was huge, more like a bench. We could even lie down next to each other and we'd fit.

I looked up at him, intending to thank him, but was caught off guard by his expression.

"You look very...pleased. Possibly smug. Why?"

Bringing his mouth to my ear, he whispered, "I like that you've never been here with anyone before."

"Did you come here with someone before?" I asked, trying to sound nonchalant.

Liam tilted my chin with his thumb, looking me straight in the eyes. "No. I don't have some standard charming program, Tess."

"Hmm...well, you almost had me fooled, what with your perfect panty-melting smile and super flirty lines."

"You think my smile is panty-melting?"

"Want to check?"

"Don't tempt me."

Holy shit, he wasn't joking.

I grinned, scooting a few inches away from him.

"What are you doing?"

"Getting the temptation out of the way."

Laughing, he pulled me right back against him so our hips were touching.

"Want to check the basket?" he asked.

I didn't need asking twice and immediately took it in my lap, inspecting the contents. I felt like a kid on Christmas morning unpacking presents.

We had a selection of cold appetizers, everything from ham and cheese to sweet spreads.

"Oooh, this is peach marmalade. It's my favorite. Mom used to make this when we were little."

Liam chuckled, kissing my cheek. "I like how excited you are."

"Aren't you? Look how many goodies we've got. I can't believe I didn't know about this place. How did you find it?"

"I asked Skye."

I stopped in the act of unpacking the bread. I wasn't sure what threw me more, that he asked my sister or that he owned up to it so nonchalantly.

We'd been here for all of ten minutes and my heart rate was already speeding up. How was that even possible?

"Well, it worked. I'm impressed."

I was grinning, and he was grinning right back. I couldn't believe how easy our interactions were, how open he was about everything.

My One and Only

"So, what shall we start with?" I asked, pointing at all the goodies I'd taken out.

"Your choice, Tess."

I rubbed my palms in excitement before digging in. I started with a roll of ham and cheese, and Liam followed suit.

"I'm saving this for last," I said, pointing to the peach jam. "It's one of my fondest memories from Boston."

"You used to live there?" he asked.

I nodded. "I was born there and only moved to New York after my parents divorced. Mom went to a farmer's market every week, and we made peach and strawberry jam every summer. I loved doing that so much. I used to think that when I had kids, I'd have designated weekends for all sorts of jam-cooking—"

I pressed my lips together before I blurted out any more inappropriate things.

"Why did you stop midsentence?"

I looked up from the glass, smiling coyly. "Fifteen years of dating taught me that mentioning kids on a date is a huge no-no."

Liam tilted forward until his nose nearly touched mine. He was grinning. "I want to listen to everything you want to tell me."

"Ha! Did you learn nothing from the 'getting to know each other' dinner? You most definitely don't want me to speak without a filter."

"That's exactly what I want, Tess." He touched my cheek with the back of his hand before moving to my lips. "I liked that about you from the beginning. What's going on through that pretty mind?"

"Lots of things. I just remembered some cute things we used to do as kids."

"It must have been difficult for your mom, moving with so many kids to New York."

I nodded, feeling a small knot tighten in my chest.

"Her sister got her a job as a teacher here, so she didn't have much choice. It was a tough time for the family. We were all disoriented for a while. Mom was trying to be strong, but I could hear her cry sometimes at night. It was just such a huge change from our life in Boston. We lived in a huge house and never had to think about money, and then overnight we were worrying about every penny. I tried to make everything fun for my siblings, to distract them by painting our rooms and sort of making toys and games out of everything."

"And you? How were you coping?" he asked.

I shrugged, pressing my palm to my chest again. "I was foolishly optimistic. I actually thought my parents would reconcile. I really believed it. Then we found out that he married someone else."

"Oh shit."

"Yeah. Luckily, I didn't have too much time to dwell on that between school, looking after my siblings, and doing odd jobs on the side."

"I have a hard time believing that."

"Why?" I asked, startled.

"Because you're a very sensitive person, very caring. When you came to my office without Skye, you had a million things on your mind and still worried if her son had something serious."

Okay, so I'd been downplaying that...but how could he tell?

Dad had been the first man who broke my heart, and I wasn't sure I'd actually given it to anyone ever since. But Liam was getting under my skin in a way no one else had. I felt safe with him.

"I'm a weirdo, I know," I said.

"No, you're very caring and sensitive, and that's nothing to be ashamed of."

I narrowed my eyes, elbowing him slightly. "What happened

My One and Only

to being tough and strict? Thought that was on the list of qualities you looked for in business owners."

"You're all that too. No one's roasted my ass like you did." He grinned, covering my hand with his on the blanket before skimming two fingers up my forearm. I hadn't even known that was a sweet spot. I was certain that Liam could turn any inch on my body into a sweet spot.

I scooted a little to the right, putting a few inches between us.

He cocked a brow. "You think these two and a half inches are enough to keep me from kissing you? Touching you?"

Could he read my mind?

"Well, no, but it was worth a try. You're looking at me like you're having devilish intentions."

"Of course I do. But I'm keeping those for later."

He skimmed his fingers up my forearm again. Heat shot through me as I caught my breath. He did it one more time, slowly trailing them down to my wrist.

"So what are you doing right now?" I whispered.

"I can't be next to you and not touch you. I'm barely keeping from kissing you, and that's just because I know I'd make a spectacle in front of everyone."

Laughing, I moved even farther away, placing the basket between us. I wanted to point out that the rows of pampas grass protected us, but who knew what he might do.

"There, that should do it," I said playfully. "Don't you dare seduce me before I've tasted everything in this basket."

"Or what?" he asked as I reached inside.

"I'm not sure. I'll think about a particularly cruel revenge."

I picked out a small jar of chili jam and immediately spread it on a slice of bread.

"Wow, this is delicious," I said after a bite. "I've never had this before. Thanks so much for bringing me here."

When he said nothing, I looked up at him and was startled to find his eyes pinned on me.

"What?" I asked somewhat shyly.

"I'm just trying to figure you out, Tess. That's all."

"What do you have so far?"

"Many notes." He tapped his temple.

"Good ones?" I asked eagerly.

"Of course."

"Tell me."

"On one condition." He lay down on the swing, patting the spot next to him.

I grinned, swallowing my remaining mouthful before scooting back next to him.

"Lie down here. We certainly have enough space."

He moved a bit, and then I laid my head on his chest, draping a leg over his. Heat speared me at every point of contact.

"What happened to distance?" he asked. I laughed at how confused he sounded.

"Well, the distance thing was so you wouldn't be tempted. You can't really touch me too much the way we're lying down. I have one of your arms completely trapped. I, on the other hand, have free rein."

I had *not* meant that as a challenge. But did he take it as one? Hell yes.

He shifted smoothly and quickly from beneath me, and before I even had time to say something, he rolled me over and completely covered my body with his. He wasn't crushing me, so he probably held his weight on his knees and forearms, which were at the sides of my shoulders.

"What are you doing?" I whispered.

"I have no idea."

"I thought you didn't want to make a spectacle."

No one could see, and we both knew it.

My One and Only

"I'm not." He feathered his lips over mine but didn't kiss me. "You just make me act on impulse."

He still didn't kiss me. Instead, he drew the tip of his nose up my cheek and temple before tracing the same path with his mouth.

I grinned, lifting my head until our lips were almost touching. "I approve."

21

LIAM

Over the next three weeks, I worked closely with Skye and Tess on their website and the marketing campaign. The radio clips were a priority. They were nothing special, just what was needed to convey their location and the website. Being direct to the consumer with that information was important.

From the day the radios started blasting their ads, we could track a hefty increase in online orders. We also revamped their Google and Facebook advertising. Usually, I was splitting my time among all the other companies we were working with, but when we signed on someone new, I liked to give them 100 percent of my time. In this case, I was giving them 200 percent—to Tess, at least. We spent a fair share of nights at her place, and I was liking it a lot. Waking up next to her? That had been the best part of today.

From there, it all went downhill. On the way to the brownstone, I got a call from our lawyer, Barney. I contacted him right after Albert showed up at the office.

"Tell me you have good news," I said.

"I have shit news."

"Okay, shoot."

I slowed my pace, venturing into a quieter side street.

"I asked around a bit. A friend of a friend knows his lawyer, and...well, turns out Albert actually wants to sell his shares."

"Fuck!" I leaned against the metal fence of a brownstone, running a hand through my hair. "He can't sell without our agreement, though. It's in the contract."

None of us could sell our shares without all the partners agreeing. It was a way to ensure that we only ever sold to a party everyone considered a good fit.

"No, but you also can't deny the sale forever."

"Does he have a buyer yet?"

"Not that I know of, but that doesn't mean much."

I unhitched myself from the railing and began pacing around the pavement, almost stepping into a pile of dog shit.

"I'll talk to Becca and David. The best way to move forward is if we buy his shares. Him selling to some randomly chosen party is not going to happen. It would be a dick move to all our mentees. They trusted the three of us with decision power, not a stranger."

When I said mentees, I actually meant Tess. I cared about all our mentees, of course, but she was more important to me than any of the others.

"I'll look at your finances, check the cash flow and the key performance indicators."

He wasn't just our lawyer but also our consulting CFO.

"Perfect."

"Look, I can tell you right away that things might get messy."

I snorted. *Yeah, especially because of that fucker.* "Can you put our options in a document and meet with us as soon as possible?"

"Sure. I'm on it."

"Thanks, Barney."

I headed to the brownstone afterward, trying to recall the wording in our contract regarding a sale. Honestly, I never paid too much attention to that part of it. When we originally drafted it, we'd all been friends, so it hadn't mattered. No one thought we'd ever sell. And when we amended the contract so Albert became a silent partner, we made no changes to that part. We barely convinced him to sign the amendment as it was.

When I arrived at the brownstone, I immediately called Becca and David into my office. It was a cold mid-October day—too cold for the rooftop, and we hadn't brought up the heaters yet. The two of them sat down. I was pacing the room.

"I spoke to Barney about Albert," I said without easing them into it, then repeated the whole conversation. I always preferred to rip Band-Aids right off.

"That fucker. He's getting a check without doing anything, and it's not enough?" Becca was seething. Her short hair was sticking out in every direction. She looked a bit like a hedgehog. It was always a sign that she was pissed.

"Barney said he'll inspect the contract and look at our cash flow," I finished.

"Thank fuck, because I get a headache every time I try to read all that law lingo," David exclaimed. He got up from the beanbag chair and grabbed the stress ball from my desk, flexing it in his hands.

"I propose we buy his shares," I said.

Becca nodded in agreement. "That's a good idea. As long as he isn't a dick and actually wants to sell to us."

Years ago, we proposed to buy him out, and he refused. Now he wanted out. This had to work.

"We really didn't need this right now when we just signed on a new mentee," David said. "I mean, getting into a legal dispute between ourselves is always a bad idea, but now, it's especially shit."

My One and Only

He kept flexing the ball in his hand, frowning.

I ran the day's schedule through my mind and made a spur-of-the-moment decision.

"Want to go for a run?" I asked him.

David turned around abruptly, looking from me to Becca, whose mouth was hanging open.

"You know it's nine o'clock, right?" he said. "You never want to go running this late."

"It helps you blow off steam," I pointed out.

David whistled loudly, tossing the ball on my desk and jamming both hands in his pockets.

"Hey, Becca. Something's wrong with him. He's becoming human. It's scary."

"Don't be a dick," I replied.

"He's not," Becca cut in. "Just pointing out a very pleasant change. You don't change your schedule even when you're sick, and now you're willing to skip a meeting to go for a run."

"I took you out for an unplanned coffee last week," I pointed out.

Becca snapped her fingers as a slow grin spread on her face. "Wait a second...I think I know what's turning him human. It's Tess, isn't it?"

"What do you mean? What did I miss?" David asked.

Becca got up from the beanbag, smoothing her palms over her black sweater.

"Our Liam here is seeing Tess."

"And you didn't tell me anything? That's a low blow, dude."

I cocked a brow. "I'm not into locker room talk."

I was like my grandfather in many ways, not used to expressing much.

"But I am." He came up to me, patting my shoulder. "And you can tell me all about it while we warm up for our run. That peep show in the bathroom really did the trick, huh?"

"Becca. Help!"

She shook her head. "Don't put me in the middle of it. You two go for a run while I actually pick up your slack." With a grin, she added, "But just saying, I'm liking this new version of you. David, we're going to have to find something else to give him shit about."

He didn't miss a beat. "I'm on it."

THE RUN WORKED WELL FOR DAVID BUT NOT FOR ME. I PUSHED myself past my usual limit, even though the cold air pierced my lungs and my thighs felt like they were about to explode. Running was addictive, especially in New York, where it was practically a religion.

We stretched again at the end of the run, and David was his usual self, still questioning me about Tess.

I didn't really blame him. I hadn't had anything else in my personal life except meaningless dates and sex for the last decade. I just wasn't used to talking about my personal life, not even with my best friend.

"No talk about Tess anymore. We do have a huge workload waiting for us," I told him in front of the entrance.

He gave me a shit-eating grin. "No, don't worry. I'll just bring her up during coffee breaks."

I snickered, shaking my head. But right before I stepped in the shower, an idea occurred to me. I made a phone call to the restaurant where I'd taken her, ordering a basket to be delivered to Tess. Pity I wouldn't be there when she received it to see her reaction, but I wanted her to know how important she was to me, how often I thought about her.

I wanted to make Tess happy. I also had a strong urge to protect her from everything—including Albert.

My One and Only

Tess

The great thing about being an entrepreneur was that I could work from anywhere. Today, I'd chosen the new store as headquarters. Well, what would eventually become the new store. Right now, it was still empty, except for the sofa, which had been delivered that morning. I was sitting on it, replying to emails in between feeling up some new fabric samples. We didn't have internet yet, so I was using my phone as a connection hot spot.

I didn't just come here for the quiet—I wanted to get used to the vibe of this place.

It still seemed a little surreal that Skye and I were already opening our second store, that everything was going so well for both of us. We had about a trillion things that needed to be done in the next two months, but we were used to the hustle.

Once I decided on my favorite fabrics, I placed an order with the supplier. I got up from the couch and started stretching a little, because my shoulders were stiff. Midway through my stretching routine, I saw a delivery guy dressed in dark-blue in the window display. He waved at me, and I immediately headed to the door, opening it.

"Ms. Tess Winchester?"

"Yes."

"I have a lunch delivery for you."

I recognized the restaurant immediately. *Oh wow. But why would they send me one? And how did they know where I was?*

I tipped the delivery boy generously and hurried back to the couch. I spread the napkin covering the basket on the couch, clapping my hands at the sight of all the goodies: freshly baked bread, a selection of cheese and ham, and peach marmalade.

I pressed a hand to my stomach, overcome with giddiness. I couldn't even wrap my mind around it, but...had Liam sent this? He had to; there was no other explanation.

I was so excited that I barely managed to keep still enough to text him a pic of the basket.

Tess: Did you send this?

His answer came right away.

Liam: Of course I did. How many others know that peach marmalade is your favorite?

He remembered! I thought maybe the restaurant had just included it as a standard package.

Tess: Thanks! This is the perfect lunch. Why did you send it?

Liam: So you know I'm thinking about you :)

I grinned at the screen before hugging the phone to my chest. I couldn't believe he'd actually written that! Or sent me the basket.

This day had already started great, but it was only getting better. My heart gave a mighty sigh while I wolfed down the food. I'd never dated anyone who treated me like this.

After finishing everything, I placed the empty basket strategically in the middle of the room so I could see it while typing at my laptop. It totally made this empty space happy. Yeah, most people laughed at my notion of happy or sad spaces, but it was just something I felt. I couldn't explain it. And this one definitely had happy vibes; it just looked a bit abandoned without any furniture in it.

The best part was that after the opening, our offices would actually be here. This layout had two back rooms, and both had windows. We were putting desks in one, and the other would be a storage room. Possibly we'd turn it into a workshop too, but we decided to wait until the room was ready to see if we were inspired while inside it or not.

God, I was so happy that I wasn't even sure what to do with myself. I moved myself lower on the couch, putting one of the fluffy pillows over my face and grinning into it.

My phone chirped with an incoming message. I moved the pillow, peeking at the screen with one eye.

Liam: How was your lunch?

My heart wasn't just sighing now; it was downright giddy.

Tess: Delicious.

Liam: Anything left over?

Tess: Not one bite.

Liam: Thought so. Are you at the new store the whole day?

Tess: Yes. It's quiet here, and some furniture will be delivered this afternoon.

Liam: I can't stop thinking about you.

Holy shit. If he keeps at this, my poor heart is just going to explode.

Liam: David just found out about us. Becca filled him in. He's mocking me. Says I'm more human since I'm going out with you, because I actually want to take breaks.

Tess: I love that you're giving me credit for that :)

Liam: I'm giving you credit for a lot more, but David doesn't need to know so many details.

Tess: Liam, if we keep texting, we're both going to fall behind on our work. You're distracting me.

Liam: I know. It's worth it, though.

To my astonishment, he stopped texting after that. I was suspicious of the sudden silence, but on the bright side, I got *so* much done.

But I missed the butterflies in my stomach every time a new message popped up.

Decisions, decisions.

If I messaged him, I wouldn't get much done. If I didn't, I'd just keep wondering what he was doing, what he was thinking.

My inner monologue was cut short by the arrival of a delivery truck. Our office furniture was being delivered!

As they unloaded the desks, chairs, and bookshelves, I snapped about a gazillion pics and sent them to Skye. The delivery company also took care of assembling the furniture, so half an hour later, our office was done.

The cherrywood desks and white leather chairs were situated opposite each other with generous space in the center. The second the guys left, I sat down in my chair, spinning once. It was super comfy, and I could lean all the way back until I was almost in a lying position.

After testing every single function of my posh chair, I took a short video before sending it to Skye.

Tess: Everything is so pretty!!!

Skye: It looks even better in our office than it looked online.

Tess: I know!

A knock at the front door caught my attention. I couldn't see who it was from the office, but maybe the delivery guys had forgotten something.

Nope, it was just Liam in front of the store, holding a laptop in one hand, wiggling his eyebrows at me. Holy hell, I barely kept myself from checking if my panties hadn't spontaneously combusted. He looked a bit different than usual, but I couldn't say why. His body language was a little stiff, and his eyes lacked the usual sparkle.

If I thought his messages had made me giddy, it was nothing compared to how I felt when he walked inside the store. I was drunk on him, pure and simple.

I parked a hand on my waist, jutting out a hip.

"What are you doing here?" I asked playfully.

My One and Only

"You told me not to message you anymore because it's distracting."

"Oh, and you think you being here isn't?"

He pointed to his laptop. "Nope. We both work. Flirt a little in between. Win-win."

"Aha. That's not distracting at all."

"It's the best I can do. I've been fighting with myself all afternoon, barely keeping from texting you all the time, and then I figured out the problem."

"And that was?"

"I needed to see you."

Oh wow. Wow.

He looked around, zeroing in on the couch. "Is that our workplace?"

"No, as it happens, the office furniture was just delivered. Come on, I'll show you."

I was ridiculously happy that he was there. It meant he missed me!

I caught myself swinging my hips seductively while I led him to the back room. I hadn't even meant to, but this sexy man had a strange influence on me. I tried to straighten up. Maybe he hadn't noticed.

When we walked inside the room, I proudly pointed each arm toward a desk. He set his laptop on one, then unexpectedly wrapped an arm around my waist. His mouth was on my neck, his hand on my hip.

"Don't swing that ass like that in front of me, or I'm going to do more than distract you. So. Much. More."

I laughed softly. "Well, if it helps, I wasn't doing it on purpose."

"It doesn't help."

Turning around, I pinched his chest. "Well, then, sit in that chair and stop tempting me."

"I've graduated from distracting you to tempting? I call this progress."

"I call it a shameless tactic."

He winked. "That too. So, which one is my desk?"

"That one. Now, let's buckle down to work, mister. It's only four o'clock."

Completing any tasks when Liam was in the same room was *not* easy. I was so aware of his presence, of that seductive energy he emanated, that I could barely focus.

When I rewrote the last sentence of an email for the third time, I groaned.

"Someone's having trouble concentrating with me around," Liam teased.

"You think?"

"Definitely." A smile played on his lips as he rose from his chair, stalking toward my desk. I swallowed, clasping my hands in my lap in anticipation. He sat on the edge of the desk, leaning in to me.

He cupped my face, pressing his fingers at the back of my head. That feral glint in his eyes gave him away—he was one second away from kissing me.

When our lips touched, my whole body lit up. His mouth was hot and relentless, and the way he moved his lips and tongue was overpowering my senses.

"Tess, I have a confession to make," he whispered against my mouth.

"Hmmm..."

"I don't actually have anything left to do today. I just brought my laptop as a way to distract myself...and it's not working."

"You're lucky, because I still have a ton of things to do."

My One and Only

"I'll wait however long you want. But only if you promise me one thing."

"And what is that?"

"That you're all mine afterward."

I licked my lips, nodding. "Yes, sir."

"Fuck, don't say that, or I'll kiss you again."

His tone was so fierce and seductive that I suspected I'd end up on my back right on this desk if I gave in to another kiss. I rolled my chair back, putting a little distance between us.

"I just need to fill an order sheet for an overseas supplier."

"I'll wait."

Half an hour later, I emailed the order sheet and jumped right out of my seat.

"I'm done," I declared, grinning from ear to ear and doing a ridiculous happy dance in the middle of the room.

Liam's eyes lit up, and he immediately rose from his chair.

"So, remember our deal?" he asked playfully, splaying his hand on my lower back, pressing his fingers against my body as if he was seconds away from slipping his hand under my dress.

"Hmmm...why don't you remind me?"

"Oh, that's how we're playing it, huh?"

I shrugged playfully.

He brought his mouth to my ear, tugging at my earlobe with his teeth.

"You're mine tonight, Tess. All mine."

I shivered and then moaned when he feathered his lips down my neck. I pushed him to sit in my chair before climbing in his lap. Dragging my hands down his shoulders, I could feel the tension in them. I looked him straight in the eyes, fidgeting in his lap.

"You're stressed about something," I said.

He swallowed, moving his palms up and down my thighs.

"I am."

"Want to tell me about it? I'm a big believer in sharing worries."

"You remember we have a fourth partner?"

"Yes, the silent one, without decision power."

"Exactly. Turns out, he wants to sell his shares."

"Oh, okay. What are you going to do?"

"We'll buy him out."

I felt a small sliver of panic right in my chest and between my shoulder blades. What if they couldn't? Of course, my mind immediately spiraled to the worst-case scenario. I just couldn't stop from picturing us closing the business, going back to finding a corporate job. That knot in my chest tightened even more. I loved what I built with my sister, the freedom it gave us. I had a fuzzy feeling in my belly every day I went into work. I didn't want to lose that.

I drew in a deep breath. As Cole always said, it's best to deal with things as they come—one at a time. And right now, this beautiful man I was straddling was all up in knots, and I wanted to unfurl every single one. I wasn't going to ask what the ramifications were or where that could lead. I didn't want to make tonight about me. It was about him.

Liam

I TOUCHED HER FACE, ADDICTED TO THE FEELING OF HER SMOOTH skin under my fingers.

My One and Only

"Ever since I spoke to my lawyer today, all I wanted was to see you," I confessed.

"Why?" she whispered, eyes wide.

"I just did. Being with you grounds me." It was mostly because nothing else seemed important when Tess was next to me. Everything faded into the background. I kissed her jaw, descending on one side of her neck. "It also drives me a little crazy," I murmured against her skin.

Tess fidgeted in my lap again.

"Hmm...just a little?" she teased.

I pushed her ass against my groin so she could feel my hard-on.

She sucked in a breath. "Nothing little about that."

"I want to take you out."

"How about we stay in and I cook us something tasty?"

"I like that. I kind of wanted to have you all to myself anyway."

"Then why suggest going out?"

"I have a whole list of places to take you to."

"What exactly are you trying to accomplish by that?"

"Wooing you."

Her mouth formed a cute O. "Wooing me? Wow. No one's done that before."

"That's a crime! But I also like that I'm the first one."

She gave me a huge smile. "You really like all these firsts, huh?"

"Hell yes. Staking my claim and all that."

Tess threw her head back, laughing. I lowered her until her back was on my thighs, leaning over her. I kissed her chest right before I tickled her right armpit. She shrieked, pressing her thighs hard against me. I burst out laughing as she tried to push my hand away.

"You're not playing fair," she said between gasps.

"I know. But I just wanted to see your reaction." I moved my hand, grinning as I helped her up. She gave me a cute pout. Her blonde hair was wild around her shoulders, and her eyes were a little watery, as if she teared up from all the laughter. Her cheeks were deep red.

Tess was bringing out a playful side in me that I didn't know I had.

"I take back all those things I said I'd do with you tonight."

"No you don't."

She tilted her head, leveling me with a challenging stare.

I kissed her right cheek, then her left one.

"Are you trying to get back in my good graces with kisses?"

"Is it working?"

I felt her smile against my cheek. "I'm conflicted."

I pulled back, facing her, tracing her lower lip with my thumb. "That smile says different."

She swatted my hand away but was still smiling.

"Fine, it's totally working," she whispered, grinning now. "I can't stay mad at someone who wants to woo me. But before you come up with any more tickling ideas, let's get out of here and start our night in."

"Let's go to my place," I said. We spent a few nights at her apartment because it was closer to the store, but tomorrow was Saturday, and I wanted to have her at my apartment, share all that huge space with her.

"Oooh...you're wooing me on your own territory now, huh?"

"Hell yes."

Half an hour later, we arrived home. Thank fuck the ride didn't take any longer, because I had a hard time keeping my hands to myself. I was done being on my best behavior. I just wanted to lose myself in Tess.

My One and Only

My woman had other thoughts. The second we stepped inside, she giggled, looking around in excitement.

"I demand a tour before I start my own wooing plan," she declared.

I laughed, taking her hand and kissing it before leading her inside the apartment. It had three bedrooms and a huge open-space living room with a marble kitchen island on one side. The black couch and home theater system were on the opposite side.

The two guest rooms only had a double bed and a dresser inside, both white. The untouched bedsheets were deep blue.

"Very minimalistic and sleek," Tess said after we left the second guest bedroom.

"Not your style."

Her own place was full of trinkets, paintings, and colors. Mine looked empty by contrast since I didn't hang anything on the white walls. I liked my surroundings as empty as possible; it helped me focus, and ever since I moved here, it had been little more than an extension of the brownstone.

"No, but it fits you. The first time I was in your office, I was actually stressed out that you didn't have any personal items."

"And now?"

"Now I just think that you're the most amazing man I've met. Sexy as hell too."

She pinched my ass. I growled at her. She looked so damn sexy in her jeans and red sweater.

"What was that for?"

"I was emphasizing the sexy part," she said nonchalantly. "Which distracted me. Where was I? Oh, I remember. So you're not just sexy but also a little mysterious and broody, but that just adds to your charm."

She leaned into me, adding, "In case you can't tell, that wooing thing totally won me over. But I was pretty sure I liked you the second you told me you let your grandma beat you at chess."

I laughed, stopping right in front of her. Before she realized what was going on, I lifted her in my arms, hands under her ass. She clenched her thighs around me, grinning.

"I just have one more room to show you."

"Oh?" she asked, tapping her chin in mock concentration. I walked us straight to the master bedroom, turning on the lights and holding Tess so she had a direct view of the bed.

"Now that's what I call a sexy bed."

It was king-sized with a leather headboard. I lowered Tess on the edge of it. Then I tugged at the hem of her sweater at the same time I leaned in, drawing my mouth down her neck. She swatted my hand half-heartedly.

"I remember saying I want to cook for you."

"Later," I said. It came out as a growl.

"But I had a plan—"

"That can wait too. I need you, Tess."

I moved my mouth up her neck, capturing hers. She surrendered to me immediately, and that just about brought me to my knees. I took my time savoring her, first her lips, then her tongue. I pushed both my hands under her sweater until I reached the hem of her bra. She hummed against my mouth. The reverberations went straight to my cock. I had a raging hard-on. Whenever I was with her, every part of my mind and my body craved her. And when we were apart, I ached to be with her.

The clasp of her bra was between the cups. I opened it, groaning at the feeling of her soft flesh in my palm, the puckered nipple. I kissed her more urgently, moving my mouth faster. She hummed against my lips again, and then her hands were on the button of my jeans. She lowered the zipper, and just feeling the back of her hand against my cock made me lose my mind. I wanted this woman with an intensity I'd never felt before.

She wrapped her palm around my erection, moving it up and down. I only resisted for two strokes before interrupting the kiss and pulling the sweater over her head. Her bra was only hanging by the straps, and I pushed those down her arms and onto the bed. With a playful glint in her eyes, Tess rose to her feet.

"I want to undress you," she declared.

I held my hands up, wiggling my eyebrows. "I'm all yours. But I have one request. You get naked first, and then you can undress me."

"Demanding, are we?"

"I want to look at your beautiful naked body for as long as possible."

She blushed but immediately pulled her jeans down. That smooth skin was my kryptonite. I kissed her right thigh while she pulled on the bows at either side of her thighs. Her panties dropped to the floor the next second, and she was completely bare for me. Parting her thighs, I dragged my tongue from her clit down to her opening. She buckled, gripping my shoulders.

"Liam," she gasped. I couldn't think about anything except bringing her pleasure. I wanted to satisfy her in every way possible. Drawing the tip of my tongue around her clit, I kept her hips firmly in my hands. I had her right where I wanted her. I sucked at her clit until the muscles in her pelvis contracted and her legs shook a little.

"Liam, fuck," she gasped. "But I wanted…"

I jerked my head back, looking up at her. "I know what you wanted, Tess. And I promise I'll dress up for round two just so you can undress me. But right now, I want to taste you until I give you an earth-shattering, sheets-pulling, legs-trembling orgasm. And then I'll do it all over again with my cock."

I pressed two fingers against her clit, watching her beautiful face change from the sheer force of the pleasure. Her eyes fluttered shut. She pressed her lips together in a thin line and clenched her fists on my shoulder. She was bracing herself for the shock of her climax. I moved the two fingers down her entrance, sliding them inside and curling them at the same time I brought my tongue to her sensitive spot. She exploded beautifully, crying out my name. Her legs were shaking in earnest now.

I held her hips firmly and guided her down the bed. She lay on her back, arms spread at her sides, taking in a deep breath. I discarded my clothes fast, not wanting anything between us before climbing over her. She gave me a big satisfied smile and put a finger on my chest.

"Don't think I forgot about my plan."

"As I said, later. I'm not nearly done with you."

I pinned her hands next to her head on the mattress while I ran the tip of my nose down her breasts, then below to her navel. I went slowly, enjoying the way she reacted to me. She rolled her hips back and forth, gasping and moaning every time I touched a part of her I neglected before.

I was so hard that I could barely think. *Condom.*

I took one out of the nightstand, rolling it on before I forgot my head altogether. Tess was watching me, lust dancing in her eyes. She moved to the center of the bed, parting her legs, teasing me. I traced my fingers up her ankles to her knees. Her eyes flashed with desire. She scooted back down, closer to me.

I raised one of her legs, hooking my elbow under her knee and positioning myself between her thighs. I entered her slowly, watching her face change the more I pushed in.

"Liam..." she whispered, arching her back when I was inside her to the hilt. She tightened her inner muscles around me, and I groaned. Pleasure shot through me, zipping along my nerve endings and pulling at my navel. My muscles clenched down. I

My One and Only

thrust inside her again and again, faster every time, nearly losing my mind when Tess brought one hand to her clit.

She looked at me like I was everything she needed. I wanted to see that every day and be worthy of that look.

A shot of pleasure gripped me so powerfully that I bucked over her, groaning.

"Fuuuck."

I stopped midthrust, trying to regain my composure. What little I managed completely disappeared when I felt her hand move between us. She needed her release, and I was going to oblige her.

I took my arm away from under her knee so we were both more free to move. Tess had more leverage now with both feet on the mattress, and she used it. We were both chasing our climax, but I wanted to prolong this as much as possible. I didn't want to give in yet. She came around me the next second, clenching so hard that I nearly gave in. She thrashed around, pulling at the sheets and crying out my name. I was fighting to stave off my orgasm, and it took every ounce of self-control I possessed. My muscles were burning, and so were my insides, but it was all worth it, watching her come apart under me. I kept thrusting even through her orgasm, intensifying her pleasure. The skin on her cheeks was red. Perspiration dotted her chest. When her breath regained a normal rhythm, I stopped moving.

Tess jutted her lip out in protest. I grinned at her and pulled out before rolling us on the bed. Now I was lying flat on the mattress, and Tess was on top of me.

"I like your sexy plans," she whispered, lowering herself on my cock. She was still impossibly tight.

Groaning, I closed my eyes, gripping her hips. I felt her breasts press against my chest as she leaned over me, kissing my Adam's apple. I intended to let her take the reins, but instinct overpowered me. I wrapped my arms around her, pushing inside her from below. Tess gasped before burying her face in my neck. I felt her soft lips on my skin, then her tongue as I thrusted.

"Liam...I'm going to come again. I can't... Oh, fuck."

I loved that she wasn't coherent, that the pleasure made her delirious.

"Yes, you can. You're going to come again."

She moaned against my neck, her breath quickening once more. I felt her come right before I gave in to my own climax. It slammed into me, filling every inch of my body. The feeling was so intense it was almost brutal. A guttural groan tore from my throat, and I was done for. I couldn't even feel my body anymore. Breathing was a challenge. Moving was impossible. I was completely spent. Eyes closed, body lax, the only thing I was aware of was Tess's warm skin.

"Are you okay?" I whispered.

I felt her nod against my chest. "Just need a minute...or twenty."

I chuckled, tightening my arms around her even more. "You're amazing, you know that?"

"Hmmm..."

We were silent for a long time, and I only moved enough to get rid of the condom. Then I resumed our position, because I really liked feeling Tess on top of me.

Just as I was about to fall asleep, she pushed herself up. She was sitting on me, tracing her fingers up and down my abs. Her mouth was set in a half smile.

"What are you thinking about?" I asked.

"The best way to make you pay for hijacking my plan."

"The three orgasms I just gave you don't make up for that?"

"Not at all. One thing has nothing to do with the other," she said seriously.

"Duly noted."

Narrowing her eyes, she leaned forward, tracing her fingers up my chest.

"Hmmm...I could tickle you."

"You don't want to do that."

Tess leveled me with a challenging stare and charged right for my armpits.

Fucking hell, this woman was something else. I roared with laughter, but I was too strong for her. I clenched my arms tightly at my side, and there was nothing else she could do.

With a pout, she lay next to me. I thought she might try to tickle me again, but she just kissed my shoulder before propping her head on one palm.

"What was the kiss for?" I asked.

She smiled coyly. "Not telling you."

"Is it because you're happy with me after all?"

"Maybe."

"I'd say you're very happy."

"You really need to hear it, huh?"

"I don't need to, but I'd like to."

She winked. "In that case, I'll make you wait some more."

"Still punishing me."

"Uh-uh. I know how to hold a grudge," she teased.

"Come here," I whispered, turning around and wrapping an arm around her, bringing her close. She smiled before burying her face in my neck. Sharing this bed with Tess brought me an inner balance I'd never known. I liked having her here, teasing and riding me.

"Just a heads-up, you've got about five minutes," she whispered.

"Until what?"

"Until I put my plan in motion, of course."

I grinned, rolling on my back. "I'm ready now, Ms. Winchester. All yours."

22

TESS

I woke up at my usual hour the next morning even though it was a Saturday. My face exploded into a big grin the second I felt Liam next to me and I realized I was in his bed. He was sleeping on his belly, completely uncovered. How could he be so damn sexy? Those muscles in his arms and legs seemed sculpted, that ass...damn, damn, damn. I barely kept from fondling it. Along his shoulder blades he seemed stiff and cramped. Hmm...I was concocting a plan to change that. First things first, I had to get out of bed before I woke him up.

I tiptoed around his bathroom, carefully rinsing my mouth with toothpaste to get rid of morning breath. I sprayed his deodorant on my armpits before sliding on yesterday's jeans and sweater. I turned the panties inside out and didn't bother with the bra. I purposefully didn't look in his direction while sneaking out of the bedroom; I really didn't think I could resist touching that gorgeous body.

Once I closed the bedroom door behind me, I darted right to the living room. It was even more gorgeous in the morning. The sun shone through the enormous windows, bathing half the room in light. I loved the shades of blue everywhere. There were

My One and Only

dark-blue pillows on the couch and a huge matching carpet underneath it, paired with silver accessories. It made me think of the ocean.

I eyed the marble kitchen island with the splendid hanging lamp over it.

Would Liam mind that I was wondering around his apartment on my own? I hoped he didn't, because my plan was hinging on exploring his kitchen.

I discovered a well-stocked pantry and went to town on it, taking out half the ingredients and laying them out in front of me for inspiration.

Okay, I know just what this morning needs.

I found a pan and a spatula and got to work. I was really hoping Liam wouldn't wake up until I was ready. That way, I could surprise him with breakfast in bed.

I poured milk in the pan, then the contents of three nearly empty cereal boxes.

"When did you wake up?" Liam asked, startling me.

"About twenty minutes ago."

He was right in front of me, only wearing shorts. The counter was high enough that I could pretend he was naked. *Oh, yum...*

"You can't stay there," I informed him in a mock-serious tone. "Remember what happened last night?"

"We didn't even make it to the kitchen. This is an actual improvement."

"But only because I snuck in while you were still sleeping. Anyway, you look as if you're naked, and it's totally messing with my concentration."

He looked incredulous for a split second before bursting out laughing. Then he came over on my side. Yeah...did I really think this was the best strategy? Having those sculpted muscles within reach was messing with me even more. I wanted to reach out and feel that sexy-as-hell five-o'clock shadow against my skin. I wanted to trail my mouth all over his abdomen. I could have Liam for breakfast every single day.

By the mischievous smile on his face, he knew exactly where my mind went.

"Should I go out of sight completely, Ms. Winchester?"

"Yes, please."

I thought his smile seemed rather smug as he disappeared from my peripheral vision, but I didn't realize what he was up to until I felt him at my back. He palmed my ass with both hands before sliding them to my hips, pressing himself against me.

"Hey, you cannot pinch my ass while I'm cooking," I warned Liam. "I could burn myself."

I was holding the spatula like a sword.

"You don't make the rules, Tess," he whispered in my ear, fondling my ass some more for good measure.

Hmmm...clearly I needed another tactic.

"I'm about to charm you with my unparalleled cooking skills, so I need you to behave."

It was a good thing he was behind me, because he couldn't see the huge grin on my face. It bordered on suspicious, but I just couldn't help myself.

Today was such an amazing day. For one, it was Saturday, which was my favorite day of the week. And the most important part: I was spending it with a delicious man. Could this get any better?

I loved his fondling, but I wasn't lying. I *was* in danger of hurting myself, because his touch was messing with my focus.

"What if I do this?" He wrapped his arms around my waist tightly, kissing the side of my neck.

"Hmmm...if you promise to keep those hands right where they are," I said, stirring the mix of cereal into oatmeal.

"You mean it's not okay if I do this?" His voice was deceptively innocent. He slid one palm down past my navel. I swatted it away before wiggling my ass right against his hard-on.

He groaned and pulled back a few inches, just out of my reach.

I looked at him over my shoulder, wiggling my eyebrows. He stepped sideways, leaning against the counter and flashing me one of those gorgeous smiles that just made my heart—hell, my whole body—sigh.

"I'd admonish you for flashing me a panty-melting smile this early in the day, but I like it, so no harm done."

He grinned devilishly, leaning in. "And you think that's gonna make me keep my hands to myself?"

I giggled. "It was a mistake fessing up to that. I'm not that sharp without coffee."

He looked at me with warm eyes. "I'll make us some."

"Yes, triple shot please."

"Duly noted. I didn't even know I had these cereal boxes," he said, watching me sprinkle peanuts and pistachios in the pan.

"I picked them because they were nearly empty."

"Why? I have some unopened ones too."

"I know. I saw them, but I didn't want these to go to waste. I bought this book when we moved to New York about how to cook cheap but nutritious meals, and it had really useful tips about how to do a week's shopping and how to make the most out of leftovers. Mom was so happy when I showed it to her. I've followed those instructions for so many years that they're honestly second nature now. I hate throwing away food."

"You manage to surprise me every time we're together."

"It was such a hard time for Mom. She's always wanted to be financially independent after that. And I think I sort of learned that from her. My family often offered to finance store-related things, but I always felt like it could get messy."

"I don't think it would. Not from what you've told me about your family."

"I know, I know. It's just been this weird pattern thought I've always been fighting. Still am fighting."

"Everything in due time, Tess. Did your mom remarry?"

"She did, actually, but only after we'd all grown up. Her husband, Mick, is an amazing guy." He handed me a cup of steaming coffee, and I immediately sipped from it.

I FELT HIM MOVE UP BEHIND ME AGAIN, HAND FIRMLY ON MY WAIST. Smiling, I plunked the cup back on the counter, pretending like nothing was happening, even as he slid his hands down my hips again. He was so naughty! And I loved it so much.

"Hey, don't distract me. I told you I need to focus on this. I've lost practice at cooking. I practically live on takeout nowadays."

He parted my hair, freeing the back of my neck and planting a kiss right there. I shuddered.

"So, you're experimenting on me?"

I giggled again. What was it about him that kept making me giggle?

"I guess you could put it like that. All right, I've finished. Let's put it on plates so it cools off a bit."

Five minutes later, it was time for the big test. I was a little nervous, because I hadn't made this in years. I just wanted to do something nice for him.

I took a spoonful and smiled while swallowing.

"This takes me right back to my childhood days. Pistachios were not in our budget, so we only bought those as a treat every two months. What do you think?"

"It's very tasty. Especially the mix of jams."

I was smiling from ear to ear now, super happy that he was enjoying himself. My plan was working! He seemed worried last

My One and Only

night, and I was hoping the Tess Winchester treatment was going to get him out of his funk.

"Why are you so quiet?" he asked.

"Oh, just got lost in my head for a bit."

"I could see that. Where did you go?"

I grinned. "Just mentally going through the plan for today."

"Let's hear it." He took another mouthful of oatmeal, looking at me expectantly.

I dangled my feet under the table, pushing a strand of hair behind my ear.

"Well, the plan is adaptable. I was actually thinking more about the goal."

"Which is?"

"You seem a bit tense." I wiggled my eyebrows. "I'm going to do something about it."

He looked at me as if I caught him completely off guard.

"How could you tell?" he asked.

"Your shoulders are a bit stiff. I felt that last night when I was exploring them." With a wink, I added, "I double-checked this morning as well, while you were asleep."

His blue eyes held a mix of playfulness and emotion I hadn't expected. We both finished our oatmeal in silence and then cleaned up the table.

"I need another coffee," I announced, heading with my cup to the coffee machine. "I want all my neurons to be awake while I put 'the plan' in motion."

The sound of the beans being ground filled the space, so I didn't hear Liam when he snuck up behind me. I didn't swat him away this time, not even when he feathered his fingers seductively from my shoulders down over my breasts. My nipples perked up.

Since I didn't have to be careful not to burn myself or the

food anymore, I could let him fondle me all he wanted. That was part two of my plan.

"I've never had this," he said quietly into my neck.

I froze a little, wondering if I crossed some boundaries, if I was being overwhelming.

"And you...you like it?" I asked, unsure.

He whirled me around, his gaze hard.

"That you woke up thinking how to make my day better? Fuck yes, I like it," he exclaimed right before covering my mouth with his. He'd never kissed me like that, with a deep and desperate urgency, as if he wanted to consume me. His lips were warm and fast, and then he pressed himself into me. I gasped, feeling his erection against my belly. He deepened the kiss until I wasn't aware of my surroundings anymore, only of him and how exquisite everything felt.

He drew his rough finger pads over the sensitive skin on the side of my neck. I moaned against his mouth, touching his arms and shoulders, wanting more and more. How was it that I was always insatiable when it came to him?

To my astonishment, he stopped the kiss, letting his hands drop to my side.

"My bad. Didn't meant to hijack your plan," he whispered.

I grinned against his mouth. "Don't worry. This was part of it. I didn't know when or how, but I was sure you were going to feel me up."

He smiled devilishly.

"In that case—" He leaned in, feathering the tip of his nose against mine. "—drink that coffee fast."

"Oh, I'd forgotten about it." I felt a little deflated. "What's one thing got to do with the other?"

"I want you to be fully awake for what I have in mind."

Oh, yum. "Yes, sir."

Taking my cup, I went to the couch, moving my hips seduc-

My One and Only

tively. I glanced at Liam over my shoulder, making a come-here motion with the finger.

I sat down on one end. To my surprise, instead of sitting next to me, he lay down with his head in my lap.

"I love your apartment," I said. "It's huge. How many bedrooms are there?"

"Four. I bought it right after selling the app. I actually thought I'd fill it up in a few years."

It took me a few seconds to realize what he meant.

"With...a family you mean?"

He nodded.

"Were you seeing someone seriously at the time?"

"No. I'd just gotten out of that relationship I told you about. But I thought it would eventually happen. Only it didn't."

"Mr. Harrington, color me impressed. I've never heard a man talk like this, so openly about actually wanting a family, instead of wincing at the idea or calling it old-fashioned."

He grinned, and it looked lopsided and adorable from up here.

"You confessed that you've been dreaming about jam day, so I feel safe around you."

I laughed, smacking his shoulder. "Hey, no judgment here. I also thought I'd have a family by now, someone to just fuss over all the time."

He frowned, playing with a strand of my hair between his fingers. "But you've dated a lot, right?"

"How do you know that?"

He immediately schooled his features. He was trying to give me a poker face! Things clicked the next second.

"Skye told you, didn't she? When?"

"When she called me once to ask me about the website design company. She also brought this up. Don't tell her you caught on. She made me promise not to give away anything she said."

"Now you're just digging your own grave. She said more? What?"

He hesitated for a few seconds before saying, "She said you always wear your heart on your sleeve."

"Oh...well, she's right."

"I'm not like you, Tess."

"What do you mean?"

"Well, to quote David, I'm a bit robotic. I think I'm taking after my grandfather. He was never one to express feelings or emotions."

"Really?"

"Yes. Whenever there was a problem, he just fixed it. Said problems are there to be fixed, not talk about. I think he would have rather kept being fired from us too, but it wasn't possible, obviously."

"So, is that why you talked to the therapist? You mentioned that once."

"Yeah. I knew there was no way he'd want to. He didn't even acknowledge the depression. So we helped the only way we could: by doing things instead of talking about them."

I laughed. "Wow. That's so different to how we do things in my family. Did I tell you how I came up with the no-secrets policy?"

"No."

"After Dad left, everyone was having a hard time, and I insisted we had to talk about it. We couldn't afford a therapist, but I knew we had to communicate." I narrowed my eyes. "I can't believe David says you're robotic. You seem so open about everything."

He lifted his head, laying a quick peck on my chin. "That's

because you leave me no other choice, Tess. I can't help but share too."

I was thrilled that I was seeing a side of him that he usually didn't show people. It made me feel special. I ran a hand through his thick hair, loving the familiarity of the touch.

"Were you never afraid of letting people in after your parents' marriage ended so badly?" he asked.

I pondered that, looking deep into myself, perhaps deeper than I ever did.

"I am afraid...but I just do it anyway. It's like I can't help myself." Even as I was saying it though, I wondered if I'd ever been so open with anyone I dated. I didn't think I'd been, and it wasn't just because they never bothered to ask. I hadn't cared to share my dreams and hopes, or my fears.

"After selling the app, it became so much more difficult to date. I was thrilled in the beginning by how much my popularity with the ladies skyrocketed."

"Hmmm...somehow I think you've always been popular."

"Yes, but after the sale, it was different. I couldn't be sure they were after me or after the fame and secure financial situation. I won't lie, I enjoyed the extra attention, but that was about it."

We both cleaned up the kitchen, and once we were done, Liam headed to the shower. I stayed behind, enjoying another cup of coffee.

Liam

Tess was still at the kitchen island after I came out of the shower. She was hunched over a notebook, pen in hand, talking on the phone. I only caught a few words, but it was enough to learn that it was about her brother's wedding.

"Look, Laney wants a shabby chic theme, and I want to make that happen for her. If you don't like it, we can just find another wedding planner. Yes, I'm authorized to let you go."

I loved this side of her too, ruthless and unforgiving.

"No, listen, I want both of them to have the best day of their lives."

What I liked most was her determination to make others happy...including me.

I snuck around her, looking over her shoulder. Her notebook was not what I expected at all. I'd thought it was a to-do list, but instead it looked like a five-year-old had gotten hold of it. It was an explosion of colors and stickers. I barely held back my laughter. Tess was still speaking, after all. She glanced at me over her shoulder, bumping her ass against me when she noticed my smile.

"Well, Honor, you have one week to get me the options Laney asked for. Otherwise, we'll part ways."

She hung up afterward, turning to face me.

"You're going to make fun of my notebook."

"Yes," I said earnestly. "I'm sorry, just having a hard time piecing together the businesswoman and that."

She stepped to one side, pointing to a page. "I have a system. Different colors for different types of tasks."

"And the stickers?"

"I put them there once a task is complete."

"Crossing it off doesn't do the job?"

She shrugged a shoulder. "It does, but it's so normal and boring."

I burst out laughing, leaning in to kiss her forehead. Only Tess.

"Hey, don't knock it until you try it."

My One and Only

"I will 100 percent not try that."

"Your loss," she said coyly.

"You have any more calls to make?"

"No, that was all. The wedding planner sent me some options, and they were no good. Laney wants a certain theme, and I'm going to get her exactly what she wants."

What would Tess want for her wedding?

The question popped in my mind out of nowhere. I had no idea why my thoughts went there. This wasn't something I'd ever thought about. Sure, there had been a time when I thought about having a family, but not recently. Not until I met Tess. And I'd *never* thought about a wedding.

"Hey...you're smiling weirdly."

"Weird how?"

"I've seen it before. What are you thinking about?"

"It's a secret."

Mostly because I thought Tess might run away if she knew where my mind just went. Hell, I was shocked too.

"Ha! The joke's on you, mister. I'm a very good detective, did I tell you that?"

"No."

"Oh yeah." She tilted her head, tapping her finger against her chin. "I'm just trying to decide what tactic to use."

"And?"

"Nah, I can't think fast this morning. But I do have an idea for today. Want to go out and explore the city?"

"Sure."

"Okay, then. I'll go put my bra on."

"I'll come watch."

Tess giggled and immediately broke free from my grasp, heading straight toward the master bathroom. I made to follow her, but she glanced over her shoulder, making a no-no sign with her finger.

"Actually, I think it's best if you wait here," she said.

"Why?"

"That glint in your eyes is a bit dangerous."

"A lot dangerous," I admitted.

"See? Stay here. I'll be quick."

I nodded, because she had a point.

I checked my phone in the meantime, going through my agenda. Very boring compared to Tess's.

Just a list, no colors or stickers. I had a new request for a meeting from my lawyer. There was a note too.

Mapped out some options. The sooner we meet the better.

He suggested several time slots. Becca and David had already agreed on one. I had a meeting then, but I'd postpone it, because I didn't want to miss this. I wanted to know every option to fight that fucker and protect everyone I cared about.

"I'm ready," Tess exclaimed a few minutes later.

I dropped the phone on the couch, heading toward the bathroom. I was determined to push my troubles to the back of my mind.

But the sight of Tess smiling from ear to ear only brought to the forefront that she could also be among those damaged by Albert's ego. No way in hell was I going to allow that. Tess was mine to protect, and I'd do that no matter the cost.

She walked to me with a seductive swing in her hips. Stopping in front of me, she frowned.

"Oh! What happened? Your shoulders are all rigid again."

"My lawyer suggested time slots for a meeting."

"Well, that's good. Means you'll know all the options."

"Exactly."

"Which also means today isn't for worrying."

"Easier said than done."

"Oh it'll be easy. Because you're going to get the Tess Winchester treatment."

23

TESS

"Should we buy something to eat? For Isabelle too? It's going to be lunchtime by the time we get there," I told Skye one week later. Ever since Josie asked us to meet up with Isabelle, we tried to find a time that worked for all three of us. Today was the day.

"Good idea."

Isabelle worked long hours, moonlighting as a tour guide as well. I wanted to pamper her a bit.

First step: getting her something delicious to eat.

Second: dish some encouragement once I was there.

Third: help plan an outing for her current clients.

The third was why we were officially meeting. Skye and I had experience planning events—primarily the charity galas our family ran. This was different from what we usually did, but we had some insights that could be helpful.

Forty minutes later, a gust of wind snaked between us the second we stepped out of the subway station, blowing my hair all over my face. It stuck a little to my lipstick, but Skye helped me untangle it.

Isabelle's practice was in a high tower in Brooklyn, and it was bathed in sunlight. She smiled as she welcomed us in. Her fiery red hair was falling in waves around her shoulders.

I loved Isabelle. She was practically family to me, as was Josie. I was also close to Josie's two brothers, Dylan and Ian. They didn't live in New York though, so we only saw them on special occasions, like Christmas and Thanksgiving, and sometimes they even showed up at the galas.

Isabelle's practice was very cozy, with two vintage armchairs in front of her desk. Black-and-white sketches of the city hung on the walls. Behind her desk was a huge golden bow lamp.

"Girls, thanks so much for coming here," she said as she set out the food containers on her desk. It amazed me that despite being from Montana, neither Isabelle nor her siblings had an accent. Then again, they all lived in various parts of the country for many years. "I just had a client, and afterward I'm off for one of my tours."

That right there was one of the reasons I was rooting so much for Isabelle. The woman just kicked ass. She wasn't making enough money with her practice, so she also worked as a tour guide twice a week. She was a dreamer but also didn't mind getting her hands dirty. A woman after my own heart.

"Okay, so tell us exactly what you have in mind for the weekend event with your clients," I said as we ate our tacos.

"I want it to be a weekend where they relax but also get to know themselves better. I found a ranch very close to the city. I've always wanted to try some sort of animal therapy. Horses are very good for this. So this weekend, they'll get individual time with me, but we'll also spend time all together doing different activities from hiking to horseback riding, or just feeding them if they don't know how to ride. I just need a daily plan. It's a small group, just ten people."

"Okay," Skye said.

I mulled this over, trying to imagine myself spending the

weekend at the ranch. How many breaks would I need? How much time would I like to spend in strangers' company and how much by myself?

"Would it start Friday night or Saturday morning?" Skye asked.

"Friday in the evening."

"Okay, so here is what I would do," I said. "I'd do welcome drinks on Friday but not dinner. Start it late enough that people will have to eat before. Sharing a meal with strangers might put them on edge."

"Oh, that's very smart. I was thinking I need an icebreaker on Friday and that putting everyone at a table might be too much. Casual drinks is very smart. They'll warm up to each other and be ready for breakfast together on Saturday."

"Exactly," I said.

Skye nodded. "I'd do the same. And then I'd alternate between group events and alone time."

My sister was right. I tried putting myself in the clients' shoes. I could imagine them needing time for themselves.

"Maybe also don't make three big meals a day where everyone has to gather. How about multiple meal times? Or even just having a permanent snack bar with some canapés or just chips and dry finger foods."

"Yes. I like both those ideas," Isabelle exclaimed. "Will that make catering more expensive?"

"A little. But we can talk to our caterer for the gala. I'll get you a good price," I said immediately. "We've been working with them for a long time. I'll talk them into it."

"Or I could talk to Rob," Skye said. Her husband ran a chain of restaurants. "Dumont Foods doesn't have a catering division, but he's had a lot of our gatherings catered lately. You have a small group, so they could do it."

"I don't want him to go out of his way for me, though. I'm happy just with an intro to your catering company, really."

Skye winked. "I'll talk to him and we'll see."

"We just want you to get a fair price," I added. "I think Rob might be a much better option."

Isabelle ran a hand through her hair, biting her lip. "Okay, talk to him. But please only tell him to agree to it if it's not too much trouble. I feel like I'm imposing on you guys a lot since I moved."

"You don't," I reassured her. "Want to talk us through the daily routine you have in mind?"

"Sure!"

Over the next half hour, we went back and forth over her tentative schedule. Isabelle obviously knew better than us how much alone time her clients needed, but where our expertise came in handy was in keeping momentum. Every event needed that, and it was even more important if it was spread over two days. You didn't want the attendees to get bored, but it was also best not to exhaust them.

"Thank you so much for coming here, girls," she said once we finished.

"No problem. That's what friends and family are for," I emphasized.

Isabelle smiled, drumming both hands on her desk for a beat before pointing a finger at me. "You know, I've meant to ask you since you came in. What is it with that...glow about you?"

I grinned. "Glad you noticed."

"Impossible not to," Isabelle exclaimed.

I'd wanted to spill the beans for so long that I was practically bursting at the seams.

"Well, since you're asking."

I swear I spoke so fast that I barely took a breath. It felt like

My One and Only

that, anyway. I was nearly lightheaded but so damn happy that my heart felt like it might jump out of my chest.

Isabelle laughed. "You totally deserve a guy who makes you happy, Tess. I think you're one of a kind. Always so optimistic in the dating world. If my clients were more like you, they wouldn't need me."

"Just your clients or you too?" I asked.

Isabelle waved her hand. "No, I'm good. Just waiting for things to settle a bit with the practice before jumping into dating waters. I can't wait. My dry spell's been so long I wonder if certain parts still work. My virginity will grow back any day now."

I burst out laughing, and so did Skye.

"But hey, if you could send Dylan some of this optimism glitter of yours, that would be great."

"Optimism glitter?" I asked on a laugh.

"That's what I call it, because optimism is catchy. Just like negativity."

"He's still disillusioned?" I double-checked.

"And grumpy as hell," Isabelle said.

"To be fair, he does have reasons," Skye added.

That was true. Your longtime girlfriend dumping you would certainly hurt anyone.

"I think maybe he needs time. And a special lady. And I can't do too much from a distance. It's kind of a face-to-face thing."

"Well, I have news. Josie and I have been trying to sell them on New York for a while now, and we've succeeded."

"Holy shit, they're moving here?" I exclaimed. Josie grew up with us, and I'd always thought of her siblings as an extended family.

"They're opening a subsidiary here of their software company since they've done so well in Washington. I think in a few months they'll be ready to come here."

That was amazing news. I clasped my hands together, smiling.

"Well, in that case, I'm gonna start spreading that optimism glitter right away," I assured her. I knew this meant a great deal to Josie and Isabelle. I could just picture how big our family events would be.

"We should go," Skye said. "Your appointment will be here in five minutes, right?"

"Oh, yes. And then I'm going to do my first Halloween tour."

I grinned. Halloween was in three days. "I didn't know there was such a thing. Does New York even have haunted houses?"

"A few. Thanks again for coming here, girls."

"No problem," I assured her.

As Skye and I left the building, I told my sister about Liam's meeting with the lawyer today. Liam said they planned to talk with all the business owners they worked with, but I wanted to tell Skye myself.

She bit her lip after I finished. "How much of a problem does he think this will be?"

"They don't know yet. That's why they're seeing their lawyer today."

"Okay, then there's no point wasting time thinking about this until we know if it's a problem or not."

Skye had always been pragmatic, but right then, I could tell she was more worried than she let on. I put on my big sister hat, pushing my own worries to the back of my mind.

"Exactly. We'll deal with this one step at a time. Want to go for cake? I have some time before I need to head back to Manhattan for the fashion show." It wasn't a terribly important show, but I'd gotten a ticket, and I always found shows good for my creativity. I'd been in a lull lately, what with splitting my time between coordinating the delivery and assembly of the furniture and lighting devices for the new store, approval of website designs, and so on.

"I can't. I need to pick up Jonas from Mom's." Biting her lip, she added, "I feel like I'm failing you, Tess."

"What? Why?" I was shocked.

"It's just that lately, you seem to do the brunt of the work, and I just keep missing out on things. Half the time, I'm not even sure where my head is."

"Sis, you have a baby. You're bound to need time to find your balance. Don't be so hard on yourself. I've got this."

"So you're not upset?"

"Do I seem upset?"

"I don't know. I feel all over the place lately. I thought I was supposed to stop being hormonal once the pregnancy was over, but it seems not."

"Skye! I'm not upset," I assured her. I was so happy everyone still lived by the no-secrets policy. So, so glad.

"Okay. Thanks for being so supportive. I'm going to start an online yoga course this evening. Hopefully it'll help me find my balance."

"Yikes. Have fun."

"One of these days, I'm gonna talk you into trying one with me."

"I did try a few, remember? Nearly broke my neck."

Skye rolled her eyes. "You and Rob are no fun. I can't convince either of you."

I nudged her shoulder. "Maybe you should try running instead."

"Hell no."

She kissed my cheek before flagging down a passing cab. Workouts were one area where Skye and I never agreed. Before she met Rob, we didn't have the same views on love either.

That reminded me of another skeptic who would soon move to New York.

After Skye left, I walked leisurely toward the neighborhood and called Dylan. It was a gorgeous autumn day, and I wanted to stay outdoors for a while longer. I loved New York in the fall—the mix of golden, red, and brown leaves, the chilly air, and the multitude of cozy wintery snacks like pumpkin lattes and cinnamon rolls. Now that Isabelle mentioned Halloween, I saw signs of it everywhere. And speaking of lattes...I couldn't resist and bought one from a mobile coffee cart while waiting for Dylan to pick up.

"Tess, what a surprise," he said instead of hello.

"What's this I hear about you and Ian moving to New York?"

Dylan chuckled. "Which sister spilled the beans?"

"Isabelle. Why did you not say anything when we were at the cabin?" We'd all been there at the end of summer.

"Because it was still in the planning phases. Why are you calling? Is everything okay with Isabelle?"

"Yes, Skye and I were at her practice, giving her tips for organizing an event for her clients. One thing led to another, and we started talking about you."

"Of course."

"She mentioned that you're still a bit moody."

"Tess..."

"No, this is just a warning so you know Isabelle is on your case."

Usually, I liked to call things like they were, but Dylan needed a more veiled approach.

"Right, and you're not?" he teased. When I didn't reply, he added, "I've heard you're seeing someone."

Wow! Had Isabelle texted him in the meantime? Because I'd only told Mom and Skye so far. Which reminded me that I

My One and Only

wasn't upholding the no-secrets policy, but honestly, the gang hadn't gotten together for a working lunch in weeks!

This was my cue to spread some optimism, as Isabelle said.

"Oh yeah. And it was definitely worth kissing all those frogs before. I cringe just remembering how many bad dates I've been on."

Okay, so this was not my finest pep talk, but it was really difficult over the phone.

"And you're still not on my case?" He was laughing now. Well, the cat was out of the bag.

"Just a little. Isabelle says my optimism is catchy."

"I see."

"I do a better job in person, I promise."

"You're welcome to try next time I'm in town. And by the way, if this guy you're seeing messes with you, Ian and I will kick his ass."

"Aww, that's sweet of you to say, but I think my brothers and Hunter have that covered."

"You can never have too many people looking out for you."

"That is true."

I grinned, pulling my coat tighter around me. I couldn't wait for them to move to New York. After ending the call to Dylan, I wrote in the WhatsApp group I had with my family.

Tess: When does everyone have time for a lunch? I have some news (not related to work)

Ryker: You can start by telling us the news.

Cole: I agree.

Tess: But I want to tell you face-to-face.

Skye: Sis...I think you just threw yourself to the wolves.

Josie: I want to know now!!

Ryker: I think she's dating someone. Tess, you can just confirm or deny.

Skye was right. I had no one to blame but me.

Tess: FINE. I'm dating our investor.

Nothing happened for a few seconds, and then the screen exploded.

Ryker: Holy shit.
Cole: Didn't expect this.
Josie: I WANT DETAILS.

Well, then, it seemed a girly evening *and* a working lunch were needed.

24

LIAM

"Gran, we always do the same thing on Thanksgiving. Of course I'm on board."

We had a traditional dinner, and Gran always cooked a small turkey for the two of us. On rare occasions, my parents were in New York for the holiday too, but so far they hadn't indicated they'd be in town.

I glanced at the clock on my laptop. The meeting with the lawyer was starting in ten minutes.

"Well, I thought since you've got that lovely lady in your life now that you're going to have other plans on Thanksgiving."

I tapped my pen against the table, realizing it had completely slipped my mind until now. I also realized I did want to see Tess on Thanksgiving. The question was did she want the same? We were spending a lot of time together, but we never planned more than when we'd see each other next. Was this too soon?

"I'd love to have her over for dinner," Gran continued.

"I'm 100 percent certain that she's having dinner with her family."

I didn't like that, actually. It felt like we were leading separate lives.

"Well, let me know."

"Are Mom and Dad coming?"

"I don't know."

"Okay. We'll see. I'll get back to you on this."

"Fine! But don't think I'll give up, young man. I want grandkids someday."

I laughed, disconnecting the call. Then I actually did something I rarely did and called my Mom. We kept in touch mostly via email because they were always traveling, and sometimes we weren't in the same time zone.

"Liam, hi!"

"Hi, Mom!"

"Is anything wrong?"

"No, just wanted to check on you and Dad and ask if you're coming to New York on Thanksgiving."

"Oh, we won't make it to the city at all this year. Not even on Christmas. We've got these cheap flights to New Zealand and want to take advantage of it."

"I think Gran would be happy if you two came. For at least one of the two occasions."

"Oh...well, she has you, right? And she's told us you're seeing someone. I'm sure she'll have her hands full. We really don't want to miss this opportunity."

I drummed my fingers on the table, deciding not to press the matter further. Mom took after my grandfather too, always a bit distant, and I accepted that. It usually didn't bother me, so why did it now? It was their way, and that wasn't going to change.

Then I realized I was the one who'd changed, and it was all because of Tess.

A knock at the door interrupted me. Becca poked her head in.

"Barney's here," she whispered.

"Mom, I'll talk to you another time. I have to go."

"Sure."

I hung up and headed straight to David's office. I was expecting good news.

That turned out to be nothing more than wishful thinking. For the next hour, our lawyer went from unpleasant scenario to unpleasant scenario, and my mind felt about ready to explode.

"You're telling us that despite our marketing valuation, we don't have enough cash flow to buy that fucker out?" David exclaimed, mirroring my own dismay.

"Not right now. If Albert were to wait four months, you'll be liquid enough again."

"And if he doesn't want to wait?" I pressed.

He pinched his nose, drumming his fingers on the table. "You can still freeze this year's investment. You have a clause in all contracts that allows you to freeze the investment for six months in extreme circumstances."

"No," I answered before he even finished uttering the last word. "That's completely out of question."

"It's an option. That would give you enough cash flow."

"No, it's not. Our mentees are putting their trust in us. We're not going to disappoint them."

He nodded but shrugged. "I'm afraid this is all I could come up with."

"Then find me something better, or we'll be employing another law firm." My voice was calm, but I was sure my rage was visible on my face. This was sloppy work. There was always more than one way to solve a problem, and I wasn't tolerating anything less than the very best from the people I worked with.

. . .

After our lawyer left, David, Becca, and I just looked at each other without saying a word.

"Let's not talk about any of this tonight," David finally suggested.

Becca nodded. "I agree. I'm too overwhelmed to actually be of any use right now anyway."

They both looked at me. If I pushed it, they'd stay for me and brainstorm together. It was a reminder that I was in charge.

"No, let's call this a day. We all need to cool off first."

They both rose to their feet before I even finished the sentence. We all left at the same time. I couldn't stand being in the office anymore. I needed to stretch my legs and clear my mind. Yet all I could do during my walk was mull the lawyer's advice in my mind. I wasn't only in charge; I was also responsible for all those we invested in. They all trusted me, and I was determined not to let anyone down. I hadn't gotten to where I was by playing into anyone's games. There was a reason I had a reputation as being ruthless and tough, and Albert was going to be reminded of that.

It wasn't the first time I was facing a roadblock. The only difference was that this time I had more people I wanted to protect. I remembered Tess's apprehension before signing, how long it took to win her over. I was afraid she would go back in her shell, and I didn't want this to drive a wedge between us.

I thought about how I was going to break the news to her as I left the office. Tess was attending a fashion show on the Upper East side, and even though we hadn't made any plans for tonight, I needed to see her.

I arrived before the show was over and waited in front of the art deco building. Soon, people started filtering out, and it only took me a moment to spot her. She came right toward me.

"Handsome gentleman, you look familiar," Tess exclaimed, a smile tugging at the corners of her lips. She looked absolutely

My One and Only

breathtaking, though I only caught a glimpse of her red dress before she buttoned up her black coat.

"How so?" I replied, giving in to her game.

She tilted her head, narrowing her eyes playfully. "I'm not sure. Maybe you should remind me."

I stepped closer, touching her lower lip with my thumb. "When we're alone."

She sucked in a breath, kissing my finger. "How come you're here?"

"To make sure no one kisses you while you wait for a cab."

She laughed softly, wiggling her eyebrows. "Not even you?"

"I didn't say that."

I dragged my thumb from one corner of her mouth to the other.

"Uh-oh," Tess muttered.

"What?"

"We really should wait until we're alone for that kiss. You give off dangerous vibes."

"You know that by the way I'm touching your lips?"

"No, actually, just from the way you're looking at me."

"You read me well."

"I actually wasn't planning on taking a cab just yet but taking a walk first. Central Park is gorgeous right now. All these fall colors."

I groaned. "But that means we won't be alone for some time. How long is that kiss going to have to wait?"

"Oh, I don't know, Mr. You're-creative-enough-when-it-comes-to-that. I have complete faith in you."

We crossed the street, heading to one of the entrances to the park.

"Do we have a destination?" I asked.

"No, I was just going to wander the alleyways."

I took her hands in mine, looking her straight in the eyes.

"David, Becca, and I had a meeting with the lawyer."

"What did he say?"

"Nothing good, but I'm going to mull that information over and find something that works for all parties involved."

"Liam! What did he say? I want to know." Her eyes were snapping fire. I wanted to protect her from this, but I should have known better.

"He can't sell to just anyone. If we find the buyer unsuitable, we can veto, but we can only do that a few times or we'll be accused of not playing fair."

"Can't you buy his share?"

"We don't have enough cash flow at the moment."

The light went out of Tess's eyes. That amazing brain of hers already put two and two together.

"But you still have time to freeze the investment you did this year."

I could practically feel her pull back in her shell. She tried to take her hands away from mine, but I held them firmly. This was exactly what I'd been afraid of. I cared so much about her that I didn't want to risk anything coming between us.

"Tess, that is not going to happen," I said with determination. "I'm a man of my word. I would never freeze an investment."

Her eyes softened a bit. "You don't have a choice, though."

"There is always a choice. You just have to be determined enough to find it. I am determined, and I will find it."

I cupped her face with both hands, caressing her temples with my thumbs. I wanted her to feel that I meant every word.

"There is no scenario in this world in which I'd let anything hurt you, you understand? You hurt, I hurt, and that's not going to happen, babe."

She didn't reply.

"Tell me what you're thinking," I said. "You have a no-secrets policy, remember?"

She smiled slowly, covering my hands with her palms.

"Too many things."

"I want to know."

"I can't believe you're willing to go through any trouble...for me."

"Fucking hell, woman, how can you say that? Don't you know how much you mean to me?"

A sliver of vulnerability crossed her face. She really didn't know.

"I've done a shit job showing it, then. I'll up my game."

A small smile played on her lips. "I've never met anyone like you."

"That goes both ways, Tess."

"I want you to keep me posted on every step, okay?"

I nodded. She narrowed her eyes.

"I mean it. Not just drip information or tell me enough to keep me from worrying."

"Why? That's a perfectly acceptable plan."

She groaned, smacking my shoulder. "No, it's not, you stubborn man. I'm not some fragile thing you have to keep in a glass case."

I tilted my head, considering this. "Actually, that's another good idea. Or just sending you to the Bahamas on an all-inclusive trip until I fix it."

She pinched my abs this time. "I mean it. I don't want you to be looking for solutions on your own. I'm part of this too. And Skye."

"I know."

She narrowed her eyes. "Aha. I'm not sure you do. Your grandmother did say you're a lone wolf."

"When?"

"While you were fixing the bell. I told her I've got this huge family and we're always in each other's business, and she said she always hoped you'd get a sibling."

It was true; I always preferred to do things on my own, but it was just the way I'd grown up, and I liked it.

"What are you thinking about?" Tess asked.

"Many things. Like what I'm going to do to you this evening."

She sighed. "You're really great at this wooing thing."

"It's more than that, Tess. I don't want you to ever doubt that you're important to me. That I'd move mountains to make you happy, keep you safe. Not just now, always. Don't doubt that."

"Okay."

I put an arm around her shoulders as we turned into a very narrow alleyway covered by ivy, which in the city was unusual but charming. There was one other topic I wanted to bring up.

"By the way, Thanksgiving is coming up. I always spend that with my grandmother, and I want you there too."

Tess elbowed me lightly. "I was hoping to convince you to come to my mom's place."

I wanted to pump my fist in the air, feeling victorious that we were on the same page. Our lives were converging in a way I hadn't planned for, but damn if it didn't feel amazing. And right.

She bit her lip. "If you want to. I mean...I don't want you to think I'm pressuring you into meeting my family—"

"Tess, I want to meet your family. Do I need to pamper you more for you to believe I want to spend as much time with you as possible?"

She grinned. "Well, no. Truthfully, you're doing a great job, but I'll never say no to even more pampering."

Then why do you keep expecting the worst? I wanted to ask, but then I realized that in the grand scheme of things, she'd only known me for a few months. She had years of disappointments.

"So should we go first to your grandmother's and then to Mom's?"

I laughed. "Two thanksgiving dinners?"

"Hey, you gotta do what you gotta do. And I've learned that you don't upset a chef unless you want to risk an empty stomach."

"I think there is zero risk of that."

25

LIAM

Over the next few weeks, I did what I knew best. I buckled down to work, reviewing all contracts and looking out for any loopholes. I didn't find any. I needed more information, the kind that wasn't easily available, so I did something I'd never done before: I asked a detective to look into Albert's personal life, get me any information he could. I didn't condone such actions usually. It wasn't my style. But desperate times...

"Holy shit, I can't believe you actually did this," Becca exclaimed on Thanksgiving afternoon. The report had been dropped off at the office because the person in charge insisted on not leaving any electronic trails.

"I just wanted more information," I retaliated.

David looked at me like I'd grown a second head. "Yeah, but usually for you, that means taking some bullshit high road. Man, I can't believe you're finally turning out to be an actual human being like the rest of us."

"Are you two done so we can look over this?" I asked.

"No, actually, I'm absolutely not done. But it can wait until later," David said.

My One and Only

Becca moved to the edge of her seat. I opened the envelope and handed each of them a stack.

"You actually asked the detective for three copies?" David asked. "Okay, time out. I do need to give you more shit. You don't even know how to be sneaky. Next time you're dealing with a detective, just let me handle it."

"David, I usually appreciate your lax attitude, but it's annoying me right now."

Becca held her hands in a T-shape, signaling a time-out. "Boys, behave. Let's read this."

"Yes, David. Let's read it."

He looked as if he wanted to add something sarcastic, but as both Becca and I started reading, he said nothing.

The report was a detailed overview of Albert's moves over the past few years—financial and interpersonal.

"Fuck, the moron's broke?" David exclaimed seconds after I just read the same information. There was no trace of humor in his voice anymore.

I saw red. My palms were itching with the need to punch something as the detective went into great detail about the amount Albert was in debt.

"Well, this is worse than I thought," Becca said slowly. "I actually assumed that he wanted to sell right now just to put us in a bad position. Turns out he's just desperate for money."

I said nothing, but I'd come to the same conclusion and didn't like it one bit. Albert was a problem even when he wasn't desperate, but now?

"I guess this means there's no talking him out of wanting to sell his side," David said through gritted teeth.

"No, I don't think there is," I said.

"So that only leaves us with pulling out of the investment we did this year," Becca said. "Our reputation will take a hit, but we'll recover. And—"

"No," I said. My voice was dangerously calm.

David blinked. Even he knew better than to joke right now.

"You have another suggestion?" Becca asked.

"Right now, no, but we've just received this information. I'm sure I can get more out of it if I have enough time to analyze it."

Becca bit her lip. "It's because of Tess, isn't it?"

David straightened in his seat at that.

"I'm not going to do anything that risks her business."

"What about us?" Becca asked softly.

"Or ours. I give you my word."

She chewed on her lip. "I trust you. You've never led us astray. But we don't have that much thinking time, do we? If we don't make him an offer until Christmas, he's free to shop around for another buyer."

"I know."

"Okay, I know we're knee-deep in problems, but...I do need to give you shit," David cut in. "The opportunity is too good to pass up. Besides, it'll lighten up the mood."

"Go ahead. We can use some of that," Becca said before I could answer. I disagreed but didn't voice that thought.

"I can't believe you're actually going all out for a woman like that. How does it feel? Is it more good than bad? Should I take notes?" David asked.

"You definitely should," Becca said.

I glared at the two of them. "That's where your mind just went?"

"It's a coping mechanism," Becca explained. "Much better than us sulking like we usually do when it's about Albert."

Okay, that was true. It was definitely an improvement over having to run laps with David and take Becca for coffee.

"I'd love to stay and chat, but I have two Thanksgiving dinners to attend," I said.

David laughed. "What?"

"Holy shit, is one with Tess's family?" Becca exclaimed. "David, you should definitely take notes, or it'll take you a year to be invited to your future girlfriend's Thanksgiving feast."

"I promise I'll give you enough material to write down after the dinners, but right now, I need to go."

David held up his hands. "I won't hold my breath. It was a rhetorical question. Since when are you taking everything so seriously?" The last part was directed to Becca.

She shrugged, smiling coyly.

I got up from the chair, bidding both goodbye. I didn't have time to linger today.

On the way to pick up Tess, I kept replaying the newest bits of information in my mind. Two things were clear. One: I was going to do whatever it took to protect everyone I love. Two: I was determined not to ruin anyone's dinner by being in a shitty mood.

Tess

"Holy shit, I can't be late." I glanced at the clock on my phone, hairbrush in hand. I was trying to multitask...and was thoroughly failing.

I was trying to keep an eye on our new online shop. It had gone live last week, and we were smoothing out all the bugs ever since. Yesterday had been a bug-free day, and I was hoping today was going to be the same, because tomorrow was Black Friday. It was one of the most important days for retail.

We were going to officially open the second store in the first week of December, and things were moving so fast I barely had time to keep up.

But today I had to press Pause. It was a big day. A happy day.

I closed the website, focusing on the here and now. I was ecstatic.

Liam wanted us to have Thanksgiving with his grandma. And then meet my whole family.

I loved Thanksgiving dinners at Mom's place. I always felt like a kid. Over the years, the crowd had grown bigger what with everyone getting married or having kids. This year, Isabelle was joining us, of course, since she now lived here. Ian and Dylan were also in the city, so they were coming too. I speed-brushed my hair, then applied mascara and eye shadow.

Once I was done, I noticed I had a message.

Isabelle: Just a reminder that Dylan's going to be there. Extra optimism required.

Tess: Oh no. Why?

Isabelle: I MIGHT have suggested he and Ian go on a double date with some friends of mine. Let's just say I am not his favorite sister right now.

Tess: Extra optimism on the way!

I grinned at myself in the mirror, pointing at my reflection. "That's right. All that frog kissing was worth it."

I just had to convince Dylan of that too. Of course, his case was a bit different. I had a string of bad dates and short failed relationships, and even that had chipped a bit at my optimism.

Dylan had a long-term relationship. He'd been in love. That left scars for sure. But I really did believe that time healed everything. I wished I knew the cause of the breakup though; it would help me come up with an angle. But no one was saying anything about it. It was still a bit of a mystery.

A few minutes later, the bell rang. When I opened the door, my breath caught a little.

Liam was wearing a very elegant coat with a dark-blue and silver scarf around his neck.

My One and Only

His cheeks were red, which meant it was definitely not a warm Thanksgiving Day.

"Well, hello there. Let me just grab my coat."

Liam let out a little growl, and I jerked my head back in surprise before batting my eyelashes at him.

"Hey, don't take this wrong. I love those growls. Very sexy. But what are they for?"

"You."

I glanced down at myself. "No, I'm wearing a sweater. And jeans. What about my outfit spells indecent?"

My sweater was even all buttoned up.

"Not indecent, just fucking gorgeous."

Before I had a chance to ask anything more, he pinned me against the open door, kissing me deeply. I wrapped my arms around his neck, instinctively pressing myself against him. He kissed me until I rose on my tiptoes, dragging my hands down his shoulders. I was resenting his sexy coat already, because I couldn't touch him properly. He really did smell like a cold winter day mixed with aftershave.

I sighed when we pulled apart to take a deep breath.

"Hmmm...I don't know what that was for, but I'll take it." With a grin, I brought my hand to the top button. It was impossible to be around Liam and not have sexy thoughts. Just the way he looked at me, with those blue eyes blazing, was enough to make me forget what day it was.

He caught my wrist even before I reached the button.

"You do that and we won't leave at all." His gaze pinned me in my spot.

"How do you know? Maybe I'm wearing something totally unsexy," I teased.

"You're wearing code red."

"Yes. How did you know?"

"You have an extra swing in your hips. You always do."

"Wow, I have to up my game if I want to keep you on your toes, huh? Wouldn't want you to get bored."

I'd meant it as a joke, but there was a bit of truth hidden in my words. A fear I couldn't shake that maybe I was doing too much or too little and all this happiness would just disappear.

"I won't tire of you, Tess. Ever. I can't believe I'm lucky enough to have found you. No way in hell am I going to let you go."

I melted, loving his warm words. But I also detected a hint of unease in his expression.

"Is something wrong? You seem to have something on your mind."

Liam shook his head. "There's always something on my mind. Let's just enjoy Thanksgiving."

"Okay..."

I didn't like that he was placating me instead of opening up, but I didn't want to cause a scene.

"You're right; there's always something going on. I was trying to keep an eye on the website while getting ready, but it's working great so far."

"Any bugs in the code?"

"None so far. It works perfectly. I love it."

He kissed me again, even harder than the first time. I felt every lash of his tongue deep inside my body. When I fisted his hair, he groaned, taking a step back.

"Tess, grab your coat and let's go or we're really not going to go anywhere tonight."

"Oh, Thanksgiving. Right."

I caught a hint of Liam's smirk as he helped me slip on my coat.

"Hey, mister. Don't look so satisfied. Any woman would forget what day it is when you kiss her like that."

"Kiss you how?"

"It made me wet," I whispered.

His pupils dilated as he exhaled sharply. "Mission accomplished. Now you're feeling as off-kilter as I do. Come on, let's hurry. I don't want to make a bad impression."

26

TESS

When Liam said he spent Thanksgiving with his grandmother, I hadn't realized it was just him. Ellen was a wonderful cook, but even as we finished our turkey, I still couldn't believe it was just the three of us.

"Ellen, this is all delicious. Thank you so much."

She beamed. "You're a darling. By the way, Liam, I spoke to your mom this morning. She said we should give them a call when we're all together."

"Sure." Liam got his phone out, and I broke out in a sweat. *His parents? Oh my God, why didn't he prepare me for this?*

I tugged at the hem of my sweater under the table, crossing and uncrossing my legs. He positioned the phone on the table so all three of us were visible. Sweat dotted my palm when the call connected and his parents appeared on the screen. His mom looked like a younger version of Ellen. His dad had jet-black hair and round glasses.

"Hey, Mom! Liam! And you must be Tess."

"I am. So nice to meet you."

"Likewise," his dad said. "Liam, how is business?"

Liam went on to explain some details about our collaboration. The whole conversation felt a little stiff and cold, at least compared to how we spoke to each other in my family. The call only lasted five minutes, and neither Liam nor Ellen seemed surprised when it was over.

"What time do you have to be at your next dinner?" Ellen asked us.

"In one hour," Liam answered.

"Oh, that doesn't leave us much time."

She started rising from the table, but Liam immediately gestured for her to sit down. "Don't get up. I'm cleaning this up."

I loved how he treated his grandmother.

"I'll help," I said.

Ellen smiled. "Well, then, I'll just be a lady of leisure. Why don't I pour us some brandy?"

"I'm your girl," I exclaimed.

Between Liam and me, we managed to carry all the plates and saucers to the kitchen.

"Liam, does Ellen have plans after we leave?" I asked tentatively.

"No."

My heart broke a little. I didn't want to leave the poor woman alone.

"You think she'd like to come with us to Mom's?" I asked just as Liam closed the dishwasher.

He straightened up, turning slowly toward me. His eyebrows were so high they were almost lost in his hairline.

"Umm…I didn't want to cross any boundaries. Just thinking about her all alone made me sad. We don't have to—"

"Tess, stop." He closed the distance to me, brushing his thumb over my lower lip. "Stop always thinking you're crossing boundaries."

"It can happen, though. You told me that when we first met. That you have a very clear line…for everything."

"Yeah. I did. Before I fell in love with you."

My heart felt about to explode. Seriously. My pulse went from normal to haywire in a millisecond.

"You love me?" I whispered. My voice sounded a bit strangled.

He brushed his nose against mine. "If this surprises you, then I really have to do a better job of showing you."

"Oh yeah. How?"

"I have so many things in my mind. None appropriate for this very moment."

Slowly, I felt my mouth curl into a smile, then stretch into a grin so big that my cheeks were aching.

I pointed to my teeth. "See this grin?"

"Hard to miss it."

"I love you so much, Liam."

His shoulders dropped a little, as if tension just left them.

I poked them. "What's this? You're surprised too?"

He tilted his head with the cutest grin, saying, "I'm just fucking happy."

I jumped him the next second, because why not put all this extra energy to good use?

He stumbled for a brief moment before regaining his balance. His hands went under my ass, and he carried me to the counter.

As soon as I was sitting on it, he took control of the kiss, deepening it until I gasped for breath. I was shaking slightly from his actions.

"You're the most amazing woman, Tess. Warm and funny, and so damn caring that it brings me to my knees. Thank you for wanting to bring Gran with us."

"You think she'll want to go?" I asked.

"Let's find out."

. . .

My One and Only

Ellen was so ecstatic that she was ready to leave within fifteen minutes. She was certainly fast for her age, and she claimed the knee injury was actually slowing her down. We chugged our cognac right before heading out the door. Liam and I had initially planned to take a train to Brooklyn to avoid traffic, but we just missed it.

Our little episode in the kitchen had sidetracked us, but it was totally worth it.

He loves me!

I was floating on a cloud so high that I could tolerate even the traffic in this city with a smile on my face.

Uber had no cars available, but Liam flagged down a yellow cab, and the three of us slid in the back seat. I was in the middle, a bit squished from both sides, but I really didn't mind.

I was still floating on my amazing cloud when I realized this was the first time Liam was meeting my brothers and Hunter. I told them more about him when we'd finally gotten around to having lunch together, but *meeting* him was different.

"Ummm...I forgot to tell you. All the male members in my family are going to pay extra attention to you. They might be a bit intense, but it's just because they don't know you."

"I know Ryker," Liam said, taken aback. "I've met him at a few industry events."

"You know Ryker the investment banker, not Ryker the brother. Big difference."

Liam cocked a brow, like he didn't quite believe me.

Ellen nudged me with her elbow. "Full of himself, this one. Always been like this. Can't wait to see your brothers in action."

"I really like you, Ellen."

She struck me as really lonely, and I immediately resolved to ask Mom to invite Ellen over often.

"Don't you two band against me," Liam warned.

. . .

To say Mom's place was packed was an understatement. The whole family was there. But honestly, I loved that we were all crammed in here. No matter where you were in the apartment, you could just hear everyone's laughter and joy. The place smelled delicious, of roasting turkey, baked apple and cinnamon, and even hot chocolate.

Isabelle, Dylan, and Ian were here too. Mom and her husband, Mick, were the first to notice us, and they immediately came to greet us.

"Liam, so happy to finally meet you. And Ellen, so delighted you could come," Mom said.

Mick shook hands with Liam and kissed Ellen's hand.

"Thank you for opening your home to me on such short notice," Ellen said.

Mick nodded. "It's our pleasure."

Mom waved her hand. "We love big gatherings, though this place is bursting at the seams. Know that you're always welcome here."

While she showed Ellen and Liam where to put their coats, I caught Isabelle's eye and waved at her. She immediately hurried over to us, checking out Liam appreciatively.

"Liam, this is Isabelle, my cousin's sister-in-law and one of my favorite people."

"Nice to meet you, Liam. Thanks for making my girl so happy and being such a sight for sore eyes. When I looked you up online, I rated you ten out of ten, but in real life, you're like twenty out of ten."

Liam's eyes bulged, and I laughed. I was used to Isabelle's balls-to-the-wall ways and sometimes forgot that others weren't.

"I just have to make sure my brothers don't scare him away. Then I'll get on with Operation Dylan," I whispered to Isabelle once Mom had Liam and Ellen engaged in conversation. We weren't even out of earshot, but the constant chatter was loud enough to cover my whisper.

She grimaced. "Right... You know what? I think that can wait. I totally forgot that hottie here might get eaten alive."

"I heard that," Liam said, turning around.

I blushed. Isabelle held her chin high. "And yet you're not cowering or even hesitating. Hmmm...can't decide if you're exceptionally brave or clueless."

"I guess we'll find out," Liam said, full of cocky swagger.

Aww, I loved him so much.

The chatter quieted down as we entered the living room.

My brothers, and even my cousin, were a bit of a wild card when it came to this. They were all welcoming with Rob, though they might have given him the talk behind Skye's and my back. That was always a possibility.

"Liam, good to see you, man," Ryker said, clapping one hand on his back.

Cole shook Liam's hand, and then Hunter did the same. I was eyeing the two closely, trying to gauge their thoughts, but it was impossible. When had they perfected their poker faces?

At any rate, they were silent, which I took as a good sign. Neither of them was glaring at my boyfriend—also a good sign.

"The turkey's going to be ready in about half an hour," Mom announced from the other side of the room. "In case anyone's hungry already, there are some snacks on the table."

I wasn't hungry, but I was *so* looking forward to Mom's cheese crates. They were my favorites. I headed straight to the table, along with Avery, Ryker and Heather's daughter. She and I had similar taste in food.

"How are you, Avery?"

"I'm so excited about my sister. I can't wait to meet her." Avery motioned to the couch, where a visibly pregnant Heather was sitting, hands crossed over her belly.

I winked at Avery. "I was very excited too when I was waiting for my siblings to be born."

She loaded her plate with a dozen crackers.

"You're going to eat all those cheese crackers by yourself?" I asked, not wanting her to get sick or ruin her dinner.

"No. I'm taking them to Mommy. If she eats a lot, maybe my sister will grow faster and come out sooner. She won't fit anymore."

Avery's tone was very serious. Clearly, she'd given this a lot of thought, and I was fighting laughter with all I had.

When she ran toward Heather, I put two crackers on my own plate. Mom had this amazing recipe where she mixed raisins, almonds, and three types of cheese. I hummed on my first bite. It was just as delicious as I remembered. As soon as I swallowed it down, I became aware that Liam wasn't next to me.

Turning around, I saw him surrounded by my brothers and Hunter, who seemed very chatty. *Really? They'd been waiting for me to leave?*

Mick came up to me, taking a few crackers for himself and laughing when he saw me watching the guys.

"It's just a sign that they take him seriously," he said. "After all, they gave me the talk too when I first started dating Amelia."

"Yeah, but I think I'm gonna go play referee anyway."

With a sigh, I put down my plate, tiptoeing toward the group. I was hoping to eavesdrop on their conversation before they noticed me.

No such luck.

"Tess is behind you," Ryker told Cole.

I rolled my eyes, putting my hands on my hips. "Really? What is this?"

"We're just getting to know Liam better," Cole said nonchalantly.

"And I can't hear that conversation?" I challenged.

My One and Only

"Well, you can. But then you might kick our ass," Hunter said.

I glared at him. "I might do it anyway. Just for fun."

Ryker winked. "Well, I think we're about done anyway."

I looked at Liam, noticing the corners of his mouth tilted up in a smile.

"Really? You didn't sound done to me. Tess, I think they're just waiting for you to leave again. They were just explaining to me all the ways they'll make me pay if I mess up," he said casually.

I ran a hand through my hair, at a loss for words. My brothers seemed proud of themselves, as did Hunter.

Behind us, someone chuckled. Dylan. He, Ian, and Isabelle were just one foot behind me and had clearly heard everything.

"You guys gave him the talk and he's not even a little worried? You're losing your touch," Ian said.

"Oh no, no. We've got enough with Hunter, Cole, and Ryker on his case. No one needs more testosterone," Isabelle declared.

Ian smirked. "Want us to keep it all for the next guy you introduce to us?"

Dylan grinned. "You don't want to bottle up the testosterone, Sis."

Isabelle gave me an apologetic nod. "Sorry. If I'd known they were going to misbehave, I wouldn't have brought them. Liam, these are my brothers. Don't pay them attention. They're all talk, no bite."

"Is that why you never introduce us to any guy you're dating?" Dylan replied.

Isabelle rolled her eyes. "Give it a rest."

"No, I'm quite enjoying it," Liam said. "The first few times I spoke with Tess, she roasted my ass. I respect that trait. Now I see it runs in the family. Even the extended one."

Oh wow. I could see my family's acceptance for him skyrocketing.

Dylan whistled. "Liam, I think you're okay."

Before anyone could say anything else, Mom spoke loudly. "Okay, everyone, sit at the table, please. The turkey's been resting enough. It'll get cold otherwise."

There was a lot of noise in the room as everyone headed to the table and pulled out chairs. I made sure Ellen sat between Mom and Liam.

I loaded my plate with a bit of turkey and a lot of cinnamon rice. Mom had experimented one year with half a dozen side dishes, and the rice had won by a decent margin. It was a staple in her Thanksgiving dinners ever since.

Hunter was pouring everyone drinks, except for Josie and Heather, who were sticking with water. I smiled to myself, feeling on pins and needles. Maybe they'd announce the pregnancy today. This was very usual in our family, waiting for the gang to be gathered for spilling important news.

As we all ate, I kept glancing around the table, listening to bits and pieces of conversation. Cole, Laney, and I spoke quite a bit about the wedding. The planner had finally sent decent proposals for the shabby chic theme, and they'd decided on a location. It was a gorgeous restaurant in a nineteenth-century mansion just outside New York.

Afterward, I turned my attention to the rest of the group.

My goal was simple: check how everyone was doing. I knew I couldn't solve anyone's problems, of course, but I was very good at listening and also at improving people's mood.

Half an hour later, I was happy to report that no one was in trouble. Heather was a little tired due to the pregnancy but otherwise perfectly healthy. Ryker seemed to be even more attentive to her than usual, which made my heart happy. He'd always been so adamant that he wanted to be a bachelor for life.

My One and Only

I caught Liam's eye. I sensed he'd been watching me for a while.

"What?" I whispered.

"You're adorable, checking in on everyone like this."

My cheeks heated and I shrugged. "I always do this."

He nodded, squeezing my hand under the table as everyone was going for seconds. I would have done the same, but I was already full when we left Ellen's place. I still wanted to save room for Mom's trademark Thanksgiving pie—a unique mix of pecans, honey, apple, and pumpkin. Also, I couldn't wait to drink punch. The scents wafting from the kitchen were strong and delicious, but we all knew better than to drink before dinner. Mom's punch was strong enough to get drunk on half a cup.

"Mom, I always forget how good your Thanksgiving pie is," Cole exclaimed a while later, when we were all indulging in the dessert.

"And the punch," I added with a wink.

Hunter cleared his throat. "Since we're all here, Josie and I have an announcement to make."

Yes! I pressed my lips together, determined not to give them away.

The table was silent as Josie spoke. "I'm pregnant. We've known for a while but wanted to wait for the first three months to pass before telling you."

She didn't get to say anything more because everyone jumped to congratulate them. I caught Mom's eye across the table. She didn't seem surprised. Perhaps they told her, or she guessed, just like me. Ian and Dylan looked particularly pleased as they hugged their sister.

"Now we have an even better reason to finalize the move," Dylan said.

Isabelle clutched at her chest. "You mean Josie and I weren't enough?"

Ian winked at her. "Not at all, Sis. Just that we're extra motivated to not drag this out too long."

"Amelia, looks like your table is going to be even fuller next year," Ellen exclaimed.

Mom beamed at her. "The more the merrier."

"You're lucky. I've been waiting for great-grandkids forever."

It took me a second to realize she was speaking about Liam. The tips of my ears felt hot. Liam looked at his grandmother as if he was seeing her for the first time.

"Okay, okay. I'm behaving," Ellen said with a grin that clearly indicated she planned to do no such thing. Then she leaned closer to Amelia and whispered for the whole table to hear, "They're so adorable, the both of them. They'll make beautiful babies."

27

LIAM

"This was amazing," Tess said once we entered my apartment. It was very late at night. We'd just dropped off Gran before coming here. "And Ellen had a great time, don't you think?"

It was endearing how much she cared for everyone's happiness.

I took off my coat before helping her out of hers. I removed it slowly, lingering with my fingers on her arms until I felt her shudder.

"She had a great time," I assured her, hanging up the coats. Then I placed my hands on her shoulders, turning her around until we were face-to-face.

"I'm sure she's going to ask Mick and Amelia to go to her place for a round of chess sometime soon. Discuss everything from more dinners together to what their grandkids will look like."

Fuck, where had that come from? I'd certainly not intended to say it, and from Tess's wide eyes, she hadn't expected to hear it.

She was blushing, just like she'd done at dinner, but she

wasn't pulling back or dismissing my words. My whole body relaxed. I wanted Tess in my life, always and forever. It had never been as clear as it was now.

"I love you, Tess." I drew my fingers over her jaw before skimming my thumb over her lips.

She smiled, clasping her fingers around my wrist before bringing my hand up her cheek and planting a quick kiss on the heel of my palm.

I moved my other hand to her neck. Her pulse quickened. Her eyes were full of emotions.

"You've given this a lot of thought, hmm?" she whispered.

"Not before today," I admitted. "But now I do have some very specific thoughts."

Her smile turned into a grin. "Care to share them?"

"No. Don't want to scare you away." I was semiserious.

"That specific, huh?"

"Actually, yes."

I'd only fleetingly thought about having a family years ago before dismissing the idea. But even then, it had been a loose sketch, more of an idea, so very different from now.

"By the way, why didn't you warn me about the call with your parents?"

"I forgot to tell you, sorry. But as you saw, it wasn't that involved."

"True."

"Before I met you, it didn't bother me as much. But now...I mean, I can't change them. But you and I can build the life we want. Together."

I could visualize our lives together in scarily accurate detail. How we'd both have busy but satisfying weeks, weekends full of laughter, games, and fun. How she'd insist on Tess-like things like making jam on specific days, and I'd try my best at being a good husband. A good dad. I thought I'd make a great one with Tess at my side.

It was a vivid image that seemed to paint itself on its own. I couldn't exactly describe it, because it was more of a feeling...but I could show her just how much she meant to me.

Cupping the back of her head, I kissed her deep and so slow that I was aware of every breath she took, every moan that escaped her. I was drinking it all in. I kissed her until her body started shaking slightly. When she began tugging at her sweater, as if she couldn't stand having clothes on any longer, I nearly lost my mind. Gripping her hips, I pinned her against the nearest wall, wanting more leverage. I got rid of her jeans. She was wearing stockings. Fuck, now I really was losing my mind. She looked at me through hooded eyelids, smiling happily.

"Come on, move it farther up." Her voice was seductive, and I realized she was holding back more than stockings.

I lifted her sweater up to her waist, sucking in a deep breath. Tess was wearing a lace bodice, connected to the stockings by thin straps running down each thigh. She was so damn sexy that I couldn't stop staring. I wanted to touch every part of her at once and didn't know where to start. Getting rid of her sweater was a sound decision, so I did. Her bodice went up to her breasts but was strapless and had buttons down the middle.

I was the luckiest man alive.

I traced the contour of her upper breasts, just where the fabric ended, while parting her thighs with my knee. She closed her eyes, swallowing hard while I undid the first button and then the next one. I didn't stop until I undid all of them. It didn't fall to the floor but hung to her curves, taunting me. She opened her eyes, placing both hands on my shoulders and pulling me toward her. She initiated the kiss at the same time I touched between her thighs over the fabric of her lingerie. I groaned at how wet she was. She moaned while I slowly rubbed two fingers over the fabric, back and forth, until she couldn't kiss me anymore because she was panting. Her legs were shaky. I skimmed my other hand around the straps and then the clips that connected the bodice to the stockings.

With two snaps, I loosened the clips. Lowering myself on my haunches, I took off each stocking. After baring her legs, I kissed from her knees up her inner thighs until I reached the apex. The lacy fabric was still in the way. Sexy as it was, I wanted it off her. I wanted her completely bare.

"Take it off," I commanded, watching her.

Tess obliged immediately, pushing the bodice down her hips and stepping out of it once it was around her ankles.

I looked up at her, drinking in her sexy naked body before rising and kissing her hard.

Then I lifted her up my body, holding her by her ass. She whimpered, pressed against me. Her clit was level with my belt buckle. Our surroundings faded as I moved through the apartment. She tightened her grip on my shoulders, rolling her hips and practically humping my belt.

She needed more friction. Fuck, I wanted to be inside her. I couldn't wait any longer.

I only made it to the kitchen counter. I lowered her on her feet, kneading her ass cheeks before letting go. I undressed in the pitch dark. Fortunately, Tess helped a lot. I couldn't even see where her hands were, just felt them all over me until I was naked.

Gripping her hand, I brought it over my cock. "Touch me. Fuuuck, touch me."

I dropped my head back, groaning when she clasped her hand around me, moving it in a maddening rhythm. I felt more than saw her lower herself to her knees. She pressed the flat of her tongue against the tip of my cock.

"Fuuuck."

My One and Only

I held her hair, needing to grip and move and thrust, barely keeping myself from moving my hips. I inhaled through my nose, exhaling through my mouth. I couldn't see anything, just felt her tongue and her lips. It was driving me insane.

"Babe, I want you." I sounded so desperate that I didn't recognize my own voice.

She clamped her lips around me even tighter. I buckled backward, letting go of her hair and pressing my palms on the edge of the counter. Tess pulled back, kissing my abs and chest. I cupped her head with both hands, kissing her until we were both out of breath.

"Condom," I muttered.

"I have one in my bag," she whispered.

Fuck no. That was in the corridor. I didn't want to let her go that long, but I had no choice.

She moved in the darkness, turning on the light once she stepped out of the room. I was so desperate that I started touching myself, squeezing my hand tight around my cock. It wasn't enough.

She returned a few seconds later, leaving the light on. It barely filtered in the room, but it was enough to see her gorgeous naked body.

"Liam..." she whispered when she looked down at me.

"See what you do to me? You make me crazy. Desperate. Come here."

She ripped open the package as she walked. I only took my hand away when she stood in front of me, rolling on the condom. Energy shot through me at her touch. Fuck. I needed to thrust into her.

Turning her around, I commanded, "Put your hands on the counter."

I spread her legs at the same time. She gasped lightly when I bit her shoulder. Gripping the base of my cock, I positioned myself between her legs, then slid inside all at once until my thighs pressed against her ass. Tess buckled forward, gasping. Leaning my forehead on the back of her neck, I breathed in her scent, covering her body with my arms, holding her, steadying her.

I moved my hips then, needing the pleasure. Tess gasped. She was coming apart in my arms, and I'd only started thrusting. We were both half curled over the counter, and I straightened us up so I could touch her better. I touched her breasts, cupping them before lowering one hand to her clit. She whimpered, tightening around me. Desire coiled through me, and I moved even faster. My legs were burning, but I didn't want to slow down. I needed more. I needed everything.

"You're mine," I whispered in her ear, wanting to voice the feeling that consumed me. "Only mine."

I held her through her moans and gasps of pleasure, thrusting inside her until I felt her come apart. One of her legs shot out to one side as the other wobbled. Even though her hands were firmly on the counter, I was the one sustaining us both. My climax formed slowly and then spread like wildfire. I'd never come like this, not ever. My whole body was burning. My bones felt liquid, and I could barely breathe through my orgasm. My legs were about to give out.

Tess leaned up a bit, resting her elbows on the counter, and I mirrored her stance, my chest pressed to her back. I rested my chin in the crook of her neck. We were both still breathing unbelievably fast, enjoying the afterglow of what we'd just experienced.

After what felt like hours, my limbs started feeling normal again. I turned Tess around, and she became soft in my arms. I lifted her up to hold her even closer to me, and she gently laid her head against my shoulder.

My feisty, talkative woman was completely quiet, too spent. I was damn proud of myself.

"Do you think you can stand in the shower?" I asked as I carried her into the master bathroom.

"Well, if I don't, I'm sure you'll do the right thing and help me," she teased.

"That's true. I'm a gentleman."

"And you never miss a chance to fondle me."

"That too."

I got rid of the condom, and after I made sure the water temperature was just right, I put her down under the warm spray. It was all I could do not to maul her against the tiles too.

Tess grinned, pointing at my mouth. "Wait, I know that look. Are you thinking about having your wicked way with me again?"

"Of course I am, but I don't want you to be sore tomorrow."

"I don't mind."

"Woman, don't tempt me."

Wiggling her eyebrows, she poured shower gel in her palms, rubbing it all over her body. I stood back, just enjoying the sight. Until she put her soaped-up hands on me. I instantly turned hard, and Tess smirked. I caught her wrists the next second, pinning them above her head against the tile.

"Don't, Tess. I mean it. I can't resist you, and I don't want you to be sore. I was an animal back there."

She smiled saucily. "I loved every second of it."

"If I let go of your hands, will you behave?"

"Hell no."

I laughed before kissing her, slow and lazy, until there was so much steam in the shower that we could barely breathe.

"Come on, sassy girl. Let's get out of here before we suffocate."

"You're going to have to let go of my hands if you want us to move," she teased.

I did let go, and she kept her hands off me...right until we dried off and stepped out of the bathroom. Then she wrapped her arms around me from behind, resting her palms on my pelvic bones.

"Tess..."

"You didn't specify until when I couldn't touch you. And these"—she ran her fingers up and down the V-line pointing to my hard-on—"happen to be some of your finest assets."

"What are some of the others?" I prompted, realizing what I'd done only when she moved her hand even lower, covering my erection. I couldn't help but groan. "Fuck, my mistake."

"I'll forgive it."

I turned around, kissing the tip of her nose.

"You sassy girl. You're not sleepy at all, are you?"

"Nope. You'd think two Thanksgiving dinners would put me to sleep, but I'm wide awake. I wonder why." She pressed her mouth in a thin line, narrowing her eyes as if thinking hard. "I know. The hot guy taking me right over the kitchen counter might have chased the sleep away."

I growled. "Don't speak about me in third person."

"Jealous again?"

"Yes. I can't explain it."

She squealed, lacing her arms around my neck and glancing at my bed. "And I love it. I have a dangerous proposition. Let's not go to bed at all. It's three o'clock, and I need to wake up at six."

"Why?"

"Tomorrow's Black Friday, remember?"

"Actually, no. Friday after Thanksgiving is always a lazy day for me."

"Not for those looking for sales. Or those offering sales."

"You're going to be exhausted if you don't sleep."

My One and Only

"I know. But going to bed for three hours will be even worse. I'll have a headache the whole day."

"Okay. I'm on board."

"So how do you plan to keep me up until morning?"

I pinched her ass. "I thought you were keeping *me* up."

"I have a few ideas. But you have to promise not to veto them."

"Can't do that now, can I? I have to take care of you, even when you don't seem to want it." I gave us both robes, tying hers around the middle tightly. She jumped in my arms, and I carried her to the living room.

"Oooh, back to the kitchen island. I like where this is going," she teased.

"No, it's the couch."

I sat down with Tess in my lap, pushing her damp hair out of her face. She yawned in a cute way.

"You sure you don't want to sleep?"

"No, sir. Why waste time sleeping when I have you to feast on? Let's call these exploration hours."

"Because you're tired."

"I'll go to bed early tomorrow. I'll have some long weeks ahead with the opening and Christmas approaching."

They planned to officially open the store on the fifth of December.

"I'll take good care of you." I started to massage her feet to prove my point, moving up on her ankles.

"You're amazing to have around." She sighed, closing her eyes and enjoying my hands on her. When she opened them again, she looked a little wary.

"You want to talk about what's got you worried? I told you I'm good at reading clues."

"And I told you that today is Thanksgiving."

"Not anymore. It's past midnight," Tess said.

"We're not wasting these exploration hours, as you called them, by talking about anything unpleasant," I replied.

"Fine, but I'm only giving in because I actually am getting a bit tired, and I want to make the most of our time together."

In fact, I didn't plan to waste any time with Tess talking about Albert. He was my mess to clean up, and she had so much on her plate that I didn't want to add any more. I was going to protect her from that imbecile, and that was that. One thing I learned from my grandfather was that problems were meant to be dealt with without burdening the ones you loved with them.

She was mine, and that didn't just mean giving her massages or orgasms or making her laugh. She was mine to protect.

"I think I know of a way to keep you up all the way until morning," I whispered in her ear.

Tess grinned. "That's your best pickup line?"

"You're saying I need one?"

She shrugged a shoulder. "I like it when you seduce me."

28

LIAM

The Monday after Thanksgiving, I did something I hadn't done in years: I went to see Albert.

I didn't ask him to come to the brownstone, because I didn't want to see David and Becca out of sorts again.

The detective had dug up Albert's personal address, as well as the fact that he spent most of his day there.

It was a hellhole outside the city, nothing like the condo he used to afford. The dumbass. If he smartly invested the paycheck we sent him every month, or at least saved a chunk of it, things would be very different.

The building's elevator wasn't working, so I took the stairs to the fifth floor. There was a coat of filth on each step. I didn't look too closely, but it was more than just dust and mud.

I knocked at number 57 a few times. When no one answered, I banged louder until I heard movement on the other side of the door. Albert opened it, finally. He looked like he'd just gone to sleep. Dark circles marked his eyes. His gray T-shirt had multiple holes in it, as did his shorts.

"What the fuck?" he exclaimed.

I pushed him out of the doorway, stepping inside the apartment.

"What are you doing here?" he asked.

"Wanted to talk to you. Didn't want you to show your face at the brownstone again."

The hallway was small and dark, but I had no intention of staying long enough to go into any of the rooms.

"How do you know where I live?"

"I had a detective look into you."

"Did you now? Liked what he found?"

"You're broke. You're actually stupid enough to waste all that money you're getting every month."

"It's not that much."

"Depends what you're used to."

His last building had a doorman and concierge services. His suits used to be five thousand a piece.

"That's why I need more. That's why I want out of the firm."

"You'll just waste that money too."

"That's not your problem though, is it?"

"It is. It requires me to do something I don't want to. I have a problem with that."

Albert narrowed his eyes. "All you have to do to get enough cash to buy me out is freeze one current investment. One."

I stared at him. "How do you know that?"

"You're not the only one who hired a detective."

"You live in this shithole and waste money on a detective? Christ, what happened to you? You used to be smart."

It was why we made him a partner in the business. It wasn't just because he'd been our friend.

"I won't freeze it."

Albert's eyes turned cold. "What the fuck is wrong with you? You've wanted me out of the business for years."

"This is a bad time."

"You're fucking one of those bitches from Soho Lingerie, aren't you?"

I rolled my hands into fists.

"The one who's not married. My detective suspected that," he continued.

"You ever call anyone a bitch in front of me again, you won't have teeth. You hired a shit detective if he didn't even confirm Tess and I are together."

"You're crazy if you think I'm going to wait on my ass until the time is convenient for you."

"Yes, you will."

"Maybe I should go see this Tess. Find out what she thinks about this."

My hands were gripping his T-shirt before I even realized it. "You go anywhere near Tess and you're done. So fucking done."

"Yeah? What're you going to do about it?"

"We never pressed charges against you."

"Because you didn't have the balls. So don't come to me with that. You're too proud to have your name tainted in any way, so don't think I'm buying this act."

"People change, Albert. You changed. I changed. Things that used to matter don't anymore."

Others did, and they mattered so much more.

For the first time, I saw uncertainty in his eyes, even fear. Good, because I meant every word.

"I'm not budging on the deadline," he said.

"I'll pretend I didn't hear that. I want a written notice that you'll extend the deadline until April, or I'll make you very sorry for trying to steal from us. I don't want an answer now. Think about it. Really well," I said.

I left before he had a chance to reply. I didn't want to hear one more word or I was liable to punch him.

I didn't know what the hell I'd been thinking, coming here.

Maybe that I could get through to him somehow because we'd been friends once? Clearly, that didn't matter to him.

And it didn't to me either. Not anymore. Albert was going to learn the hard way not to mess with me.

29

TESS

The week after Thanksgiving was slightly insane. I mean, it usually was, and not because Black Friday was the following day. Once the town was full of Christmas decorations, tourists flocked to see them. All the main shopping streets were crowded, and we could barely find our ass from our elbow in the store the whole week. This year, I had a bit more on my plate than I could handle, splitting my time between the two stores while supervising the last-minute repairs at the new location.

Unfortunately, on the second of December, the furniture company announced that our order had arrived damaged. The replacement order wouldn't be here for two weeks. No way could we open without shelves and couches and chairs.

"You know what? I have an idea," Liam said after we both read the apologetic email. "Why don't you have a pre-opening party with the family? That way you still have something to look forward to."

"That's a great idea," I replied. "I'll text Skye to see what she thinks, but I'm sold on it. Oooh, we could also invite our VIP clients. We can make it seem like a very exclusive event, where they also get a peek at the new collection."

"You're a genius."

I grinned. "I love it when you sing my praises."

"It's true."

We were at the new store in the back office. Liam was expertly massaging my neck, and I could feel my stress melting away.

"Why are your hands so amazing?" I whispered.

He brought his mouth to my ear. "I'm amazing. My hands, tongue, lips. Cock."

I spun my chair until I was face-to-face with him. The tips of our noses were almost touching.

"How can you say that with a straight face?"

He straightened up, winking. "Again...because it's true."

I rolled my eyes playfully. "Did you finish your emails?"

We had a very cute routine going where he came to the store every day after everyone left the brownstone, and we worked in companionable silence until at least one of us was done.

"No." With a frown, he went back to sitting behind his desk.

My stomach jolted. Lately, even with all the shit going on, I was still done before he was. He could just about make me melt into a puddle with nothing more than a kiss or those magic hands, yet I was failing miserably at helping him relax.

Liam typed on his laptop while I texted with Skye.

Skye: I'm SO on board with this!! It's one hell of a good idea. I'm also going to give Sam a piece of my mind. I don't care if he has to deliver the furniture personally; this is unacceptable.

Tess: You do that.

Skye was great at putting the fear of God in everyone, though to be honest, this wasn't Sam's fault at all. Still, extra motivation never hurt.

My One and Only

I quickly drafted a newsletter, specifically aimed at our VIP segment. Once I was done, I looked up at Liam. He was frowning at his screen.

I got up, sashaying my hips in an exaggerated manner as I went over to him, hoping to catch his eye. I didn't. He only noticed me when I sat at the edge of his desk, mirroring his earlier pose.

"Mr. Harrington, you're so focused lately that my attempts at seduction go unnoticed. I'm losing my touch," I said in a mock serious tone.

"Not at all. I just have a lot on my mind."

I sat in his lap, shimmying a little. "Tell me."

"It's not worth it." He waved a hand, planting a quick kiss on my chin. He trailed his fingers down the sides of my body before attacking my armpits. I shrieked with laughter, hanging on to him for dear life.

"Stop. Stop! How did you know I have ticklish armpits?

"Because that's where you tickled me. Figured it was your weak spot too."

When I straightened up, I noticed he was still not in playful mode. He was still thinking about his troubles...which he wasn't sharing.

Lately, he was evasive whenever I asked him about his day. I didn't want to insist too much, though. What if he got sick of my questions? No, no, no. I didn't want to go down that negative path of thinking. He didn't have to share every thought like I did. Maybe I couldn't help him relax right now, but I could love him with all my heart and hope that was enough.

"Well, okay, since you're so secretive, I'm just going to have to try all my tactics to get that sexy smile I like so much."

He leaned back in the chair, wiggling his eyebrows. "All of them?"

"Every single one."

"How will you start?"

I traced my finger in a small circle around the top button of his shirt. "I could start here..." Then I quickly moved to the last button right over his belt. "Or here..."

He groaned a bit, rocking his hips a few inches forward. I pushed him back playfully.

"Nah...I don't think I'll start here after all."

Something flashed in his eyes, and I knew I was close to unleashing all that passion inside him. I leaned in, kissing the side of his neck, then his Adam's apple.

"I love you," I whispered.

"I love you too, babe. If you go on like that, this desk is going to see some very inappropriate things."

I smiled against his skin, shimmying some more in his lap. "Just the words I was hoping to hear."

On the day of the pre-opening party with the family and our VIP clients, I was in a complete frenzy. To be honest, I'd been like that ever since we decided on the idea. Thankfully, a certain sexy man doted on me all the time, as if he knew it was just what I needed.

It was practically impossible for me not to be in a good mood. Proof of that was the fact that even though I was bone-tired and mad at the furniture company for messing up, I was still grinning from ear to ear, watching him walk through the door with a seductive smile and a pizza. His coat was covered in pristine white snow, as was his hair. It had been snowing all day.

I sashayed to him, relieving him of the pizza box.

"Wait a second. I don't even get a kiss?"

"Now that you mention it..."

I rose on my tiptoes, giving him a quick, chaste kiss, but

Liam immediately turned it deep and dirty until I was breathless and squirming in my spot. I was blushing when we pulled apart, gesturing with my head toward the crew setting up the buffet for tonight. It was low-key, but we still wanted to offer something for everyone.

Liam shrugged, those smoldering eyes trained on me.

"We can eat in the back," I said, leading the way. Usually, I liked to eat in the front, people-watching and enjoying the Christmas decorations on the street, but now it wasn't too relaxing with the crew bustling about.

"Oh, I forgot I have napkins in the front. I'll get them."

We sectioned off the front, setting up tables against the wall next to the entrance. We left enough space for people to be able to move about. Since a lot of the furniture was missing, the store was half empty anyway. We had three mannequins we dressed up in nightgowns in the display and a few racks with lingerie in the center. I found napkins on the buffet table the guys had set up.

I heard the front door open and turned around. It wasn't anyone I knew.

"Can I help you?" I asked.

"Tess Winchester?"

"Yes."

"I'm Albert McDowell. I'm—"

"I know who you are. Liam told me about you. What are you doing here?"

I narrowed my eyes, inspecting him. He seemed a few years older than Liam, Becca, and David, or maybe his bald head just gave me that impression. His large green eyes scanned the room. Clearly, he didn't like that I had company. By the way he swayed in his boots, I suspected he was a bit intoxicated.

"Where's Liam?" he asked. "I saw him come in."

He followed Liam?

"What are you doing here?" I repeated.

"Can we speak somewhere more private?"

"No. No offense, but I've just met you, and you don't exactly come recommended. I don't trust you."

"You're a piece of work, aren't you?"

"Excuse me?"

"If it weren't for you, Liam would have given me what I wanted."

"Bad luck. I can't help you."

"Yes, you fucking can."

"You don't come inside my store and talk to me like that." I pointed to the door, barely able to keep my temper in check. "Out."

Footsteps echoed behind me.

"Babe, what's—what the fuck are you doing here?" Liam bellowed the second he noticed Albert.

"I want to talk to you."

"Then you make an appointment and come to my office. Get out of here."

"I don't think so." He stalked toward us, and when he was less than a foot away, he confirmed my suspicion. He was drunk. "What happened to you, man? The Liam I knew would never risk his business for anything, let alone a woman."

My heart sank. *Risk his business?*

"Shut up."

"You told me to think really hard about my next steps when you came to see me," Albert said, which made me wonder if this was what Liam had been so tense about. When had Liam seen him? And why hadn't he mentioned this?

"And I did," Albert continued. "If you don't buy me out by Christmas as the contract stipulates, I'm shopping around for another buyer."

"Get. Out." Liam barely moved his lips as he spoke.

My One and Only

Albert lifted his right arm. I brought my hand to my mouth when I realized he was aiming his right hook in Liam's direction. Liam caught his punch in midair, pushing it to one side before shoving Albert, who stumbled back, barely keeping his balance.

"You piece of shit," Liam bellowed as Albert regrouped. He wasn't going to take another shot, was he? He was far too drunk, and Liam was far too sharp and fast. "You don't come in here and threaten my woman."

Liam took Albert by the collar with one hand and blocked his second attempt at a punch with the other. I shrieked, looking around at the crew, who just stared at the scene.

This time, Liam turned Albert around, keeping his right arm behind his back.

"Get the fuck out." Liam marched him toward the door. Opening it, he tossed him in the street. Albert stumbled and nearly collided headfirst with the nearest lamppost. Instead, he managed to break his fall by clinging to it. He looked over his shoulder, frowning at us through the thick curtain of falling snow before turning around and leaving. Liam remained at the door until Albert was out of sight.

Then he turned toward me. "I'm so sorry about that. Are you okay?"

"Yeah. He didn't do anything, just babbled until you arrived. How are you?"

I hurried to him, oblivious to everyone else in the store, even though they were still staring at us.

"I'm okay, Tess," he said softly. My heart was still hammering in my chest. He looked at the guys surrounding us before taking my hand and walking with me to the back office. The smell of melted cheese filled the air, but I didn't feel like eating. I just wanted to make sure he wasn't hurting—in any way.

"Tess, babe, what is it? You're shaking."

He placed his hands on my neck, and I covered them with

my palms. "What did he mean about you risking your business?"

Liam shook his head. "Don't worry about that. I'm dealing with it."

"No, we're in this together. I want to know."

"You already know he wants to sell his shares, and I'm going to find a solution so the shares remain in our control."

"What aren't you telling me?"

He sighed. "If I don't make an offer before Christmas, he can sell them to whoever he wants."

I closed my eyes, trying to rein in all my emotions. "Why didn't you tell me there was a clock on it?"

"I didn't want you to worry."

"Do I seem like I can't handle things?"

"Not at all, Tess. But you have so many things going on with the opening of the store and the inauguration of the new digital platform. I didn't want to take away your joy or add more to your plate."

I melted at his words, pressing my palms over his hands even tighter.

"This isn't right though, Liam. I need to know everything."

"Do you? Why? So both of us can worry instead of just one?"

"Yes. Exactly."

He frowned. "I disagree. Seeing you worrying wouldn't help one bit."

I blinked, taking a step back. "So, what...your solution is just not telling me things?"

Liam looked like he very much wanted to say yes. Before he had a chance to voice that thought, we heard a knock at the door.

"It's me," Skye said.

"Come in," I replied, holding Liam's gaze. Neither of us said anything more as my sister came in.

My One and Only

"Hey. Oh, Liam. I didn't know you were here. Am I interrupting you two?"

"No, not at all," Liam said smoothly. "I brought pizza for everyone."

Skye laughed, peeking at the box. "You mean for you and Tess, but it's huge enough for all of us. Let's dig in. I'm starving."

We all leaned against the desks, eating while standing. I wanted to continue the conversation with Liam, but I honestly didn't know how. He was disarming me with his charm and beautiful words, and I wasn't sure how to make him understand that this was very important to me. I believed communication was the basis for everything.

Skye seemed to pick up on the unease floating in the room, because she kept looking between us.

"This was delicious," she said once the pizza was gone. "Liam, are you staying the whole afternoon?"

"Can't. I just came for lunch. I'll be here for the party later."

"Okay, then get your charming self out of here so Tess and I can prepare everything. And no cute or sexy messages. Those always distract her."

He chuckled. I smiled too, even though what I really wanted was to pull Liam to one side and discuss things with him until we were on the same page. But since I had no plan, I stayed put.

He gave me a quick peck on the forehead, looking me straight in the eyes.

"See you later," I murmured. "Thanks for lunch."

After a beat, he nodded and bid Skye goodbye before leaving.

Once he was gone, my sister eyed me suspiciously. "Okay, so maybe my detective skills aren't as sharp as yours, but there seemed to be something weird in the air."

I sighed, walking over and leaning on her desk right next to her. I laced one arm with hers, resting my head on top of her shoulder.

"You're right."

I then proceeded to tell her everything.

"Wait a second. Of course this isn't right. You're supposed to know. *We're* supposed to know, since this affects the business too." Skye chewed on her lower lip, frowning.

"I have an idea. Let's talk to Becca," I suggested. "I keep feeling that Liam is downplaying everything, and I'd like to hear all the facts."

"Good idea," Skye said.

I called from my phone, which I put on speaker.

"Tess, what a surprise," she greeted. I had little contact with her and David since Liam was our official mentor.

"Hi! Skye's here too. Do you have a few minutes?"

"Sure. How can I help?"

I pushed a hand through my hair and told her everything about Albert as quickly as possible. She swore when I was done.

"Becca, what's going on?"

"You and Liam spoke about this?"

"Yes, but I don't think he's telling me everything."

"Tess," Becca said softly. "He's doing everything he can to find a way out that doesn't involve freezing the investment."

My stomach dropped. "But that's still the best solution?"

She hesitated.

"Becca?" I pressed.

"At the moment, yes."

"Shit!"

"Listen, we've had our fair share of crises over the years, and we always came out on top—"

"I don't want to bring on a crisis!" I exclaimed. I felt heavy all of a sudden. "Becca, thanks for taking my call. I won't keep you any longer. Have a great day."

"You too, girls."

I hung up and hugged the phone to my chest, pressing my forehead against a wall. I needed to think, and I needed to stop panicking, but I didn't know how.

My sister hugged me from one side. "We'll figure this out. Just let me go hunt down some cake and cheese."

I chuckled despite everything. "You sure know how to lift my mood."

"And let's ask the clan to come in earlier. Emergency working lunch before the party. They always give good advice."

"I love that idea."

30

LIAM

"*Fucking* Albert," David exclaimed. We just had a meeting with one of our other mentees, and I only got around to telling him about that imbecile's visit after we got out.

"Are you coming back to the brownstone?" he asked, ordering an Uber.

"No, I'm going to Soho Lingerie's pre-opening party, remember?"

David grinned. "You party, I work. When did the tables turn?"

I grunted. He grinned even more. "That's it. Brood some more so I don't feel like I'm turning into you...too much."

"Tess wasn't very happy that I didn't tell her how pressing the issue with Albert is."

David held his hands up. "Man, don't ask me for relationship advice. Most of my relationships last between one night and one week."

"I wasn't asking for advice," I assured him. "Just thinking out loud."

"Good luck at the party, then."

My One and Only

I nodded as he got in the Uber he ordered. I flagged down a cab and headed to SoHo. When I arrived, I did a double take when I noticed the store was already full. I checked the time. I definitely wasn't too late.

I pushed the door open and was immediately greeted by Cole, Josie, Hunter, and Ryker. The store was filled with the entire Winchester family plus Isabelle. Since the furniture wasn't here yet, the sound of voices was amplified. I felt like I just stepped into a stadium. Amelia and Mick waved to me from next to the buffet.

"When did you all arrive?" I asked. "I thought it was supposed to start in ten minutes."

"It was, but Tess and Skye asked us to come earlier. Emergency family council," Ryker said.

Josie grimaced. "You weren't supposed to give that away."

Ryker cocked a brow. "They never said it's a secret."

"I think my wife is right," Hunter said, putting an arm around Josie's shoulders.

Emergency what? My pulse sped up. "Where is Tess?"

"Some of their VIPs saw that the party started earlier and came in too. They took them to the changing rooms, where we're not allowed," Cole said. "But don't worry, she'll come out eventually. We can entertain you in the meantime."

I rubbed a hand over my jaw. It wasn't that I didn't want to spend time with them, because I did. But I needed to talk to Tess first. I had a bad feeling when I left the store before, and now it was just getting worse.

I shrugged out of my coat, intending to take it easy and enjoy a drink with the Winchester clan while Tess tended to her customers.

Five minutes later, I broke down and asked Josie to tell Tess I wanted to talk to her. She headed to the back and returned with Tess, who'd changed into a black wraparound dress that was driving me crazy even from a distance. It was tight around her body, molding perfectly around her breasts and hips. And those heels...fuck.

I met her halfway.

"Babe, you look beautiful," I said, leading her a bit farther from the group, near one of the mannequins.

She gave me a small smile. "Thanks. Josie said you need me."

"Can't I compliment my gorgeous woman?"

She tilted her head, smiling even wider. "Compliments are always welcome, but we have customers out there."

"Ryker said you wanted an emergency family council."

"Ummm, yes." She averted her gaze.

My stomach clenched, but I wanted to keep things light.

"Never heard you mention family councils. Is that more serious than a meeting?"

Tess sighed before nodding.

"Babe, talk to me," I said.

"Can we do it after the customers leave?"

I stepped closer, cupping her face. "You want to torture me that long?"

I looked her straight in the eyes, watching her determination melt until she shook her head.

"I think Skye can handle the customers for a few minutes. Let's go in the back office," she murmured.

We passed the changing rooms, which were shielded from the store by a huge black curtain. Tess closed the door behind us in the office.

"Tess, talk to me."

She paced the room, arms over her chest as she bit her lower lip. I grabbed her shoulder, steadying her so we had eye contact. I touched her lip where she bit before.

"You're worried."

My One and Only

"I am. Hence the family council." She was smiling, but her eyes were still full of unease.

"Is it related to our conversation before I left?"

"Yes. I'm still processing it, but I wanted to process it with my family."

"You're mad at me?"

"Not exactly...but I don't understand why you didn't tell me everything."

I pressed my thumbs gently in the nape of her neck, deciding to lay all my cards on the table. "Because when I talked to you on Thanksgiving about this, you closed up. I could practically feel you slipping away, and I didn't want to risk that happening again."

Tess dropped her gaze to my chin. "You've been so withdrawn and silent during these past few weeks instead of letting me in so we could work through this together. I thought..." Her voice wobbled a bit. "I thought I'd done something wrong."

Fuck!

"Tess...babe. I was just trying to protect you."

She swallowed, nodding. "But I don't want you to do that. You're taking all the tension on yourself all the time, and that isn't good, you know? You'll get tired of it...of me," she whispered.

"No, I won't. Ever. I love you."

"I spoke to Skye, and we'd like to tell you to please not handle the situation with Albert any differently than you usually would. If we weren't together, I mean."

"What are you saying?"

"I spoke to my family, and if you were to freeze the investment for a while, they could extend us a credit line until things work out."

"You'd rather borrow money from your family, which you've told me you don't want to do, than trust me to fix this?"

Her eyes flashed. "No, I'm looking for options so you don't have to put your business in danger. Because I love you, Liam."

Fucking hell, this woman. She was infuriating. Did she really trust me that little? That was worrying me more than anything else. I knew Tess loved her independence. I knew her dad leaving when she was a child affected her more than she let on. She'd practically told me that one of the reasons she'd always been so self-sufficient was because she hadn't wanted to depend on anyone else financially—not even her family. I wasn't asking her to depend on me, just to trust me.

"You can't go rogue. We need to decide these things together," I said in a measured tone.

Tess threw her hands up in the air. "You're the one who didn't involve me in your decisions."

There was a knock at the door. Isabelle poked her head inside.

"Sorry to interrupt, but the customer is asking for you, Tess. Also, we can hear your voices a bit. I propose you continue the conversation later on. Liam, we have plenty of goodies outside. I will have Josie stop by the changing room with snacks for you too, Tess. Things make so much more sense once your belly is full and you have some sugar in your system."

Tess chuckled. I smiled too. Isabelle was something else.

Tess hurried outside the room to her customer.

"Come on." Isabelle laced an arm around mine, practically dragging me from the room. "I wasn't joking about the sugar."

"Is that your official therapist advice?"

She laughed as she led me to the buffet.

"Hell no. That would be to not push things tonight. Tess and Skye are running on adrenaline. Once everything's over and they've rested a bit, I'm sure they're going to see things more calmly."

My One and Only

"Listen to Isabelle. She knows her stuff," Hunter said. He was right next to us, helping himself to snacks.

"Awww, thanks for being such a supportive brother-in-law," Isabelle replied with a wink.

Ryker and Cole approached us too.

"You survived," Ryker said seriously. "I'm impressed."

"Means he doesn't even need the talk, does he?" Cole added.

"I wouldn't go that far," Ryker said quickly.

Hunter patted my shoulder. "Liam, full disclosure. I completely agree with your approach."

"So do we," Cole said.

Ryker nodded. "But a lifetime of dealing with our sisters taught us that we actually have no clue what to advise you."

Isabelle groaned. "You lot are no help."

Hunter smiled at her. "No. Hence why we suggested he listen to you."

"Why don't we all listen to me and actually eat some of these goodies? Maybe we can come up with better advice after that."

I loaded my plate, not really caring what I was eating. I looked over my shoulder, willing Tess to come out of the changing rooms. I just needed to try talking to her one more time tonight. Isabelle's advice made sense, but I didn't want to let this evening go by without making things right with Tess.

But at five o'clock on the dot, the rest of their VIP customers came running inside the store. Skye and Tess only emerged from the changing room to walk customers out before heading back.

I was forced to admit defeat. Isabelle was right. This was not the time to talk to Tess. I wanted nothing more than to wait and take her home once the evening was over, take care of her in all the ways I knew. But the longer the evening stretched on, the more I realized that wasn't likely to happen. The party just refused to end. Their VIP customers didn't show any signs of wanting to stop shopping.

As an investor, that was excellent news. But I just wanted to be alone with her.

As the family started to filter out, leaving Tess and Skye with their customers, Josie and Isabelle approached me again.

"Oh no, no. That's a determined look," Isabelle said.

"I'm calculating the risk of Tess still wanting me if I throw her over my shoulder and take her out of here," I replied. I was only half joking.

Josie patted my shoulder. "You don't want the answer to that. Why don't you focus on what you'll do next time you see her instead?"

"Just a tip, but having her favorite food around might not be a bad idea," Isabelle added.

Josie nodded. "Like ice cream."

"And cheese," I said.

Josie grinned at me.

Isabelle nodded approvingly. "I think you'll do just fine."

31

TESS

The next morning, I woke up with a pit in my stomach. My head felt heavy. Last night had stretched until the morning hours. Our customers had so much fun that they hadn't wanted to leave, and there was no way we could chuck them out.

It had been a glorious evening, and only one thing had kept it from being perfect. Whenever I thought about the pre-opening night, I envisioned Liam by my side, unable to keep his hands off me—of course— whispering sweet and naughty things. Instead, we fought in the back room and then barely made eye contact the rest of the night.

My poor heart was hurting.

I dragged myself out of bed. Those orders to the factory couldn't wait just because I'd gone to bed late, or because it was Saturday. The shower didn't really help wake me up, and neither did the first cup of coffee.

As I made myself a second one, I noticed a text on my phone.
Isabelle: Are you awake?
Tess: Yes.

She didn't write anything back.

Tess: I just need to drink another coffee to wake up my neurons, and then I can help with whatever you need.

Isabelle: I don't need anything, silly. Was just checking on you. Do you have any plans today?

Tess: Yup, I need to send all of last night's orders to the factory.

Isabelle: Wow. I know we both live by the motto #HUSTLE, but you can probably take a day off.

Tess: I will, don't worry. AFTER I send the orders :)

Isabelle: So you'll be home all day?

Tess: Yes. But we can plan something in the afternoon.

Isabelle: Let's talk after you're done.

Tess: Sure :)

The second coffee didn't help as much as I hoped either, but then again, what could mere caffeine do against that hollow feeling in my chest?

Armed with a third cup and my laptop, I turned on the Christmas lights on the balcony before sitting in my armchair. Yep, it was one of those days when I needed all the holiday spirit I could get. Except the lights didn't do the trick. I needed just a bit more Christmas in my home.

Setting my laptop aside, I brought out my box of decorations from the storage room.

I could do this very quickly. I was a pro at decorating under every circumstance. Even the year Mom moved us to New York and had neither space nor money for decorations, I turned our little apartment into Christmasland. All I needed was a trip to Goodwill, scissors, paint, and glue. And I'd done it all before Mom had even come home from work. I'd known it would lift everyone's mood, and I'd been right. Even Mom smiled that day, and I'd rarely seen her smile since the divorce. Christmas was magic—for me at least, it had always been.

My One and Only

I was only going to need ten minutes.

Half an hour later, I was sweaty and swearing, because I couldn't untangle the last set of Christmas lights.

I only stopped because my doorbell rang. Had Isabelle decided to pay me a visit after all? Or was it someone from my family? Come to think of it, I could do with some Winchester love right now. My apartment was cozy, with the Christmas lights, fake tree, silvery garlands, and painted globes hanging everywhere, but I still would love a bear hug from one of my brothers or Hunter.

"Come in. The door's open," I said loudly, still trying to untie the Christmas lights. I heard the door open and only looked up when footsteps approached, then promptly stopped.

Liam.

He was wearing jeans and a blue sweater that molded perfectly around those steely muscles and brought out the depths of his eyes. He sported a five-o'clock shadow, and his hair was messy. He just rolled out of bed and looked drop-dead sexy. I felt very self-conscious in my old yellow sweater and leggings. They were the first things I found in my closet, and I'd put them on without giving them a second thought, even though they looked like rags.

He stared at my hands, then swept his gaze around the room before focusing on me again.

"Liam, what... Was I supposed to know you were coming?" I asked.

I hadn't looked at my phone since starting Operation Christmas and didn't hear it chime with a message or a call.

"No. It's supposed to be a surprise."

My heart was beating so fast. Last evening, I'd told him so many things and hadn't given him time to say much. I was afraid of what he had to say now.

"How did you know I was home?" It quickly occurred to me. "Oh, Isabelle."

He smiled at last, and my stomach unclenched a little.

"You asked her to spy for you?"

"No, just to find out if you were home. And keep the rest of your family from showing up."

"Why would you want that?" I really wanted some Winchester love.

"So I can have you all to myself."

He moved from the doorway, making a beeline for me. Even though I was sleep-deprived, I couldn't help but drink him in. I couldn't decide what was sexier: those deep blue eyes, the stubble, or the stance of his shoulders.

"Liam...I don't want to fight again."

"That's not why I'm here."

"Oh."

He was so close to me that I could smell his deodorant.

"Tess, the only reason I didn't throw you over my shoulder last night and carry you someplace private was because you had customers."

"How thoughtful of you," I said with a small laugh.

"I didn't think you'd forgive me if you missed your event because of me, and I didn't want to give you more reasons to be upset with me."

I clutched the string of lights tighter, waiting with bated breath for him to continue.

"I love you, Tess. I love you so damn much that I didn't even hesitate to put you first when deciding my next steps. It felt natural to me. Was I wrong for not including you? Yes, I was. But also...not really."

The corners of my mouth twitched, but I said nothing. For one, my heart just about jumped out of my chest when he said that putting me first was the only thing that felt natural to him.

And I wanted to know why he thought he was wrong but also *not*. Sounded like one of my brothers' lines—maybe that was why they liked him.

"You'd been in over your head for weeks with the store and everything else. I didn't want any of this weighing on you. It was my mess to fix." He took one of my hands in his and then reached for the other. "It's the way I was raised. Solving problems, not talking about them."

"But that's not okay with me. I want us to communicate. No secrets, remember?"

"We're very different when it comes to that...but I promise I'll do better. I'll try." Swallowing hard, he added, "It's not the only reason I didn't tell you everything, though. I didn't want anything getting in between the two of us. Just in case there was any chance this could drive us apart. Last night, seeing that wary look in your eyes, the anguish...it fucking slayed me. It was like my worst fear coming true, and I couldn't take it, not even for a few minutes. And I won't. I'm not leaving here until we figure this out."

"We?" I whispered, smiling. I dropped the light strings, touching his face with both hands. His whiskers lightly scratched my palms. "I'm sorry I was harsh last evening. I just didn't know how to react or how to deal with all of it. I've gathered so much tension over the past few weeks, and I was so afraid you were pulling away from me... I was putting you first too, you know. When I spoke to Becca, the first thing I thought was 'I don't want him to harm his own company because of me.'"

He kissed me the next second, hard and deep and with so much urgency that I couldn't help but respond with all I had. I wrapped one hand around his neck, running the other through his hair. His body was vibrating lightly, or maybe it was mine; we were so entangled that it was impossible to tell.

He wrapped an arm tightly around my waist. I finally felt like

I could breathe again. I never wanted to not kiss him again. And I had no idea how it happened, but I completely agreed with his view that he was wrong but also *not*.

"I still want to talk, but I can't stop kissing you," he whispered, trailing down my neck now. His arm was still firmly around my waist.

"Then kiss me. Do whatever you want with me."

He groaned, moving his lips back up my neck and capturing my mouth. His kiss was even deeper than before, even more urgent. When he finally released the arm around my waist, it was only so he could lift me up by my ass with both hands. I wrapped my legs around him, laughing against his mouth.

"What?" he asked, pulling back just enough to look at me.

"Nothing. I'm just happy. That you care so much about me. That you spoke with my family just to make sure no one interrupted us today. You're everything to me, Liam."

He closed his eyes, pressing his forehead against mine. I loved feeling him this close, knowing he was mine. I loved him with all I had, and I never wanted him to doubt that.

"I love you," he said.

"You know, you keep saying you do, but if you thought this problem was going to drive a wedge between us, then I have some things to prove as well," I said.

His eyes were like fire as he traced the contour of my mouth with his thumb, parting my lips slightly. I leaned in, brushing my mouth against him. I did it slowly at first, just wanting to soak in his nearness, the fact that he was here. But before long, I grew too hungry for him. I kissed him, smiling against his mouth when he took control of the kiss. He walked me backward, right until we bumped into the box of decorations.

I giggled. Liam grinned before tightening his grip on me. Oh, how I liked this position, where his hands were firmly under my bottom. I could explore him all I wanted without his touch distracting me.

I kissed down his neck. My fingers were already working on the best way to get rid of his sweater. I was so focused on pulling it up that I didn't even realize we reached the bedroom until he laid me down on the bed. I didn't let go of his sweater, so he tumbled right on top of me, bracing himself on his forearms and smiling down at me.

The way he looked into my eyes was just surreal, as if I was the only thing that mattered to him.

He covered my mouth with his, kissing me gently and without hurry. The slow strokes of his tongue drove me crazy. I was vibrating as my fingers fumbled on his sweater, and I clumsily pushed it over his head, yanking it down each arm.

"Slow down, babe."

"No, I'm greedy today." I really was. I wanted him completely naked. I got rid of his pants and boxers with his help.

"Happy?" he teased.

"Almost."

I slowly pulled my sweater up my belly. He scooted closer the next second, pulling my sweater higher, then getting rid of it before moving to my leggings and throwing them somewhere in the room.

I was wearing simple white lace underwear because I hadn't been paying attention to what I put on this morning, but Liam's eyes grew darker still. He spread my thighs wider, coming closer before drawing one hand down my navel, then lower still. The muscles in my belly clenched as he trailed two fingers over my panties, touching me over the fabric until I soaked it through. I rolled my hips, pushing myself harder against his fingers, gasping. I needed more.

He took his hand away, and I groaned in protest before grabbing his hand and pulling him down completely over me. I felt more than saw his smile before we kissed, just as slow and as deep as before I undressed him.

Except now I was ten times hungrier for him. Feeling his hot skin against mine was just exquisite. The weight of his body and all those delicious muscles pressed against me, and I was hyperaware of every move he made.

And when he pressed his cock right across my opening, I moaned. He was so damn hard, and I was so turned on. He gyrated his hips. The shock of pleasure reverberated through my entire body, making my toes curl.

"Close your eyes, Tess."

I pinched my eyelids closed, simply giving myself to him. I meant it. He could do whatever he wanted; I trusted him completely. He unhooked my bra, taking it off. I felt him move off me and suddenly felt cold...but not for long. He placed a wet kiss on my belly at the same time he hooked his fingers in the elastic band of my panties.

My entire body felt like a sweet spot as he pulled the fabric down my legs and moved his mouth even lower. He kissed down the length of my legs before exploring my upper body with his mouth too. He was moving slowly, almost...reverently.

I felt him hover just over my clit, and I fisted the bedsheets in anticipation.

He blew cold air over my sensitive spot before pressing his hot mouth against it. I bucked off the bed, crying out as his tongue teased me mercilessly. Still, I didn't open my eyes. Every sensation was heightened like this. It was glorious.

He alternated between blowing cold air and feasting on me until my whole body was shaking. Then he just...stopped.

I blinked my eyes open, locking my gaze with his.

He smiled wolfishly, kissing my thighs before pushing

himself to his knees. Then he got up from the bed, pulling me to the edge of the mattress.

He reached across the bed for pillows, and I couldn't help but place quick little kisses on his chest. I wanted to shower him with kisses, but Liam was too impatient for that. He pushed one pillow under my back and the other under my ass, lifting me up a bit.

He spread my thighs wide, positioning himself between them, then drew the length of his cock slowly up and down my entrance, driving me crazy every time he touched my clit. When he finally put on a condom and slid inside me, we just stayed like that for a few seconds without moving, simply enjoying our connection. He took one of my hands in his, interlacing our fingers as he started thrusting. My nerve endings were already so on edge from the foreplay, my body so close to a climax from having had his mouth on me, that I wouldn't last long.

I dragged our hands down his abs, needing to touch more of him. I abandoned my exploration when he increased the rhythm of his thrusts, though. He was desperate for his release, and I was going to give him just what he needed. I pushed myself on my heels and one elbow, moving against him. I only just started feeling him widen inside me when my inner muscles clamped down. I was lost to the world after that, overcome by pleasure. I could barely breathe through it, but I did feel him come apart violently, thrusting and pushing until I was spent.

I was putty in his hands as he moved us on the bed so he was lying on his back, arm under my head, and I was half straddling him. He drew little circles on my back with his fingers.

"Maybe we should fight more often," I teased. "That was...incredible."

He immediately rolled me over so I was under him. He clearly wasn't as spent as I thought.

"Are you implying it's usually not incredible?"

"It's always amazing, Liam. Always. I think I just felt everything more intensely because I'd been afraid of losing you before you showed up." I swallowed, clearing my throat. "I don't want to ever feel that again. I hope we never fight again. I don't like it."

He kissed my cheeks softly, then my temple.

"I'm on board with that. I don't like fighting. I like this." He kept showering me with kisses until I was giddy.

"I like it too," I whispered.

"I love you, Tess. And I'm not letting you go. Ever. Life probably won't be smooth sailing, but I'll be a happy man knowing I get to spend every day with you."

My breath caught. His gaze turned playful before he added, "And that I can make you mine every night."

I grinned. "I bet that's your favorite part."

"Hell yes."

I traced a line from one shoulder to the other before skimming my fingers up his neck. I couldn't stop touching him, but I had to.

"Why the cute pout?" he asked.

I hadn't even realized I was pouting.

"I don't want to get out of bed, but I need to send the orders to design and production. I'll feel guilty if I don't do it."

He tilted his head to one side as if seriously considering my words.

"I have a solution for that."

"What is it?"

With a mischievous smile, he clasped my wrists, pinning them above my head.

"I'm just not going to let you leave the bed. Then you have nothing to feel guilty about."

"I see. I'm your prisoner, huh?" I lifted my head, stealing a quick kiss.

"You're mine to take care of and make happy. And I have so many ideas about how to make that happen."

I laughed, feeling my heart just soar with joy. I attempted to wiggle underneath him but couldn't. I smiled coyly before stealing another kiss.

"Go ahead, Mr. Harrington. Try out all your ideas."

32

LIAM

"You're a bad influence," Tess murmured later that afternoon.

"We've already established that."

I was kissing the back of her neck while she tried to email the order sheet she worked on for the past hour. We were still in bed.

"There, all sent! Only took me five times longer than it should have. But I'll take this distraction every day."

"Good, because I don't plan on behaving anytime I'm around you. Especially if you're wearing this."

"I'm naked."

"Precisely." I put her laptop away, pulling her in my lap.

"But I'm at a disadvantage. Why are you dressed up?"

"You insisted. So I wouldn't distract you."

"Oh, that's right." Grinning, she tugged at my sweater. "Just saying, it's not that much of a cover. I can still see all these gorgeous muscles through the fabric."

I ran my hand through her hair, enjoying how smooth it felt between my fingers. I was lost in thought, wanting us to talk about the issue at hand.

My One and Only

"You're frowning. Let's talk about the elephant in the room," she suggested. "But wait, I want to cover up first."

"Why?"

"I don't know, just feels like I should be covered." She looked over her shoulder, then pressed herself up on her knees. "You bad man. What did you do with my dress?"

I lifted her off me, putting her on the mattress before getting out of bed and hunting for the dress. I found it on the floor at the foot of the bed. Tess held her hands out, but I swatted them away. Leaning with a knee on the mattress, I pulled the dress over her head.

"Oooh, you want to put my clothes on. That's a first."

Five seconds later, it became clear I was much better at taking them off. I got her arms tangled in the fabric, but between the two of us, we sorted it out.

She looked adorable with her hair plastered to her face, blowing it out of her eyes.

Sitting next to her on the bed, I cupped her cheeks. "Tess, I promised you I'll try to be more open about everything, so let's sort out a few things. I don't want you to borrow money from your family."

"And I don't want you to risk your business."

She put a finger over my mouth, scooting away from the mattress. "I know I told you before that I don't feel good about getting family finances involved because it makes me feel dependent. But...I don't know how it happened, but my perspective about that has changed, and although it still wouldn't be my first choice, I don't think trusting those I love with all things, including financial, is a bad thing. I'd always been wary of that, ever since Dad left us, I guess, because it was just so devastating. But if you can't trust family, who can you trust? Am I making any sense?"

"Yes, you are. I'm proud of you, babe. Your family deserves you to trust them in all things."

"I know. I told them that. You're a big reason behind my change of heart, you know."

I grinned. "Can you mention it to Ryker and Cole? They were saying something about giving me the talk."

Tess laughed. "I'm on it."

I toned down my grin, because what I was about to say was serious. "But I still don't want you to do that, because we won't freeze the investment. I'm not giving that asshole what he wants. He doesn't deserve it. I have a plan, and I want you to trust me on it."

"Okay, so what's the plan?"

"Something I never considered until you. I'm going to make it public that we caught him trying to embezzle years ago."

Tess gasped. "But you always said that wouldn't bode well in the industry. That it might look poorly on Harrington & Co. too."

"Yes, that is the concern, but I don't care about that anymore."

"What do Becca and David have to say about this?"

"They're both on board. I spoke to them this morning. Between that and him showing up at your store making threats, we have enough to push him out of the company with very little money. We even have eyewitnesses in your shop, so he can't fight that claim. There's a clause about foul play. It's not enough to put him away, but he'll be ruined for good, and I don't think he'll fight it. This may be the more discreet way to shut him down. He'll accept the smaller buyout. And after he does...after his ties with Harrington & Co. are severed, we'll give him to the justice system."

"Well, well. There's karma, and there's you," she said.

"I don't mess around when someone wants to hurt those I love."

"You certainly don't."

She climbed in my lap again, wrapping her arms around my shoulders. She tilted her head from one side to the other.

"Your neck is stiff." I immediately pressed my fingers at the side of her neck. She sighed, closing her eyes. "I wanted to do this last night too."

"You can make up for that now." She smiled, lying down on the mattress and moving her hair to bare her neck.

"Who said I'll start with your neck?" I wiggled my eyebrows.

"Oh, what do you plan to attack first, then?"

Before I got a chance to answer, the doorbell rang. Tess frowned.

"I ordered food," I explained.

Her eyes widened and she leapt out of bed, heading out of the bedroom. Chuckling, I took my time, knowing she would already be elbow deep in the basket by the time I was out.

"You ordered a cheese basket," she exclaimed when I stepped inside the living room. I could tell she was smiling, even though her head was bent and she was rummaging through the contents.

"Apricot jam too."

She giggled, taking out the jar. I went over to her, wrapping an arm around her waist.

"You're a keeper." She looked sideways at me. "You have more surprises for me?"

"Just a few."

She had no idea.

Five days later

"Let's drink to that bastard no longer being part of the company," David exclaimed as soon as we stepped into the brownstone. It was late in the afternoon, and the interns were already gone. We'd just come from the meeting with Albert's lawyer.

David immediately took out a bottle of champagne from the cooler. I hadn't even known he bought one, but I should have figured as much. He never missed a chance to celebrate.

We all got out of our coats. They were drenched from the rain and snow. New York was really messy when it poured like this.

"He's not out yet," I replied.

David rolled his eyes. "Well, no, but we just kicked his ass. Everything else is a formality."

That was true. That bastard was getting exactly what he deserved: a package so small that it was practically nothing. But he agreed to it on the count of not going to jail. I was going to let him believe that, until he was officially no longer part of Harrington & Co., and then a judge was going to get all the paperwork about him trying to embezzle from us all those years ago. Back then, we were a young company, and a scandal would have damaged us irreversibly. Now, it was different. We were established and well respected, and an old incident wouldn't hurt us as much.

Albert wasn't going to bother anyone again. Ever.

"We only have coffee cups, but they'll do," David said, pouring champagne for Becca, Tess, and the two of us. We needed Tess there, because we wanted his drunken incident at her store on record.

David clinked his cup to Tess's first. "I'll drink to Tess, who managed to make our friend here not just human but a happy

My One and Only

human instead of the broody robot Becca and I have known for...a long time. Don't want to say how long. Makes me feel old." The last part was directed at Becca.

"Fine, I'll have mercy on you today," she replied, clinking her cup to ours. "I'll drink to finally getting rid of Albert, and to the best investment we've ever made. I've crunched some numbers last night, and Soho Lingerie has the highest acquisition rate of new customers out of every investment we've ever made."

"Wow. Good thing we're officially opening store number two next week. We're really bursting at the seams," Tess said.

"You crunched numbers last night?" David asked Becca, crestfallen. "Please tell me you're not turning into Liam."

Becca rolled her eyes. "Please go get laid. You're becoming more intense by the day."

David choked on his drink. Becca, Tess, and I burst into laughter. Becca then inspected the bottle of champagne, smoothing one thumb over the label.

"You know what? I actually have wine in my office that I've been keeping for a special occasion. How long do you guys think we'll be here?"

I looked at Tess, who said, "We don't have plans tonight."

"I'll go get it before the bubbles mess with my ability to walk straight."

"I'll come help you," David said. I snickered. Becca looked at him suspiciously but shrugged. I foresaw a future where Becca really did take my place as David's favorite person to give shit to. They bickered all the way up the stairs.

The second they were out of sight, I put an arm around Tess's waist. Sitting at the edge of one of our intern's desks, I pulled her toward me.

"You're quiet," I said.

"Just processing everything," Tess replied. "That there's no threat hanging over our head anymore. That you're mine and we're kicking ass together."

"This is just the beginning."

"I like that. Sounds like a promise."

"It definitely is." I kissed her forehead, gripping her hips tighter. "And I'm going to make good on it every day."

"Starting today?" she teased.

"I'd start right now, but Becca and David are in the building."

"Oh I see. So this plan of yours begins with something dirty."

"Every plan begins like that. It's brought us good luck until now."

She laughed but nodded. "You're right about that."

I debated giving her a taste of the dirty plan I had in mind, but I heard David and Becca coming down the stairs. She was holding that bottle of wine like it was her firstborn.

"This is my pride and joy," she explained. "Got it from a very special someone a very long time ago. But let's have another round of champagne first."

"Should we open it up or wait for Skye to arrive?" David asked.

"She texted that she's going to be here in a few minutes," Tess. "No clue why she's late."

She pouted, turning around to face David and Becca.

I leaned in to kiss the side of her neck, trying to hide my smile from everyone. I had a good poker face in business, but this was definitely unchartered territory. Skye was coming from a certain shop on Fifth Avenue where she looked at the ring I wanted to buy for Tess. I was planning to surprise my woman soon. I couldn't wait to see her reaction.

EPILOGUE

Tess
One week later

The official opening day was finally here! We'd chosen a Saturday, because we intended to make an event out of it, and most people shopped on the weekends. We invited all our existing customers, enticing them with gift cards. It was going to be a huge party. It started at noon. We reserved the morning for showing our family around. During the pre-party, half the furniture had been missing, and we wanted to show them the final version.

"You did such a great job with this space," Isabelle exclaimed.

"Thanks," I said. We were in the back office. Josie, Laney, and Heather were also here. My brothers, Mom, Mick, and Ellen were in the front with Skye. We were doing tours in groups; otherwise, we'd barely have space to move about.

"I'm so happy for you girls," Josie said, patting her belly. She wasn't showing yet. Heather was sitting next to her, and her belly was huge in comparison. They looked very cute, but Heather was a little sad that none of our super-sexy lingerie fit her properly. Ever since Skye's pregnancy, I toyed with the idea of developing a line for expecting women, something that would accommodate the body's changes. Now I was more convinced than ever that the project needed to happen.

"I'm so proud of you two. You're such kickass businesswomen," Isabelle said.

"You're doing amazing yourself," I replied.

"The event with the clients went well, and it gave me all sorts of ideas."

It was so good to see Isabelle happy. As usual, her hair seemed to reflect her mood. It was bright red and fell into a silky curtain around her shoulders.

"Well, if we can help with anything, just let me know," I said. I felt like I had a lot of free time, though it wasn't really true. The wedding planner and I wrapped up the most pressing issues for Cole's wedding, but there was still plenty to do.

Josie and Heather nodded too.

Josie was a shark in all legal things, and Heather's skills as a reporter came in very handy at writing press releases as well as website texts. Between all of us, we had expertise in all sorts of things.

"Let's go to the front," I suggested. Everyone agreed, so we returned to the group. Rob had the party catered, so we had everything from miniature sandwiches to scones in one corner of the store. Since we were serving champagne, we thought it was best to also have some food to help soak up the alcohol.

The family was milling around the small buffet, chatting with each other. Even Ian and Dylan had come for the opening, which I really appreciated.

We put a huge Christmas tree in the display window. It was a

My One and Only

snowy mid-December day, and it all looked so magical. I was pleased with how the decorations turned out inside the store. We only had Christmas lights in the display window and on the tree. Keeping it simple prevented guests from tripping over cords—but as soon as the party was over, I planned to unleash myself and really decorate it all up.

I spotted Liam chatting with Rob and Hunter, and my heart just soared. He turned around, as if he felt I was watching him. He held out his hand for me, and I immediately walked over to him. Who could resist those baby-blue eyes? Not this girl.

"Hey, beautiful," he said, kissing my hand, then pulling me close enough that I thought he'd kiss my lips too. Only he didn't.

"Ready for the toast?" he asked.

"Yes. Everyone's had the tour."

He led me toward the second small table dedicated to drinks. They already poured champagne in all the glasses.

"Attention, everyone. We'd like to make a toast," I said.

Everyone shuffled around the room, grabbing a glass. Skye came to stand next to me.

"Thank you all for coming here today," she said. "We couldn't have done this without all of you. Thank you for all your support, for always being here for us."

"It's all been a crazy ride, so thanks for putting up with us," I added. I was so happy to be surrounded by everyone I loved. I turned to Liam. "Also, a huge thanks to this wonderful man I'm lucky enough to call my boyfriend. He's the best partner we could wish for. The best man I could wish for. Thank you for being part of my life."

I looked at my mom, a bit surprised at her misty eyes.

"Mom, why are you tearing up?" I asked.

"I'm just so proud of you. All of you. It's a parent's biggest wish for their children to do well, to be happy."

Oh no. Now I was tearing up too.

Liam tapped his fingers against his glass. "I'd like to say a few words too."

I nodded, happy someone else was taking over, because I was sure my voice would come out a little wobbly. He brought one hand to the side of my waist, pulling me closer.

"When I met Tess, my first thought was 'I'm in trouble.' I could barely focus on anything that wasn't her. Then as I got to know her better, I realized I was in very *big* trouble."

Everyone laughed. I felt my cheeks heat up. I loved the way he held me as he spoke.

"Babe, I love your passion and dedication, your determination to fight for what you want." He paused and took in a deep breath, cocking his head to look at me. "And I'm so damn lucky that you want me."

He let go of my waist, and I immediately felt cold and wanted him to touch me, but my man seemed to have a plan. I tilted my head toward him, and a strand of hair came loose from my braid. He pushed it behind my ear before taking a step back.

Someone in the group started whispering something, but my ears became fuzzy the second I realized Liam was lowering himself to one knee. My heart started beating so fast that I couldn't even breathe. I pressed a palm to my stomach when he pulled a ring from his back pocket. No box, just the most beautiful ring I'd ever seen. The band was a mix of platinum and gold, and there were three stones in the center: a ruby, a sapphire, and an emerald.

"Tess Winchester, after today, I no longer want to be your boyfriend. I want to be your fiancé."

His hand was shaking a little, so I took a step forward, cupping his outstretched hand with both of mine.

"I want you to be my partner in all things, the mother of my children, my wife. You're an amazing human being."

His voice was strong, his eyes determined, and all I could do was nod. My hands were shaking now, and he was the one steadying me as he slid the ring on my finger. I jumped in his arms before he even finished rising to his feet, but my strong man didn't even wobble. My ears started working again, and I heard everyone cheering and clapping. I hugged him tightly, hiding my face in his neck and breathing him in for a few moments. I couldn't believe this was real, that he loved me so much.

He lowered me to the floor carefully. I gave him one hell of a smooch, trying—and failing—to keep it from being too hot.

He was grinning from ear to ear when we pulled apart.

"I love you," I whispered.

"You're my whole life, Tess."

He kissed both of my hands right before I felt a bear hug from behind. I didn't even have to turn around to know it was Cole. Everyone hugged and congratulated us, and I was looking for Mom in the crowd, because I thought she might need a hug right now too. I couldn't see her though, not until everyone but her, Mick, and Ellen had congratulated us. They waited in the back. Mick just wordlessly hugged me, then shook Liam's hand. Mom was even more misty-eyed than before.

"Liam, take good care of my girl," Mom said.

"Every day of my life. I promise."

"You have a good man there, Tess. Love him always just as you do now," Mom added.

"I will," I promised her, nodding in excitement.

Ellen smiled at me. "I'm biased, of course, but I agree with your mom. You're perfect for him."

"Thank you, Ellen."

"And don't keep us waiting too long for those grandkids," she told Liam.

"Gran, don't start."

"If I can't start on the day you propose, then when can I? You know what, don't answer that. I'm eighty. I'm at the age where I can officially not care about permission anymore."

Liam and I both started laughing, but I was pretty sure Ellen wasn't joking. She'd lobby for grandkids even more openly than before.

But that was okay, because I was completely on board with that plan.

I glanced at Liam, trying to read his expression. He was looking at me with a very smug smile.

"I know what you're thinking about," Liam whispered in my ear as we went back to the buffet table.

"Oh?"

He winked. "We're going to start working on that very soon."

I felt the tips of my ears heat up and then my cheeks. Isabelle, Ian, and Dylan were currently at the buffet, arguing in a brotherly and sisterly way I knew only too well.

"What are you bickering about?" I inquired.

Isabelle waved her hand in the air, pointing from Ian to Dylan to herself.

"Well, with all the Winchesters now officially off the market, I was just wondering which of the three of us will make it out of the bachelor club next."

"And let me guess, these two are firmly insisting they like being in the club?'

"We're right here," Dylan said with a smile. "We can hear you."

"If anyone asks us, we think—" Cole started, but Ian interrupted him.

"No one is asking," he said loudly, and I cracked up.

"I am," Dylan said.

Ian stared at him. "Man, don't do this. It's like a jinx."

Cole cocked a brow, looking between the brothers. "I don't

want to start a war between you two, so I'm withholding my opinion."

"I think it'll be me," Isabelle declared loudly, swinging her fiery red hair to one side and winking at her brothers.

We all burst out laughing, but then Skye groaned.

"Oh no, we're supposed to open now. It's already eleven o'clock."

I glanced out the window. It was snowing in earnest now, and SoHo looked even more magical than usual. The day was so dark and cloudy that the lampposts were already glowing, as were the Christmas lights hanging up and down the street.

I headed to the door, still chuckling at Isabelle's proclamation that she was going to be next as I turned the sign from Closed to Open. I totally believed it, though who knew? Maybe her brother would be next. Someone may steal Dylan's heart.

Finding love in New York wasn't always easy, but with a little luck, anything was possible.

The End

ALSO BY LAYLA HAGEN

The Bennett Family Series
Book 1: Your Irresistible Love
Book 2: Your Captivating Love
Book 3: Your Forever Love
Book 4: Your Inescapable Love
Book 5: Your Tempting Love
Book 6: Your Alluring Love
Book 7: Your Fierce Love
Book 8: Your One True Love
Book 9: Your Endless Love

The Connor Family Series
Book 1: Anything For You
Book 2: Wild With You
Book 3: Meant For You
Book 4: Only With You
Book 5: Fighting For You
Book 6: Always With You

The Lost Series
Book 1: Lost in Us
Book 2: Found in Us
Book 3: Caught in Us

Standalone

Withering Hope

Printed in Great Britain
by Amazon